Mute

Richard Salsbury

First published in 2023

www.richardsalsbury.com

ISBN 978-1-7394794-0-4

A CIP catalogue record for this book is available from the British Library

Typeset by the author in Adobe Garamond Pro and Adobe Myriad Pro

Cover design by The Art of Communication artofcomms.co.uk

Printed and bound in the UK by Biddles Books Ltd, King's Lynn, PE32 1SF

Richard Salsbury is a novelist and award-winning short story writer based in the south of England. His work has appeared in *Artificium*, *Flash Fiction Magazine*, *World Wide Writers*, *Portsmouth News*, the Fairlight Books website and on BBC Radio. He is an editor and website designer for environmental writing project *Pens of the Earth*. He also plays the guitar and brews his own beer. *Mute* is his debut novel.

www.richardsalsbury.com

For Heg

'It is difficult to believe in the dreadful but quiet war of organic beings going on [in] the peaceful woods & smiling fields.'

Charles Darwin
Fourth Notebook on Transmutation of Species

'Civilization advances by extending the number of important operations which we can perform without thinking about them.'

Alfred North Whitehead
An Introduction to Mathematics

'Those who believe in telekinetics, raise my hand.'

Kurt Vonnegut

Friday

SOME people had criticised Wes's blog for being too cynical, but the fact that a man had just tried to murder him in the office toilet validated everything he'd written in the past three years: *we're living in a madhouse.*

The weirdest thing was that he didn't feel more scared. He should be razor-edged, revved into the red. But years of martial arts training seemed to have dulled his reaction. He practised being assaulted every week, and now it had actually happened, his body was reacting like it was just another Monday evening. It was ready to settle into the familiar pattern: a curry from the Jewel of India on the way home and a night in front of the telly with Alex.

A bit more abject terror might have persuaded PC Bennett to take him seriously, instead of dumping Wes in an interview room and buggering off. He imagined Bennett at this very moment, sipping tea from a Hampshire Constabulary mug and chuckling to his colleagues from under that wispy attempt at a moustache, 'I've got a right one in room four.'

The interview room's walls were a flat grey, and a single energy-saving light bulb struggled to push the shadows back into the corners. It was designed for anonymity, for deniability. The only object of any note was the poster, showing a torso wearing a black T-shirt and leather jacket, the edges blurred to suggest motion. A fist at groin level gripped a flick knife. The caption: 'If it's longer than three inches, it's illegal.' Definitely one for the blog.

In fact, this whole episode was. In some cloistered part of Wes's mind he was already deciding how he was going to write this up when it was all over. Like a journalist who hid his delight in disaster, he was already thinking what a terrific story this was going to make. Astonishing that he could be so flippant after a murder attempt. If Wes himself couldn't take this seriously, why should they?

But it wasn't like he'd had the chance to express any of this. Where the hell had PC Bennett gone? Shouldn't he be taking his statement? Wes thought he'd made his situation – and its urgency – clear, but now the doubts began. Communication had never been his strong point. There was always room for people to misunderstand him, and the likelihood increased with those who were busy or impatient. His phone was out of his pocket and blinking to life before he remembered the bloody thing was still on the fritz. No way of texting Alex. Although, given their argument this morning, maybe speaking to him was not her top priority.

It was these two things – the argument with Alex and Bennett's non-appearance – that stirred up the first real feelings of fear. It was the old fear, reaching back into childhood and beyond, the fear of being misunderstood, of being ignored. Many times throughout his life he had thought this a thing of the past, something he had conquered. Every time it found a way to return.

The door opened explosively. Wes's feet jerked, and the chair screeched across the lino. A policeman stood there, framed by the door, but it wasn't Bennett. This man was tall and grey-haired, his face sheer as a cliff. The diamonds on his epaulettes marked him as someone with clout, unlike Bennett, who had seemed hesitant and distracted.

'Right,' the policeman boomed. He strode across the room, two quick paces, and took the chair opposite. 'My name is

Inspector Selvidge. Let's hear what you've got to say, then.'

Blunt. To the point. Maybe that wasn't so bad. At least things were now moving. Wes fished out his notepad and a tiny mechanical pencil, and displayed the message he always wrote in thick felt-tip on the first page of any new notepad:

I'm Wes Henning.
I'm unable to speak
but I'm not deaf.

Selvidge's mouth moved, as if he were chewing gum. He took out a notepad and pen of his own.

'And your address?'

No, the bureaucratic niceties could come later. Wes flipped to the sheet on which he'd written his summary of events:

A man tried to kill me at work at about 18:00 today.
I've never seen him before.

Selvidge scanned the lines, then turned his eyes on Wes. He pursed his lips, tilted his head to one side. 'Okay, let's not jump the gun, Mr Henning. I need to ask you a couple of basic questions. The sooner we get past them, the sooner we can get to the nature of the incident. Is that acceptable?'

So, more delays, more faffing. It was a way, he supposed, for the police to deflect the frivolous claims, the weirdos, the nutters.

'So, if you could give me your address, Mr Henning.'

He bit his lip and wrote on the pad:

7 Oak Rd.

'Strathurst?'

Wes nodded. Yes, bloody Strathurst. Where else?

'And the incident occurred at your work, you say? Which is?'

J+H Web Design, Weaver's Down Business Park.

He paused, then added:

Strathurst.

Selvidge's pen moved across the surface of the paper, its whisper the only sound in an otherwise silent room. He took his

3

time, as if the formation of the letters was more important than the information they conveyed.

'Very well. So, this man – how did he get into your office?'

It has an open reception area.

'With no staff?'

It's a small business.

'We deal with a lot of scuffles and altercations here, Mr Henning, especially on a Friday night. What makes you think this was something more serious?'

He said 'I'm going to kill you.'

'Well, that's very … straightforward.' Selvidge placed the pen down on top of his pad. 'People are usually more cagey about murder.'

Christ. Surely even gallows humour had its limits.

'What sort of weapon did he use?'

None – bare hands.

'Bare hands? If he wanted to kill you, why would he just use his hands?'

How the hell should he know? Couldn't Selvidge get off his arse and *do* something? Wes put his hands flat on the table and tried to slow his breathing. This kind of thinking was not going to help. He broke eye contact with the policeman in an attempt to reel in his frustration. There was nothing else to look at but the poster – the actor holding a flick-knife and trying to look threatening. And now Wes thought about it, his attacker's lack of a weapon did seem strange. He had also passed up the opportunity for a surprise attack and waited until Wes was ready to defend himself. Why? Selvidge made him question his own story. And yet there was no doubting the ferocity of the attack.

A balaclava torn off to reveal a face he didn't recognise. Blows coming in – a jab, a roundhouse.

He saw Selvidge frown and realised he must have flinched.

'Would you like a glass of water, Mr Henning?'

4

Wes shook his head. He didn't want Selvidge leaving the room, getting diverted by a colleague who had mislaid the office stapler, and only coming back half an hour later when he remembered he'd left someone in interview room four.

'So, am I right in thinking this occurred in the reception area of your office?'

Well, no. Actually it occurred in the toilet cubicle, some of it on the toilet itself. Wes decided Selvidge didn't need to know this. He nodded again.

'Okay, so let's examine the question of motive. Why might someone want to murder you?'

Well, that was the crux of it. He could anticipate Selvidge's line of questioning because he'd already asked those same questions of himself, over and over. Could he put a name to any person he considered an enemy? No. Had anyone shown aggression to him recently? No. When was the last time he'd upset someone? Well, that would be Alex, this very morning. As he left the house, he could tell she wasn't happy – he'd never met anyone whose expression more accurately telegraphed their feelings – but he had gone anyway, the regret building up in him throughout the day. But there was no way he was going to volunteer this information to Selvidge. He knew how keen the police were to link murders to family members. It could only mean more dead ends, more wasting of time. Which left him with what? Although he had failed to dig up anything plausible in the last half hour, he had to offer something to divert Selvidge from his scepticism.

My blog?

'Your ... blog.'

It was a long shot. While *In Absurdia* was sardonic and biting, it was never aggressive. There were plenty of things in life worthy of scorn – corrupt politicians, vacuous celebrity culture, people's steadfast belief in idiocy – but Wes skewered them with a playful good humour. Granted, he had ruffled a few feathers on occasion, but he resisted the temptation to rant, and made sure his mocking never developed into a sustained personal attack. The blog was open for comments, giving anyone a chance to correct him or give their own perspective. Any arguments were short-lived. Or that's the way it seemed. Perhaps, somewhere away from the Neverland of the web, he'd kindled a seething resent-ment.

'You think a man tried to kill you because of something you wrote on the internet?'

Wes gestured that he needed time to think. The first thing that came to mind was his latest post:

Mrs Mute cracked a fingernail last week while hacking her way into the plastic clamshell containing her new headphones (she needs something to shut out my incessant jabbering). Why does pack-aging have to be like this? The answer came to me in a flash:

Company's desire for profit -> paranoia that products won't survive shipping -> vastly over-engineered packaging -> my wife's broken fingernail.

Another damning indictment of capitalism.

Mute

It was an observation capped off with a silly joke. Who could possibly be offended by this? People who designed packaging? Capitalists?

'Mr Henning?'

On the other hand, he *had* taken the piss out of people – the guy who took BT to court, claiming 'an unreliable broadband connection is suppressing my freedom of speech'; or the woman who had expunged a particular shade of red from her life because it had a wavelength of 666 nanometres and was therefore scientifically proven to be the colour of the devil. These kind of stories were *In Absurdia's* bread and butter, and he expected a few people might be annoyed by them. But that was fine. Being told he was an arsehole every once in a while was part of the job, and something he was prepared to take on the chin. Being murdered in the khazi wasn't.

'Mr Henning?'

We're living in a madhouse. It was the first thing he'd written on the blog – both a fundamental belief and a mission statement. But in the last hour that sentence had taken on a very different meaning. It was the difference between watching a wrestling match from the sidelines and being pitched into the middle of it. Given that none of this made any sense to Wes, how was he supposed to rationalise it to anyone else?

'So, I'm assuming you can't think of a suspect.'

There were too many, that was the problem. Everyone looked like a suspect now, all of them equally improbable.

'I understand PC Jackson has examined you?'

Reluctant to be dragged away from his line of thought, but seeing no other option, Wes nodded. It had been a perfunctory check from a woman with all the bedside manner of a refrigerator. She had seemed unsurprised with his injuries – abrasions on the knuckles of both hands and the scalp above his left ear, some bruising on the chest. 'Been drinking?' she asked. 'Taken any drugs or medicines?' He shook his head. Her final comment to him – 'You'll be fine, dear' – had seemed more like a dismissal than a reassurance.

'You'll forgive me for saying so,' Selvidge said, 'but your injuries don't seem consistent with a potentially fatal incident.'

He was <u>unarmed</u>.

'And that's what I'm struggling with. If it was genuinely a murder attempt, he wasn't exactly trying very hard, was he?'

7

Oh, yes – easy to make light of it when you weren't on the end of those fists. Did Selvidge want the facts, or some idealised scenario that fit his idea of how things *should* have happened?

'You're afraid this man might have another go at you?'

Wes gestured that yes, of course he bloody was.

'All right, then,' Selvidge said. 'I have a proposal for you. We put you in one of our cells while we sort this out. We lock you in. No-one will be able to get to you there. You'll be absolutely safe.'

Wes had misheard him. He must have misheard him. The guy wanted to lock him in a tiny room, no bigger than a toilet cubicle, with no exits. Had no-one explained the purpose of the police to this man? The idea was to get the *criminal* behind bars.

Selvidge leaned back and folded his arms. 'Not so keen? Is that because it would prevent you from leaving the station as soon as you get bored?'

Wes shut his jaw once he became aware that it was hanging open.

'That's an impressive look of shock, Mr Henning, but let's review the facts, shall we? You claim that someone has tried to kill you, but (a) you have no evidence, (b) you can't suggest any-one who might have a motive, and (c) PC Jackson has singularly failed to find any knife wounds or bullet holes in you.'

So he had to be bleeding to death before they would take him seriously? Right. And presumably if the guy had attacked him with a knife less than three inches long, that wouldn't count either. Wes flipped over the page and wrote as fast as he could.

Selvidge didn't do him the courtesy of waiting. 'This is Stra-thurst, Mr Henning, not Syria. Do you really think we've got nothing better to do?'

I need your _help_.

When he looked up and held the page out to be read, Selvidge was leaning back, balancing the chair on its two rear legs. He glanced at the page, then back at Wes.

'Mr Henning, I have been absolutely fair with you. I've listened to what you have to say, just on the off-chance that it bears any resemblance to reality. Now I'm going to level with you. How many more times is this going to happen?'

They were confusing him with someone else. It was the only explanation. Wes had never been in this building before in his life. But as soon as he put pen to paper to explain, the chair thumped back down and Selvidge snatched his notepad away. Wes stifled his natural impulse: the curve of the arm into taan sau – palm face up, elbow in – that would deflect the policeman's arm away before he had the chance to grasp the pad. It was a reaction hard-wired into him from years of Wing Chun training, the sort of reaction that, less than an hour ago, had saved his life. It would do him no good here.

'Let's not waste any more time. This is your last chance to tell me the truth.'

Wes looked at the pad, caged under the officer's right hand, and his attitude set like cement. So this is what you got when you asked for protection – a silencing, a gagging. If you can't complain any more, there can't be any complaint. It was a shock, but not entirely a surprise. Part of him expected the world to be like this. Part of him said, 'See? I told you.'

'Very well,' Selvidge said. 'Because I'm a man of infinite com-passion and kindness, I'm going to give you a choice: either you can go and tell your friends to stop this little game, or I can have you arrested for wasting police time.'

What friends? What game? Was Selvidge mixing up his cases, or was he jumping to conclusions without the faintest shred of evidence? It hardly mattered. Wes had run out of patience with this bullshit. He stood and jabbed a peremptory finger at his pad. Selvidge skimmed it across the table and Wes scooped it up. They glared at each other, and Wes had it in mind that he would make

Selvidge break eye contact first, that he would win at least this small victory. But after a few seconds he began to feel like an idiot. The policeman was reclined in the chair, arms folded, perfectly still. You can't outstare geology. Wes turned, yanked at the door handle and headed for the exit.

From behind him he heard Selvidge's raised voice. 'Please do ask about the Independent Police Complaints Commission on your way out, Mr Henning.'

Back in the reception he saw PC Bennett leaning against the wall, arms folded, eyes tracking him as he strode to the door. Wes flipped him the middle finger and burst out into the night.

2

Ten hours earlier

ALEX made another attempt to get through to him during breakfast, while Wes was dipping a finger of toast into his boiled egg. The yolk, displaced from its bed of white, rose up and oozed down the side of the shell. She stood behind her chair, grasping its back and towering above him. He glanced up at her with the beginning of a frown.

Come on, girl, bite the bullet. 'I went to see Dr Clayton yesterday.'

He looked up. The frown deepened into a look of concern.

'No, no – nothing like that. I just asked her about ... you know, what we were talking about.'

He shook his head slowly, and she suspected he was being deliberately obtuse. She put one hand on her belly and saw understanding creep across his face. He took two substantial bites out of his toast.

'I, uh ... I put your concerns to her.'

He focussed on his egg. Another plunge of the bread – another yellow uprising. Okay, perhaps she should have consulted him first, but it would only have made things more complicated.

He took the pencil and notepad out of his top pocket and wrote:

We discussed this last week.

Discussed, yes, but he didn't seriously believe they'd reached a conclusion, did he? Things had petered out after an hour and a half because they were both frustrated by the conversation, but that was in no way a conclusion.

'She said it was highly unlikely that any child of ours wouldn't be able to speak. Those were her exact words: highly unlikely.'

Speculation – she doesn't know.

'But what she said made complete sense. There's nothing physical about it, so genetically speaking there's little chance our child would inherit your ... problem.'

Even after three years together she still didn't feel right referring to it this way, although he'd assured her that words like 'disability', 'problem' and 'limitation' were all fine. The euphemistic approach was anathema to him. In one session with a psychologist he had lasted no more than ten minutes before walking out because the man kept describing him as 'speech free'. This was nothing to do with freedom – it was a hindrance, an obstacle to be tackled, every day.

Mental problems can be inherited too.

'I didn't mean that,' she said.

He shrugged.

'You know I didn't.'

Wes scraped out the egg white with his spoon and gulped it down.

'Don't be absurd, Wes. There's nothing wrong with you mentally, nothing at all.'

Evidently not true.

And technically, she supposed he was right. After years of examination doctors had found no evidence of a physical cause for his speechlessness. They concluded it was an inability to make the muscles of his vocal cords function, in the same way that most people never learn to move their toes independently. But that constituted a mental problem? Pure melodrama.

He was so difficult to argue with, all his communications so edited. With him, she missed the rapidity of normal conversation, because in amongst the jumble of words a truth could come out, something that might not otherwise have been spoken. It didn't have to be angry, just ... from the heart. And although it might be awkward in the short term, later you'd be glad of it. You'd move one step closer to agreement, or an acceptable compromise, or ... something. While Alex was quite capable of blurting things out – her overactive mind always ready to supply some random topic for discussion – Wes's thoughts always had the calm authority of the written word. She was sure it was her love of literature that lay at the root of the problem; his side of the argument always looked like Shakespeare next to her clumsy verbalisations. As soon as something was written down – even on the screen of a mobile phone or scrawled across the back of an Indian takeaway menu – it somehow acquired more firmness, more authority.

Out of nowhere, she was struck by a sudden desire for an onion bhajee – crispy on the outside, tender in the middle. What a perfect summary of where they stood: he was stalled on the very idea of having kids, while she was already jumping ahead to the food cravings.

And that's only half the problem.

'The other being that you wouldn't be able to talk to our child?'

He nodded.

'But I'd be happy to babble away enough for two. It would be no worse than being brought up by a single mother. I mean,

Joanne copes fine with the twins, doesn't she?'

That's different.

'How?'

Kids emulate their parents.

'So our child would be a warm, lovely human being, just like their dad. I don't see the problem.'

A mistake: Wes had always been impervious to this facile kind of flattery. For him, praise was unearned without effort, without hardship.

You don't appreciate how I feel about my past.

It had been a long journey for him, to be sure, from bullied schoolboy to part-owner of a small business, but he'd conquered all problems in the end, leaving her in no doubt about his courage and persistence. So, having come this far, why this reluctance to take the next step with her?

Her own childhood had been considerably easier – a sun-drenched time in which her parents gave her boundless encouragement, love and indulgence. Having received such gifts, she longed to be the one to bestow them. Even if their baby was born without speech, they would be more prepared than Wes's parents had been. And if bullying became a problem, they could always opt for home schooling. For each of his fears, there was a solution. She saw the potential for joy and fulfilment where he saw only problems.

'Look, if we could remove these concerns of yours, then how would you feel about it?'

You can't do that.

'Of course we can. There's always a way.'

You can't just change reality to suit you.

'You make it sound like these problems are insurmountable. We're not trying to defy gravity, Wes. You didn't let a darned thing stop you when you were setting up the business. What's so different about this?'

13

Everything.

'I know what you're thinking – you might not put it on paper, but it's as clear as day to me. You think I'm being whimsical and flighty and … you know I wouldn't be that way about something as important as this. The reason I gave up the tennis lessons and the accountancy course is that they weren't right for me. This – *this* – is the direction and purpose I've been looking for all along. There comes a time when a woman just *knows*. To hell with piecemeal secretarial work or trying to find a nice hobby. This is what I want. I've never been more sure of anything. What could be more important, more wonderful, than bringing a new person into the world? And now is the right time, Wes. Even if we started now, I'll be fifty-two before our child is out of their teens. Can you imagine that? Fifty-two!'

She was saying too much. He had taught her the art of the short sentence, the thoughtful pause, but still, sometimes she couldn't help it – the dam broke.

She finished her speech rather feebly. 'I don't think you know how I feel about this.'

He made a double-quote mark in the air. *Ditto.* When he wanted, his face could be as expressive as a silent movie star's. But in the last few moments it had hardened into blank neutrality, the doorway to his feelings closed. He was retreating, hiding behind his disability.

What if Wes shut down the discussion, said no, never, not under any circumstances? Was she pushing him towards this? And what would it mean for their relationship? She had not experienced doubts like these since the early days, when she had asked herself if it could really work with a man like this. Now they sprouted in her mind again, stretching out their tendrils like some virulent weed.

We've got very good reasons not to have kids.

'You mean *you* have.'

14

He stood up, and for a moment she really thought he'd lost his temper. He gulped down the last of his tea, tapped his watch and jerked a thumb over his shoulder, indicating that he was late, and he had to go. The clock on the wall took sides with Wes – no, he wouldn't make it in for nine o'clock, but given that he co-owned the company he could surely spare a few more minutes for her. It was an arbitrary deadline, another way of avoiding the issue. And meanwhile the hands on the clock kept turning, marking out the seconds, the hours, the years. She heard the scratch of his pencil and turned to see what he'd written.

We'll talk later.

Later. Always later. She wanted to discuss it now. He formed his index finger and thumb into a circle, raised his eyebrows. Okay? The clock told her how unrealistic she was being – you couldn't resolve an issue this big between breakfast and the drive to work. Why had she thought now was an appropriate time? Because it was an emotional decision rather than a rational one. She'd woken from a hazy, half-remembered dream in which her breasts were swollen, her belly gloriously full with new life, and Wes, without recognising the reason, had complimented her on managing to put on some weight. On waking, she was left feeling thin and hollow.

She followed him to the hallway, where he put on his shoes and coat. He gave her only a brief nod before he went out, closing the door behind him. So, no hug this morning.

Through the frosted glass of the front door she saw him dawdle on the step. He wasn't all that late, then. After a few seconds the letterbox opened. A folded sheet of notepaper drifted onto the doormat and his blurred outline diminished as he walked off to the car. She picked up the message and opened it.

I love you.
I love you.
I love you.

It wasn't fair. It wasn't fair because it was true, and she knew it, and it made her feel ungrateful.

She spent the day in a distracted, aimless mood, achieving nothing. It had been this way since she'd been made redundant from Spurling Wilcox, and the feeling would remain until she got another short-term job. There would be a period of interest when everything was fresh, but soon the work would become familiar, and then boring, with only the companionship of her colleagues to keep her going. Either she would leave in search of something new, or be culled through the vagaries of modern business.

She didn't just want a change, she needed it. And perhaps he did too, even if he wouldn't admit it. The problem was that her argument was with his perception of himself, with his inability to see Wes Henning as a good father. How do you go about changing someone's self-image?

There was no more contact from him throughout the day. She began to wonder, with increasing annoyance, whether he thought that he had made amends with that final note. As the sun set, and she realised she was watching her third episode of *Come Dine With Me* in a row, she lost her temper.

She stabbed the TV remote's off button and reached for her phone.

3

IT was the waiting that got to Keiran, the endless fucking waiting. It was probably all part of the test, but still ... His eyes strayed to his mobile, sitting on the dashboard, but he didn't dare reach for it again. Instead he said, 'Tell me what it was like when you did it.'

Grant turned in his seat, one arm braced against the Renault's steering wheel. 'Why do you want to know?' A challenge. Always a challenge.

'Preparation,' Keiran said simply.

The word was a shield. Behind it was the desire to bite a nail or jiggle his legs to relieve some of the nervous energy that had built up. Grant's eyes probed for these signs of weakness, but there would be no deviation from the path, no reason for Grant to report negatively on his performance. Keiran would earn his brother's respect; he would make him proud.

'Okay, then,' Grant said.

Another emotion to hide: surprise. His brother had never told him any of the details before. Perhaps now, on the eve of his Ascension, Grant had decided to honour him with a little more trust. In the weeks that followed – assuming he covered his tracks well enough to avoid the police – Keiran anticipated a slew of answers being delivered by virtue of his new rank. It was about time.

'My target was one of the Surrendered,' Grant said. 'Or at least he was very close to becoming one.'

'What was his name?'

'Ascension first; answers later.'

Keiran swallowed a tut of frustration. He had heard this too often.

'He had always been arrogant,' Grant said. 'He began to say, even in DA meetings, that he thought the Doctrine should be modified.'

There was a pause, and Keiran saw an opportunity – an expectation? – to demonstrate his commitment. So he came straight out with it. 'He might as well have tried to change when the sun rises and sets. You can't make a fact any more factual.' He hoped it wasn't too obvious he was fishing for approval. Better to say it, however clumsily, than to let the opportunity pass.

'We tried to reason with him,' Grant said. 'We gave him every chance, but he kept pushing back. He was trying to convince the

17

other Novices that a modified version of the Doctrine would be better, and Novices can be –' Keiran didn't miss the significant look '– impressionable. We had to act. At this point, I was nearing readiness for Ascension, so it was decided that he would be my target.'

'So it was Brad who gave the order?'

'Yes. It was critical that it was done quickly. Although he hadn't actually left DA, it was clear that he was Surrendered. If he went to the police or the press, things could have got very complicated.'

'How did you deal with him?'

'With my bare hands. How else do you think I did it?'

'No, I mean … when and where? Did he fight back? That sort of thing.'

Grant stared at the windscreen, as if his memories were being projected onto it.

'I went to his house. He let me in, thinking I was there to try and persuade him. I said, "You've been given fair warning. I'm here to kill you." And he said, "Okay, do your worst." Like I said: arrogant.'

'Did he injure you?'

'Not a scratch. It was over in ten seconds. I broke his neck.'

Again Keiran experienced a vivid premonition of the fight to come, of bruised flesh and blood and broken bones. He accepted this. He had rehearsed every eventuality in his mind. There was nothing left to do except the act itself.

He wanted to open the door – the air in the Renault was humid and stale. 'How did you feel about it?'

'That's a shrink's question.'

'I didn't mean it that way.'

'Analysis means paralysis,' Grant said. 'The man of action wins through.' Grant seemed to take a deliberate pleasure in misinterpreting him.

18

'I mean, how did you feel about the achievement?'

'How did I feel?' He tilted his chin upwards, though his eyes were cast down at the dashboard. 'Powerful. Dominant. Ascended.'

No new insight, then. Keiran was disappointed with the words, even though he was impressed, as always, by his brother's iron self-assurance. Since coming back into his life, Grant – the new Grant, the transformed Grant – had not betrayed a hint of doubt in his words, actions or body language. This was what Darwin's Army did to a man. This was why it was worth all the hard work, all the pain.

'Do it right,' Grant said, 'and you might feel the same. But that's not for me to say. It's different for everyone. You *will* be challenged by it.'

'Good,' Keiran said. 'That's what I want.'

He wriggled his hands inside the thin leather gloves. He'd been wearing them on and off all week, softening them up to give maximum flexibility. These stretches of the hands and fingers had become habitual. To demonstrate that the movement was not an indication of nerves, he thumped each fist into the other hand a couple of times.

'You could have got a pair of cheap work gloves,' Grant said. 'They're only a few quid.'

'I didn't want to leave anything behind, like a bit of fabric or rubber residue. You know what these forensics guys are like.'

'What if they can pick up traces of leather?'

'Leather varies. Artificial stuff is more traceable – it has, like, a chemical fingerprint.'

Grant shrugged. 'You're in charge.'

What did he mean by that? Was there an implicit disapproval in the words, or was it a simple statement of fact?

'Yes, I am,' Keiran replied.

Grant dipped his head in a half nod, and Keiran felt a glow of pleasure. His brother's approval was all the more valuable for its

19

rarity.

Was Grant aware of Kieran's admiration? Was he aware how close it strayed into friendship, even brotherly love? Keiran could only hope that as he progressed these feelings would dwindle, that he would eventually become his brother's equal, rather than the follower he knew he was now. It was easy to believe that Grant would always be one step in front, his head-start unassailable, but if Keiran Ascended today it would be the start of a new balance in their relationship – the first step towards purging these emotions, vestigial as an appendix. In the meantime he had to mask them, even if Grant knew he was doing it.

Two weeks ago Keiran had questioned the need for Novices to be accompanied during Ascension, thinking he would appear stronger if he did this alone, but now he saw the wisdom in it. He wasn't there yet. He was still evolving.

'You know it might not even be today,' Grant said.

'Of course. I'm prepared, whatever happens.'

'You may have to make the decision to proceed or abort in an instant.'

'I know.' Why was he saying this?

'And you're ready to make the decision? Like *that*.' Grant snapped his fingers.

'Brother,' he said firmly, 'I am ready.'

It surely wasn't possible that Grant was nervous too. Keiran glanced at his brother, who wore a half smile and appeared on the verge of dozing off. No: it was a provocation – another test of his mental strength, his focus.

He looked out of the windscreen. The sun was already behind the roof of Bailey & Wicklow, Accountants – long shadows reaching out to swallow the cars. Soon the sun would sink further, into the grave of the horizon, its light fading to a feeble strip of orange, and then to the nothingness of night. The car park was emptying now, people desperate to outrun the shadow, to get home to the sorry façade of their lives after another day of servitude. Keiran was too hard on himself sometimes. At least he was not like any of these people, wilfully ignoring the Harsh Truth. None of them had gazed into that abyss and had the strength to let it change them for the better. What, for example, did the people in Bailey & Wicklow think they were going to do after The Collapse? Count Keiran's livestock for him? Broker a trading deal with the neighbouring survivors? There would be no need for deals, perhaps no need even for counting, at least in the short term. The resources would go to the strongest. The bean-counters would end up as slaves, and after so many years of growing fat on good living, the shock of hard labour would probably kill them.

A phrase popped into his mind from another life: 'woe unto you that are rich, for ye have received your consolation'. His mind supplied the verse – Luke 6:24 – without his permission. He grinned at the irony of it. Perhaps not everything his parents believed had been bullshit after all.

Until The Collapse, though, the world was governed by the flow of money and information, and while he loathed this falseness, he had adapted to it. It was information, he supposed – or rather misinformation – that threatened DA. No sane, rational person who read the Doctrine could deny it. And yet they were still an underground organisation, committed to secrecy because society was in denial about the Harsh Truth, despite it being public knowledge for over 150 years. Amazing, mankind's capacity for self-delusion.

He turned his attention back to Henning's office, with its blue plastic J+H logo. It was part of a red brick building consisting of four single-room units – two up, two down – each of which housed a different company. A shared reception area with seating and a toilet was accessible to anyone until the security guard came round to lock up at seven o'clock, but the offices them-

21

selves were badge-locked. The windows were tinted, enough to prevent someone reading text off a screen, for example, but not to conceal the blurry shapes of the people working within. Difficult to tell which of the two people remaining in J+H was Henning, but it didn't matter. Unless he deviated from his usual habit – staying late on a Friday to coddle his precious business – he would soon be the only one left in the building.

Where had Henning got his information about DA? A mole within the organisation was the favourite theory, and plans were in place to root out any traitors. They would clamp down hard, as Grant had. No mercy. Tonight Henning's website would be removed from the internet and Henning himself would be removed from the face of the earth. No amount of martial arts skill would help him – although these things looked impressive in the movies, they were fuck all use in a real fight.

Still, Keiran wanted this all to be over. But no, he shouldn't want it to be over. These were the thoughts of a man lacking confidence, a man unwilling to face the challenge. He should be able to embrace this moment, to accept it, to own it. He wondered whether the other Novices felt this shame, this urge to push things away, but there was no way to ask them without betraying his own feelings. He could not know if he was unique in wrestling with this cowardice. He put his hands together, fingers laced, in his lap.

This heart is mine – I control its beat. This mind is mine – I control its thoughts.

As a distraction, he thought of the reward he had promised himself: a night with Amber. She was expensive, but had every reason to charge so much. He remembered how her hips felt under his hands, the undulations of her spine, her tight-throated moans. He shifted in the passenger seat. No, this was not the best way to calm down.

He allowed himself to pick up his phone, just to check the

time: 17:32. As he looked up from it, he saw their contact leave the building and pass by, not three metres away, unable to see either of them through the Renault's tinted glass. Henning was now the only person left in the building.

Keiran sat up. This was it. It was going to happen. Sixty seconds later, the phone vibrated. He read the message, then passed the phone to Grant.

'So,' Grant said, and placed the phone on the dashboard. 'Say it with me, brother.'

Keiran nodded, eyes fixed on the brick building. They recited the Doctrine together:

Life or death: the only question
Adaptation: the only truth
I will cure myself of the burden of choice, for it tempts me to weakness;
deliver myself from the illness called love, for it makes me dependent.
There is one path and one choice.
I will take it.
The survivor evolves.
The evolver survives.

Grant said, 'The next time we meet, you will have Ascended.'

Keiran kept his mouth shut. Grant hadn't always shown such confidence in him. It had been a hard road, for sure. But now his brother's faith was a fire in his heart. He put on the balaclava, checked his gloves once more, looped his fingers round the door handle. Timing would be critical. He wanted an absolute minimum of things to do when the window of opportunity came, when Henning was between the badge-locked office door and the entrance to the car park.

'Remember to protect your stomach,' Grant said. 'Too often

23

you leave your stomach exposed.'

Keiran didn't need to be told. Hans had exploited this a couple of months ago during a DA meeting, a one-on-one deal in which the vicious little bastard had driven a fist so deep into his guts that Keiran had no choice but to curl up into a ball on the floor. The referee hadn't called a stop to the fight because Keiran's mistake was obvious, and he needed to be punished for it. Hans had piled in gleefully. The bruises healed, but the memory remained. Memory of pain was the best kind of education.

His body hummed like an electricity pylon in the rain, but he still had to wait in an agony of anticipation until 17:57 before his opportunity came.

'There he is,' Grant said.

He had already seen it: the silhouette had stood and was heading for the office door. Keiran felt the pulse of life in his chest – a pounding that shook his whole torso. One of the Unseeing might have described this feeling as fear. Not Keiran. It was his to direct, to control, and in this sense it was not a weakness. He would master it, as he would master the man in the brick building. He made the mistake of looking once more at his brother – a mistake because it was a hesitation, where there should be none.

Grant punched him on the arm and said, 'Now – go!'

Keiran filled his lungs to capacity and opened the car door.

4

AT half past four Wes decided a takeaway would be a good idea, maybe that new Thai place on Woodland Road. For the whole day he had found it impossible to ignore the issue of Alex for more than half an hour. As soon as he turned his focus away from his screen or Tom or Marcus, there it was, in the corner of his mind, squalling for attention. He would drop by Sainsbury's and get her a bunch of flowers too. Whatever the outcome of tonight's tête-à-tête, it was important to start out with the right kind of statement.

This positive frame of mind was soured when he tried to text her about the takeaway. The phone had no signal, something he had never experienced in the office before. After all the problems with syncing his calendar and trying to roll back dodgy software updates, he really should have bought a different phone.

He was just taking his earphones out when Tom said, 'Cup of tea, chaps?'

Wes nodded. When Marcus didn't respond, Tom said, 'Oi, cloth-ears!'

'Uh?' Marcus said.

'Tea?'

'Oh, yeah, cool.'

'Don't tell me you still can't hear properly.'

Wes gave a questioning frown and Tom elaborated: 'Ah, you didn't hear about our debauched young colleague's gig last night, did you?'

Wes shook his head. Marcus was only five years younger than them, but he sometimes seemed to be from a different generation entirely.

'Tom has never heard of battlecore,' Marcus said.

Wes shook his head blankly. Neither had he.

Marcus was blessed with the wide eyes of a man used to expressing astonishment. 'Both of you? For real?'

'Go on,' Tom prompted, 'tell him.'

'It's a subgenre of metal where the music is like the sound of war. Drums like machine guns, guitars like explosions, yeah?'

'And tell him what the singer does.'

'Gives orders, screams,' Marcus said, as if this were the most obvious thing in the world. 'If the band's good – and Tet Offensive are seriously good – you're, like, shellshocked by the end.'

'It's just occurred to me,' Tom said. 'Is this something your "make me cool" company told you to do?'

Marcus tutted. 'I've told you before, it's a lifestyle and brand consultancy service.'

'And I've told you before that you can't afford to pay a company thirty quid a month to tell you what your tastes are.'

'Increase my salary, then.'

Wes grinned at this display of nerve and Tom said, 'Not a convincing argument for a pay rise.'

Wes had established a rule concerning Marcus: no blogging about him. Which was a shame – there was enough material there to keep *In Absurdia* going for months. But for all his odd behaviour, Wes didn't regret their first, and so far only, hire. They threw work at him and it got done. Marcus was also the only person they interviewed who asked about Wes's speechlessness in an unembarrassed way, showing genuine interest as Wes explained that he could just about manage the voiceless plosives and fricatives, but preferred not to; that gestures and writing were his preferred means of communication; that, no, he didn't really have any use for sign language.

Returning to his phone problem, Wes found a pen under the drifts of paper that persistently covered his desk, and wrote:

Are you seeing this – no phone signal?

He demonstrated the problem to them. Tom had the same model and was on the same network, but when he phoned Marcus' mobile as a test, he got through without a problem.

'Weird,' Tom said, and handed his phone over. 'Here, use mine.'

Wes waved the idea away. It seemed simpler to skip the takeaway and just opt for the flowers.

*

Tom left on the dot of five o'clock. 'Need to be ready for my first date with Ursula.'

Wes was on his phone at the time, double checking the layout of a web page on a smaller screen. He switched to the notepad app.

What happened to Becky?

'Becky? That was over weeks ago.'

Weeks?

'Days, then.'

You are a bad man.

Tom flashed his Han Solo smile. 'Perhaps Ursula will be the one to reform me.' He shrugged on his coat. 'Wish me luck.'

Marcus stayed another half hour before he too was on his way out. 'See you Monday.'

Wes raised his hand in a wave, checked the time – 17:32 – and went back to work. Or at least he tried. Normally he found a certain satisfaction in putting the business to bed on a Friday evening, but today was different. Now that his colleagues had gone he felt strangely distracted.

At 17:51 he turned away from his screen with a sigh. The world outside was a deep blue, dark enough that the windows were more reflective than transparent, expanding their office into the car park and giving the appearance of three ghostly extra desks. A premonition? If Alex got her way, and they had kids, there would be no choice – J+H would have to expand. Tom had brought up the idea before, suggesting they could go after the larger, more lucrative corporate contracts. As a businessman it was what Wes should have wanted, but he'd never been happy with the idea that things had to grow. You didn't have to look far to find the wreckage of businesses punctured by ambition. And all the extra profit would be ploughed into bringing up children. It was a selfish thought. He shouldn't resent that kind of expenditure, but … there it was. And if Alex did go back to work, her income would be neatly absorbed by childcare. It would be a zero sum game.

But that wasn't the only problem. In an office twice the size, dealing with people more difficult and less industrious than Marcus, how would he cajole them into a decent day's work? The fact was, management was never going to suit him. Without the ability to speak to his employees he could never have any real authority. So, how would this work out? Tom would be in charge and Wes would be his underling? But right from the beginning they'd agreed it would be an equal partnership. That was the whole idea. And then he would go home to a wife so distracted by their baby that she would no longer have time for him. He saw how it worked with his sister's kids – it was barely possible for anyone to get in a whole sentence without interruption. In a competition between his hastily scrawled notes and a child's insistent wailing, he would always be sidelined.

His thoughts looped and circled – a fly returning to butt its head against the same window, over and over again.

17:57.

He got up and headed for the door, past the table in the corner with the coffee maker and teapot, the whiteboard with its multicoloured splurge of brainstorms and page layouts and in-jokes. He felt a fondness for these otherwise mundane objects. After all the years of struggle, just as he was finding some comfort and stability in his life … She didn't know what she was asking of him.

He left the J+H office, turned left past the visitor's sofa and headed for the toilet. All the other offices were dark now. Everyone had gone home or was off out for a drink down the pub to mark the start of the weekend – a ritual he'd never much cared for. As a convenience for wheelchair users the toilet door wasn't spring-loaded, and with no-one else in the building Wes didn't bother to close and lock it, he just pulled it to. He unzipped his flies. And that was as far as he got. Although he heard nothing, he felt a change in air pressure, as if someone had just opened the main door. Someone returning to the office for something they'd left behind? He hesitated, stranded between continuing regardless and locking the door after all. The sliver of light falling across the cistern expanded. He turned round and the toilet door was wide open, framing a man dressed entirely in black and wearing a balaclava.

He had come from the ghost world with the three extra desks, that was his first thought. No, it was one of his Wing Chun partners, playing a practical joke. But he was the wrong build – too much upper body strength. A burglar? But then why not wait until all the lights in the building were off? Wes spread his hands and frowned, going for a look of 'do you bloody well mind?' The man thumped one gloved fist into the other, and Wes's hands assumed a position of readiness through sheer habit – one in front of the other, protecting his centreline. The man nodded and stepped forwards.

The first punch came in: a jab to test his defence. Wes's hand made contact at the wrist, ready to deflect the blow, but the fist was immediately withdrawn. The man's stance didn't give away his fighting style, but from the couple of steps he'd taken it was clear that he was agile and pumped up. His movements lacked discipline, yet his arm positioning was good, ready to cover his stomach and face. Probably a street fighter – someone with experience, but without any of the good conduct instilled as part of formal training.

'I'm going to kill you.' The voice was a monotone. 'Do you understand that?'

Wes shook his head rapidly. He didn't understand shit. The man punched again without any hint of telegraphing. Wes's left arm shot out in taan sau and he instinctively stepped forwards and to one side to get past the blow, ready to step back in for the counterstrike. But the door frame halted him mid-manoeuvre, and the gloved fist skimmed his cheekbone. His opponent leaned to the side and Wes's palm passed millimetres from his head. Wes closed his fingers, trying to get a grip on the neck, but all he got was the balaclava. He withdrew his hand, pulling the headgear clean off. The man's head sprang back. Wes had never seen him before. His face was round, the skin slightly blotchy, hair light brown and shaved down to a grade one or two. At this distance Wes could see every pore, the beginning of stubble, the blue radial fibres of the iris. The eyes stared with a wild determination.

Wes made a cardinal error: he stepped backwards. He heard his sifu's disappointed yell: 'Always, always go forwards!' But what could he do? The door frame would channel him straight onto his opponent's fists. The retreat gave him no breathing space: his attacker closed the distance immediately.

I can't die here, he thought wildly. *I haven't finished my argument with Alex.*

Wes found himself stepping backwards again. The edge of the toilet seat caught him on the calves, forcing him to sit down heavily on the bowl. Another punch came in without delay – a big, jaw-breaking roundhouse. His left arm came up in a corkscrew defence that deflected the blow just past his nose. In his eagerness to land a good, hard punch, the man had overcommitted. Wes hooked the arm with his other hand and pulled hard to the side, adding to the man's momentum, making his body twist and topple backwards until he was sitting on Wes's lap. He caught a whiff of sweat and cheap deodorant.

Wes snaked his left hand underneath the man's armpit, striking upwards with his palm to the chin. The neck snapped back, accompanied by a gulping sound. Wes held it there to increase his opponent's sense of disorientation. An elbow came back hard at his ribs, fingers reached over for his eyes, but they only found a handful of hair to wrench. The man twisted his head to one side, releasing himself from Wes's grip and tried to stand. Wes hooked his left hand over one shoulder and pulled him back to sitting. With his right hand he took the mechanical pencil from his top pocket – the sturdy metal Staedtler Alex had bought him for his last birthday. Fingers gripping the knurled barrel, thumb over the cap, he stabbed the steel tip into the front of his assailant's rib-cage twice in rapid succession. The scream bounced off the tiled walls, loud enough to hurt his ears.

Flailing arms knocked the pencil from Wes's grasp and the man bent over in pain. Wes drew back both fists as far as he could, elbows skimming the cistern until they hit the wall behind, and punched him in the kidneys. A tortured cough erupted from him, desperate and pathetic. Well, tough; you don't start what you can't finish.

Wes pushed at his attacker's buttocks, sending him sprawling onto the floor, and launched himself off the toilet, trampling and grabbing for the door. He felt a hand on his leg, and couldn't open the door without hitting the man's arms and head, so he did just that, keeping him down with one foot and bracing an arm against the wall while he pulled the door repeatedly into his skull. Bang, bang, bang. The hand let go. The crack in the door widened and Wes launched himself through, out into the reception and heading for the doors and into the cold air and across the car park.

His breath fogged as the air burst from his lungs. There was a car between him and his Mini: a blue hatchback with tinted windows. The driver's door opened and another man in a balaclava got out. Fuck – there were two of them. He veered off to the left, between the accountants and the charity for cystic fibrosis, leaped the ditch and vaulted the fence bordering the edge of the business park. Turning at right angles and sprinting along the pavement parallel to the dual carriageway, he crossed right in front of a van – a deliberate manoeuvre to slow down anyone who was following. He cut it very fine. The van screeched to a halt in front of him, its bonnet dipping and the back wheels skewing to one side in a cloud of vaporised rubber. Behind the windscreen, the driver's eyes and mouth were wide. Wes jumped the railing on the central reservation and crossed the other side of the road.

'What the hell are you doing?' the driver yelled through his open window. 'You're gonna kill yourself!'

Wes looked back. No-one seemed to be following, but 'seemed' wasn't nearly comforting enough. He was heading instinctively towards home, but it was on the far side of town. They could easily catch him in the car. They might even have two vehicles at their disposal.

He needed a sanctuary, somewhere they couldn't follow him. The police station near the town centre seemed his best option. Yes. If he could make it there he would be safe.

5

KEIRAN had been lying for several indulgent seconds, the tiles cold and hard against his face, when he heard the low thump of the outer door opening. Footsteps on the reception carpet, increasing in volume. He levered himself up into a crouch, curling over his punctured chest, and by the time the toilet door was open he had stood fully, doing his best to force aside the sensations of pain and the even more wounding sting of defeat.

He raised his fists in a show of readiness. As suspected, it was Grant who stood in the doorway, not Henning. Grant's mouth opened, as if he were about to say something but thought better of it. His face hardened, and Keiran lowered his arms. After one humiliation, there would now be another.

'What happened?' Grant said.

Keiran felt something in his chest that was nothing to do with the two stab wounds – a lump, a knot. He tried to swallow it down. Grant had been right: the fight had been different, fundamentally more chaotic than any of his bouts at DA. Those matches had not seemed like practice at the time, but that's exactly what they were now revealed to be.

'Tell me what happened.'

'I –' He coughed, and fresh fire blossomed in his kidneys.

It wasn't the pain that angered him – pain was simply a test, a lesson – it was what the pain represented: evidence of Henning's superiority over him.

'It wasn't a fair fight. He had a weapon.'

'That's always a possibility you face.'

'What was I supposed to do?'

'Disarm him.'

Would he still be saying this if *he* had been the one facing Henning? But no. Grant was right – there was no excuse. It was ironic: if Henning had been holding a knife or a baseball bat, Keiran's course of action would have been clearer. He had practised knife defence, and would not have blundered in with an overcommitted punch in the hope of ending things as soon as possible.

He was glad Henning hadn't had a knife.

'What did he use?' Grant said.

Keiran's gaze darted towards the bloodied metal implement lying on the tiles. A pencil. A fucking mechanical pencil. He waited for Grant's snort of contempt, but it didn't come. Sometimes his brother did show a little mercy.

'He was stronger than you thought, then?'

'This won't happen a second time.'

'But he was stronger than you thought,' Grant said.

He wouldn't let it go until Keiran accepted the blunt truth of it. 'Yes.'

'So we move to plan B.'

'I wanted the clean kill.'

'I know.'

'I wanted it to be perfect.'

'I know. So we move to plan B. This is still in your control. This is why we prepared everything so thoroughly.'

'But it wasn't supposed to be like this! I –'

'There is one path and one choice.'

Keiran clenched his teeth, hard. As long as he clenched his teeth he couldn't come out with any more bullshit whining. He was straying, allowing emotion to derail him. His feelings were no longer serving him – he was serving them. Unacceptable.

'Listen,' Grant said slowly. 'These are the facts.'

Just nod. Listen to your brother and nod.

'He didn't kill you. You've learned something about how he fights. If he's gone to his house, we can follow him there. If he's gone to the police station they won't be keen to help him after Sean and Jamal's good work. We can get to him through his wife or his best friend. These are the facts. This isn't even close to being over. More opportunities will follow.'

Keiran saw again the wisdom of his brother, the clarity, the certainty. When he spoke again, he was calmer. 'I tried for the clean kill.'

'And you failed.'

He felt a muscle near his eye twitch. 'I failed.'

'So what do you do now?'

'Learn, adapt, plan for success.'

'And if you fail again?'

'Learn, adapt, plan for success.'

Grant nodded. 'You see? In this moment, this very moment, you have taken another step towards Ascension.'

He could have hugged his brother. He bent his head to conceal any evidence of this disgusting surge of gratitude. Then, knowing even this action would make him look weak, he made a pretence of examining his chest wound. Two glistening trails crept down the sweater towards his navel. Grant was right to berate him, and right to praise him. Impatience had cost him the kill, but he was still standing, still strong. Against the black of his sweater, his blood was also black. Dragon's blood. Demon's blood.

'Could have been a lot worse,' Grant said.

'Yeah.'

Grant used some toilet paper to wipe the blood off the mechanical pencil and the floor tiles, then flushed the red wad down the toilet. After confirming there were no other signs of the struggle, he pocketed the pencil. It gave Keiran time to bring his thoughts to heel, so that when his brother turned to him and said, 'So?' he was ready to act rationally once more.

'Back to the car,' Keiran said.

They put their balaclavas back on and Keiran made sure he was the first to stride out of the building. Grant unlocked the Renault and Keiran lowered himself into the passenger seat, clutching the top of the door frame with one hand while he cradled his ribs with the other.

'We need to … get this cleaned up,' he said, indicating his chest.

Grant turned. 'We should get away from here first.'

'Yes, that's what I meant – find a quiet place.'

Grant drove them out of the business park, onto the B3023, then off into anonymous residential streets east of the town centre. Keiran noticed him checking his mirrors.

'Anyone?'

'No. It's Friday night. They're all down the pub, destroying their ability to function.'

He parked the car on the pavement outside a Victorian terrace and killed the engine.

'Right. Let's see what he's managed to do to you.'

Keiran grunted as he took his sweater and T-shirt off, trying to ignore the friction of the fabric as it dragged across the puncture wounds. Grant opened the first aid kit.

'It hurts?'

'Yeah.' No point denying it.

'Enough for us to abort?'

'Not a chance!'

He caught a faint smile on Grant's lips.

'It's not serious,' Grant said, probing at the ribs. 'No broken bones.'

He cleaned up the blood, then taped gauze over the holes. Keiran managed not to make any more noise, but he couldn't stop his body tensing whenever Grant fingers got near the source of pain.

'I'm going to bandage this to keep the dressing in place and stop any spots of blood leaking through.'

Keiran leaned forward so that Grant could wind the strip of fabric round his chest, just under the arms. It brought back a memory, of his mother bandaging his chest in the same way after … was it a football injury? It was so hazy – another time, another life, before her grief and the influence of the church had swept all rational thought from her mind, back in the days when she was still capable of showing some compassion towards her sons.

But this was different. This was dealing with damaged tissue, nothing more. Why did his mother have to pop into his head at a time like this? What use was it to him? To drive a stake through the heart of this sentimentality, he gave his brother another reason to be angry with him.

'The balaclava came off,' he said.

'What?' Grant stopped tying the bandage.

'He tore it off. I didn't … there was no chance to –'

'So he saw your face?'

'Yes.'

'Shit,' Grant said. 'That makes things more difficult.'

'I'm sorry.'

36

Grant's head whipped up. 'What?'

'I meant –'

'Don't you dare say that. Make it right or get out of the game, but don't fucking apologise to me.'

Keiran lifted his chin. 'I'll make it right.'

Grant stared at him, eyes dark except for two tiny points of light where a nearby street light was reflected. 'Good,' he said finally. 'Don't bloody forget it.'

'I'm still learning,' Keiran said by way of excuse. 'I'll get there.'

Grant finished another circuit of Keiran's chest and fastened the bandage with a couple of safety pins.

'I think your pride is hurt more than your chest. Both will heal. Any other injuries?'

'He pulled the door into my head.'

Grant felt his skull under the stubble of hair. 'There's a lump. No bleeding.'

'He punched me in the kidneys, too.'

'How the fuck did you allow him to do that?'

Keiran opened his mouth to offer an explanation, then closed it again. Offering himself up for constructive criticism was all well and good, but admitting that he'd ended up sitting on his opponent's lap? He said nothing.

'You might be pissing blood later,' said Grant.

Keiran winced.

'Serves you right. When I said protect your stomach, I didn't mean turn your back and let him have a go at that instead. Lean forwards.'

Keiran did so. Tilting his face to one side while Grant prodded at his back, he saw a telegraph pole at the end of the road, a black T against a purple-grey sky. A bunch of crows sat on it – a murder of crows, that was the word. They shuffled, looking down disdainfully from their perch, knowing they were safely beyond reach. No – *thinking* they were beyond reach. Cut down the telegraph pole and the crows will flee in panic. A shotgun would show them the error of their arrogance. New ways of thinking. This is what he had to do with Henning – find another way, a better way.

'Kidneys don't seem too bad,' Grant said.

Keiran leaned back into the seat. 'So. Plan B.'

'You're ready?'

'I am.'

Without warning, Grant flicked his fingers into Keiran's chest, right over the wound he had just dressed. If he didn't know his brother so well, Keiran might have let out a yelp of pain. Instead he looked straight ahead, tensing all of the muscles in his torso while he waited for the flare of pain to subside.

'Yeah,' Grant said. 'You're ready.'

6

WES burst from the police station, striking the door hard as if it – rather than Selvidge or Bennett – had offended him. Tossers, the lot of them. His momentum carried him into the pedestrianised High Street, into the coloured-light chaos and heaving hedonism of Strathurst on a Friday night. People were clustered round the pubs and bars, and they were all shouting at each other. It was all so raucous and deafening and unnecessary, such an excessive way to celebrate a mere two days of freedom from work. Some of them, it seemed, had already been going for hours: half a dozen lads sloshed out of the doors of the Crown in front of him, slewing and yawing and pitching while somehow managing to stay upright. He saw close-cropped hair and found it impossible not to jerk backwards.

'Chill, mate,' one of them slurred affably and clapped him on the shoulder.

They broke round him and reformed on the other side, a multi-celled organism oozing its way across the precinct to the next pub. 'Chill' was exactly right – Wes had left the office wearing nothing warmer than a T-shirt. But he could not in any way afford to be relaxed; he should be alert to the point of paranoia. He should be checking every passer-by and assessing their level of threat. He should be watching doorways and the edges of buildings. The slightest lapse of concentration and they could be on him.

The police were out here too, he noticed – a pair at either end of the High Street, watching for trouble. Wes had offered it to them on a plate, but no, apparently they had to find it for themselves.

He shouldn't be here at all, but somewhere dark, hidden, alone. He found himself heading homewards again, through instinct rather than any kind of plan. He saw in his mind's eye a cascade of dark hair; a ready smile; eyes alive with intelligence, enquiry, compassion. Of course, he was doing the only thing that made any kind of sense – he was going back to Alex.

He would write a simple note, something along the lines of:
We're in danger. We MUST leave the house NOW.

He would grab the keys to her Citroën, usher her into it, and drive out of Strathurst. But where would they go? Tom's house in Alton? His parents' down in Portsmouth? How far would be far enough? And if they decided to hunt him down, would he not be endangering the people he loved? Better: once he and Alex were sure they weren't being followed they would park in a lay-by on some country road and figure out where to go, what to do. Two heads were better than one, especially if one of those heads was not fizzing with adrenaline. He needed her. He needed the sharpness of her mind.

At the end of Strathurst's main drag, he turned right and the Friday night crowd thinned. He jogged through the subway under the roundabout where the two dual carriageways met, then turned left onto a quieter street just before the fire station. He decided to cut through the playing fields rather than take a winding route through the residential roads. A car couldn't get to him here. The park was locked at night, but that had never stopped cider-fueled adolescents using it as the venue for a late night gathering – perhaps the authorities shouldn't have installed a gate with so many convenient footholds. But there were no teenagers here now; no-one at all. The grass squelched underfoot after the rain of the last few days, but the darkness and broad field of view were unquestionably an improvement over the town centre. They calmed him, and the openness of the park gave his mind the space it needed to function properly.

His thoughts turned back to his blog as the only plausible reason for all this to have happened. It was the article in which a kid claimed that remembering things was obsolete now the internet existed. Or the one about the problems Wes had experienced updating the software on his phone, much to the howling from the brand's fanboys. Or perhaps the one about the woman who claimed that winning the National Lottery had ruined her life and was therefore suing them ... for money. No, no and no. Who in their right mind could justify murder over something he had written? And so the only conclusion was that he was dealing with someone not in their right mind. It was, in a strange way, the most comforting explanation he'd come up with yet. There was no need to rationalise the irrational.

Mentions in places as diverse as *The Independent*, *The Telegraph* and *The Huffington Post* had brought increasing numbers of visitors to his blog. Now, for the first time, he wondered whether this was such a good thing; whether a smaller site might have passed under the radar of the furiously offended, the mentally unbalanced.

Once he reached the far corner of the field, by the cluster of old oaks, he finally had the opportunity to relieve the urgent pressure on his bladder. Why hadn't he gone in the police station? Reaching down to unzip his flies, he discovered they were already undone – he had never zipped up after the assault. Maybe *that* was why the police hadn't taken him seriously.

Letting go was a problem. He looked over one shoulder, then the other, wondering why this was taking so long. He had read somewhere about snipers shooting their enemy while they were relieving themselves, so that everyone else in the platoon was afraid of going to the toilet. After a couple of fruitless minutes trying to relax, he resorted to thumping himself just below the navel until at last his urine began to hiss into the grass. When he was done he zipped up with a defiant tug. Screw them, whoever they were – if he wanted to take a piss, he would take a goddamned piss.

He quickened his pace now he was nearing home, but on turning into his road, he jerked to a halt and stepped back behind the brick wall of the first house. In the space on the drive where his Mini should have been was the blue hatchback with the tinted windows. It should have occurred to him that they might do this. Shit. Even now he wasn't thinking straight. They still wanted him, and were prepared to get to him through Alex. Were they interrogating her right now? Kidnapping her? In a night prickled with uncertainty and confusion, Wes experienced his first truly unambiguous thought: if they laid a finger on his wife, he would kill every last one of them.

He broke cover and approached the house. The kitchen blind was down. The frosted glass of the front door and toilet windows gave no visibility, either in or out. That left only the bedroom as a potential problem, but he would soon be close enough to be out of view. Hearing a car door open, he thought for one horrified moment they were still inside the vehicle. He was ready to turn and run, but the car remained motionless. He refocussed on Mr Stevens at number 17, levering himself out of his BMW. He

41

was in his eighties and partially deaf, but there was nothing wrong with his eyesight – as he stood, he spotted Wes immediately.

'Hello, Wes!' he bellowed. 'How are you? Glad the weekend's started, I reckon.'

Wes put a finger to his lips and shook his head vigorously. He glanced up at the bedroom window. Still empty, for now.

'What's that?' Stevens said.

Wes put his hand in front of his groin and mimed urinating, then crossed his legs and bounced up and down with a grimace of discomfort, just in case Stevens didn't get the message.

'Ah!' the old man said, tapping the side of his nose. 'If nature calls, one must answer. I'll leave you to it, then. See you later!'

Stevens padded towards his front door, fumbling for his keys. Wes turned his attention back to his own house, skirting the car on the drive and noting every detail he could without actually stopping: Renault Mégane, dark blue, HL64JCN.

With no way to see into the kitchen or hallway, he needed to head round the back and try the lounge. Alex had an annoying habit of not drawing the lounge curtains fully once it got dark. He had developed a gesture to encourage her to do it properly: pinched fingers drawn together, accompanied by a frown. Hopefully she hadn't taken any notice of him. He had oiled the wrought iron gate a couple of months ago, and was able to lift the latch and slip through without making a noise. He considered shutting it behind him, but decided that quick access to the front of the house would give him more options. Rounding the corner, he could just make out voices, muffled and wordless, but enough for him to recognise calm conversation, not an argument or a struggle. And another reassurance: a slice of light from the patio doors where the curtains failed to meet. That's my girl.

As long as he stayed at the back of the garden, near the flower bed, it should be too dark for anyone in the lounge to see him.

He moved slowly sideways until the curtains framed two men sitting on his sofa. He recognised the nearest one as his attacker, dressed in a suit now for some reason, but definitely the same man. The other one was taller, but looked similar, as if they'd been pressed from the same mould. Possibly he was the one who had emerged from the Renault when Wes escaped from J+H.

The taller one was pocketing his mobile phone while talking to someone on the opposite side of the room. Wes crabbed across the lawn and Alex came into view. She didn't look terrified by her guests, not even intimidated. In fact, the more he watched her, the stranger the situation seemed. His wife, normally so effusive and open, looked every bit as serious as the two men. It was her interview face, her business meeting face. She nodded and stood, meeting the taller man in the centre of the room. He passed her something whitish and flat – possibly a business card or folded banknotes; it was impossible to tell – and they shook hands firmly. Alex brought her other hand in to cover his. It was what she did when she didn't feel enough connection to hug a person, but still wanted to radiate warmth and sincerity.

Wes felt a plummeting in his chest, as if a cavity had opened up and his heart had dropped six inches. He retreated to the far corner of the garden, near the bamboo tripod for the runner beans, where it was darkest. *Alex, Alex, what are you doing?* Framed by the edges of the curtains, the two men headed back through the lounge towards the front door, followed by his wife. And that was where Wes's unease was supplanted by a new and more urgent fear: they might notice that the gate was now open; they might want to have a look round the rest of the premises. It was the office loo all over again – a dead-end, a trap.

From the other side of the house, he heard the front door opening.

BOOKS on astronomy and the Pre-Raphaelites. A novel by Carlos Ruiz Zafón. An iPad, displaying a web browser with a dozen open tabs. A copy of *The Guardian*. The TV remote control. Next to it, an untouched cup of tea, slowly cooling. Alex had figured out what Wes was doing. He was staying late tonight to avoid the discussion. He'd made a deliberate decision to eke out the work at the office, and when he came home he'd say he was too tired to talk.

Her phone call earlier with Joanne had been an attempt to alleviate some of her frustration, but it had ended far too quickly. Once one of the twins started acting up, the other soon followed and any chance of conversation flew out of the window. She had texted Wes, but there had been no reply. Either he had decided to ignore her, or he'd switched his phone off for a bit of peace and quiet. It was the sort of obstinate silence that drove her nuts. It had taken her a long time before she felt comfortable giving him an earful over using his speechlessness like this, but when he came through that door that's exactly what she would do. For a moment a fantasy overtook her: of him returning home with some eloquent written apology which he expected to win her over, and her saying: 'Oh, don't worry about that. I got someone else to pop a bun in the oven. It's all sorted now.'

She would never say such a thing. Of course she wouldn't. It was his cynicism infecting her, and that was exactly the sort of thing she had to resist.

It was half past seven before the doorbell rang – a full hour after he was usually home. She yanked the door open to two men with dark suits and very short hair. Her indignation slipped from her fingers and shattered. Oh, God. He'd died in a car crash, was on his way to hospital after a sudden collapse, had been stabbed while stopping off at the newsagents by someone trying to empty the till. All of these thoughts occurred to her in the time between the door swinging to the end of its arc and the shorter of the two men beginning to speak.

'Mrs Henning?'

Guilt struck her like a blast of wind blowing in through the doorway. All these mean-spirited thoughts about her husband and he could already be lying on a slab in the hospital mortuary.

'Can we come in?'

Textbook. Absolutely textbook.

'Yes, of course,' she found herself saying.

The shorter one flashed his badge. 'We're from MI5. I'm Agent Kavanagh. This is Agent Groves.'

They moved like funeral directors – slow, practised movements; nothing abrupt. They had done this a thousand times before, and had learned not to get emotionally involved.

'Would you like a – a – a cup of tea or coffee or something?' she said.

'No. Thank you.'

'Or … we have other things.' *We*. 'If there's anything else you want. Fruit juice, lemonade, cocoa?'

Cocoa? What the hell was she saying? She was babbling, and immediately understood why: for every moment she delayed, there was still hope that something terrible hadn't happened. Until they told her, it wouldn't really be true.

'No, that will be fine, Mrs Henning. Could we …?' Kavanagh gestured towards the lounge, though his gaze wandered between the kitchen, the bathroom and the stairs as he said it.

Alex nodded, ushering them through and taking the chair near the TV while they perched on the edge of the sofa, stiff, business-like, utterly unrelaxed. Kavanagh, she noticed, had lowered himself onto the sofa like a much older man.

'It's about your husband,' he said. 'We'd like to speak to him.'

This last sentence elicited such a tingling ecstasy of hope that for a moment Alex was unable to say anything.

'Your husband, Mrs Henning?' he prompted.

'He – he's not here at the moment. I, uh … I thought you were going to tell me that something had happened to him.'

Kavanagh glanced towards Groves, just for a fraction of a second. 'No.'

'Well, that's a relief.' She let out a muted laugh, quickly stifled. 'So, what's this about, if you don't mind me asking?'

'I'm afraid we can't tell you.'

'Why not?'

'It's a matter of national security.'

'National security?' she parroted. 'Are you saying you think he's done something illegal?'

'We're not at liberty to discuss the details of the case.'

The only thing that came to mind was the graffiti during his college years. Wes had assured her it was just the fallout from a difficult adolescence – a consequence of frustrated self-expression, and not the habits of a career criminal. After the initial shock, she had decided that dating a man with a slightly colourful past was not without its attractions. As long as it didn't happen again. But it wasn't a matter that required the intervention of the intelligence agencies. Which meant there was something worse, something she didn't know about.

'But he wouldn't …' she said. 'Surely the police would have contacted us if there was anything …'

'This is above the police. Involving them would only complicate matters.'

Above the police? And they couldn't tell her anything about it? But if Wes was innocent – if he just had access to sensitive information, or a lead they wanted to follow – surely they would offer her some kind of reassurance. She expected them to ask where her husband was now. It was the obvious next question, and yet they remained silent, which meant they had probably

46

already been to the office and Wes wasn't there. He must have stopped off on his way home for something, and would be walking through the door at any moment. Either that, or he was trying to avoid them. Having wanted Wes to come home for hours, now she fervently hoped he would stay away, at least until these two were gone. She was assuming, of course, that they would go. They might insist on setting up camp until he arrived.

They sat and stared at her, oblivious to any concept of social awkwardness. The only thing that spoiled the perfection of their posture was Kavanagh's tilted head. She knew, from the massage course she'd done a couple of years ago, that this was probably a cricked neck or muscle imbalance. She imagined working her fingers into his neck – not without a shudder – and finding that the problem was a misalignment of metal plates, something that required not a healing touch but a screwdriver.

Kavanagh's eyes wandered to the A4-sized box on the coffee table into which she threw Wes's various scribblings: suggestions about what to do on Saturday evening, a snarky comment about someone on the TV, a discussion about the best combinations of ice cream flavours. All these conversations were one-sided, Wes's parts recorded in his muscular but graceful handwriting, while her spoken replies had already retreated into the past, prey to fickle memory. Had it been pistachio and hazelnut or pistachio and mint choc chip? The idea of the box was to keep the coffee table neat. The idea was that it would be emptied frequently. It was close to overflowing.

Kavanagh picked up Wes's last note, the one he had posted through the front door this morning, and turned it to read the words:

I love you.
I love you.
I love you.

He tossed it back into the box and Alex felt a fundamental shift in her mind. Who did these people think they were, barging into their lives like this? It was this simple movement of his fingers, more than anything else, that put the idea into her head – maybe they weren't who they claimed. And now the possibility was broached, other things began to make sense: their failure to reassure her, the long silences that a professional would know how to fill. They were intruders in her home. Now she looked at them again, they seemed a bit rough for MI5. Their identical buzz cuts made them look more like military than secret service. How easy was it to fake an MI5 badge? It was irrelevant: she didn't know what an MI5 badge looked like. In the whoosh of terror that accompanied their appearance, they could have flashed her a Pets at Home loyalty card and she wouldn't have questioned it. No matter how official these men claimed to be, she was not going to trust them over her own husband. Since Wes wasn't here to defend himself, she would do it for him.

'If you think my husband has done something wrong, I can assure you you're mistaken. He's a law-abiding and peaceful man. He wouldn't be mixed up in anything –'

'Peaceful?' Kavanagh interrupted, his voice rising. 'Your husband has got himself mixed up in something –'

Groves put his hand on Kavanagh's arm and muttered his first words since entering the house: 'There is one path and one choice.'

Kavanagh was silenced instantly, although his lips continued to move against each other. The reality of the situation struck her: these men were physically strong, they outnumbered her, they were in her house. Perhaps it wasn't Wes that was facing the most immediate danger after all. Would the neighbours hear a shout for help? Mr Stevens was nearly deaf, and Sharon was probably out toasting the weekend with her mates and half a case of prosecco. Alex tried to remain still and emotionless, containing the pressure that was building up in her throat, pushing at the roof of her mouth.

Groves took his mobile phone out, glanced at it, put it away. He stood, looking down at his colleague, and said, 'We have to go.' It was clear now that Groves, not Kavanagh, was the one in charge.

Kavanagh rose slowly, pushing air out noisily through his nostrils. Thank God – it was coming to an end.

'If you see your husband,' Groves said, handing her a business card, 'call us. It's very important.'

What did he mean 'if'? He meant 'when', surely. She ignored the signals of panic from her brain. Her face was, she hoped, a mask. She took the card, careful not to make contact with his fingers. But he reached across with his other hand to shake, and she made the split-second decision to grasp it. His grip was firm – too firm for shaking hands with a woman. She kept her jaw clamped shut. To convince him of her honesty she brought her other hand into the shake, making it as solid as possible, squashing the business card against the back of his hand. As she did so, the sleeve of his suit rode up and she noticed a tiny tattoo on the inside of his left wrist: three lines, making up three sides of a rectangle:

⊏

'I'm sure this is all a misunderstanding,' she said. 'We'll both cooperate fully to get things resolved.'

She was an actress delivering her lines. She forced herself to look him straight in the eyes, into that blankness, that mannequin stare. After a few seconds he nodded.

She saw them out. Their car was on the drive – another intrusion – and she memorised its details: a blue Renault, registration HL64JCN. Closing the front door gently behind them, she sat down on the hall carpet and the trembling started.

49

8

AFTER a two step run-up, Wes planted both hands on one of the concrete posts bordering his garden and attempted to vault the fence panel. The effortless arc of a high jumper, that's what he was aiming for. But the wet soil of the flower border sank underfoot and what he achieved instead was a cat-like scramble, the fence panel acting like the skin of a drum as his foot struck it. Managing to get a leg on top, he levered himself over and dropped. He fell straight into a bush and curled defensively, but it was softer than he expected. A billow of scent announced it as rosemary.

If they'd heard this racket they might look over the fence. He disentangled himself from the bush and carried on down his neighbour's garden. Their curtains were pulled tight, allowing him to slip unnoticed past the house and onto the street – a quiet cul-de-sac. Unless the two skinheads were prepared to go door-to-door through the neighbourhood, they would have no reason to come here. He waited for the telltale clunk of his front door shutting or the sound of someone else scaling the fence, but neither came. It was difficult to make out sounds at this distance; there was more background noise: a dog barking incessantly, a couple arguing in a nearby street, traffic. After a few seconds he heard the thump of two car doors closing and the cough of an engine coming to life. A tree provided him with some cover while he watched the T-junction with Castle Street. If they were heading towards the town centre, or back towards the J+H office, he would see them pass the end of the road.

He gave it plenty of time, and there was no sign of them. They had gone in the opposite direction. Wes began the walk back to his own front door. Alex had some serious explaining to do. Maybe he would stick to the original plan – bundle her into the car and head east, up Midhurst Road, then picking up the A3 heading towards Liphook, Hindhead, Guildford, however far he needed to go. Would she refuse, resist? Would he be taking the journey alone?

Before he reached the end of the street he was stopped by the sight of the blue Renault turning into the road towards him. He was paralysed by disbelief, by the sheer injustice of it. He had escaped; they had no reason to drive down here – it was a cul-de-sac. The car stopped, the passenger door opened and the man who had assaulted Wes jumped out. A flashback to the fight in the toilet closed a circuit in Wes's mind. He turned and ran. Behind him he heard footsteps pounding, the car door shutting, the engine revving. He hit the end of the road at a sprint and curved into an alleyway. At its entrance were a set of steel railings, designed to prevent cars from going through. He leapt them head-on like a hurdler, making a much better job of it than the garden fence. Behind him there was a gravelly stutter as the car braked hard under ABS. The note of the engine rose and fell as the driver performed a three point turn.

He had to get off these quiet streets and lose himself in the safety of the crowds. Yes, he would head back to the centre of town. But wasn't this the exact opposite of his plan on leaving the police station? He was improvising wildly, hoping that at some point something worked. How long before this led him into a mistake?

The end of the alley opened out onto a crescent. Wes turned left onto the pavement, then realised this would take him further away from the town centre, so he took the next right onto Woodbridge Road. A glance over his shoulder at least reassured him that the distance between him and his pursuer was increasing. Those two holes in his chest couldn't have been helping.

The driver obviously knew his way around these streets because the car made another reappearance right in front of him, two wheels briefly leaving the road as it turned. There was no way of avoiding it, and Wes wasn't about to turn back and face the man on foot, so he carried on towards it, aware that the rules of chicken generally assumed that both of the participants were in cars. He was intending to leap aside at the last minute, in front of the dark green telecoms cabinet at the side of the road that would hopefully absorb most of the car's impact, but for some reason the driver slammed on the brakes rather than trying to run him down. Wes passed by on the passenger side to prevent a rapidly opened door from taking him out, and turned left into another narrow alleyway.

He expected the driver to get out and follow, but he put the car into reverse, accelerated until the engine screamed, skidded into a J turn and carried on in the opposite direction, out of sight. Was the car trying to herd him towards the guy on foot? If they wanted him dead, why did it matter how it was done? Surely a car accident would be ideal.

This time, rather than squelching across the playing fields, he skirted them, wanting to maintain his speed. By the time he had gained the other side there was no sign of the man on foot. He made as many abrupt turns as possible, favouring minor roads, ready to divert onto alternative routes in case the car reappeared. Once the road opened up again, he made a sprint for the town centre. The subway would have been quickest, but it was dark and enclosed, and he took his chances with the traffic instead. As he reached the beginning of the pedestrianised High Street he glanced back. Nothing. He turned right abruptly, straight through the doors of the Green Man. It was every bit as busy as he'd hoped – noisy and humid and roiling with closely packed bodies. He squeezed through the crowd of drinkers and headed to the back of the pub, so there were plenty of people – plus the large central bar – between him and both of the pub's exits.

Some kind of plan would have been nice, but for now all he could do was find a space in the darkest corner and take a few moments to regain his breath. He kept an eye on both doors, more from a healthy paranoia than any actual expectation that they would find him here. Every time someone came in or out, he made sure that it wasn't ... and there he was. He had shed his suit jacket and tie somewhere during the chase, and looked like a businessman who had just knocked off for the weekend, but it was definitely him. This was insane. They couldn't just keep finding him like this. It was ridiculous. It was ... unrealistic. The man glanced down at something in his hand, then up to scan the crowd, then down again. A phone. They were using it to track him.

Using his arms as a wedge, Wes parted the crowd before him and made for the other exit. He expected complaints from his shoving, but most of them were too busy enjoying themselves to care. He was out of the pub before he'd been spotted, and started running again.

How were they doing it? Had they slipped a tracking device onto him somehow? But if they'd managed to get that close, they would have killed him there and then. He rummaged through his pockets and the first thing his hands made contact with was his smartphone. Shit: that was it. A phone could be located through GPS, or by triangulating its position from phone mast signals. This was not supposed to be something any random person could do without your permission, but ... what other explanation could there be? So: shut the phone down completely, maybe remove the battery to be absolutely sure. No, wait. He had a better idea.

He turned into one of the narrow shopping alleys, dark now and closed up for the night. Halfway along, he locked his phone and put it into a public bin attached to a shop wall, then headed a few metres further on and stepped into a recessed doorway. It was an all-glass shopfront, but he was able to half conceal himself behind a – he squinted – a vampish mannequin wearing suspenders and a crimson bra. It was the Anne Summers shop. Well, whatever. He tried to quiet his breathing while he waited. A couple walked past and glanced at him, so he pretended to be having an intense – if silent – conversation with the mannequin. They moved quickly on.

A patter of steps and the skinhead came straight past the bin and into Wes's view. Christ – he hadn't counted on that. But he was looking down at his phone, and turned away from Wes before heading back towards the bin. Wes filled his lungs, rounded the corner and closed the distance as quickly and quietly as he could. The man was just becoming aware of him – the beginning of a glance over the shoulder – when Wes stamped on the back of his calf, making his legs buckle and his knees hit the ground.

'Fuck!' he yelled, and Wes followed up with a rolling series of palm strikes to the back of his skull, following him as he went down. The man's arms came up behind his head in defence and he curled into a ball as he hit the ground.

Wes heard a gasp from the couple who had just walked by, but ignored them – they wouldn't interfere. His opponent's phone was buried somewhere underneath him. Wes booted him in the side, but it just caused him to grunt and curl up even more tightly, so he stood back, planted one foot against the man's ribs and pushed hard. He rolled over, arms and legs coming up defensively, his face screwed up in pain. The mobile was on the ground next to him – a black rectangle against the grey of the paving slabs. Wes scooped it up and bolted.

'There! Over there!' shouted a voice behind him.

He looked round to see the couple who had seen him in the shop doorway. The man was pointing, the end of his scarf flapping out horizontally from the movement. A stocky policeman had appeared from one of the passageways connecting to the High Street, and was following the line of his finger. Wes swerved right into an even narrower alley, heading back in the direction of the Green Man and the library. Behind him he heard the slap of shoes on stone. While he ran, he swiped his thumb at regular intervals across the screen of the stolen phone to keep it active. If it locked, it would be useless to him. He turned left onto the dual carriageway, crossed the road in a gap between the traffic, turned right opposite the cinema. It was clear that he was faster than the policeman – he was warmed up, fitter, lighter. Still, he didn't slow his pace until he was a comfortable distance away.

In a quiet street near the Roman Catholic church he crouched down in the lee of a brick wall and turned his attention to the phone. He had to do this fast and get rid of the thing as soon as possible. If they could track his phone, he had to assume they could also track their own. There was almost nothing stored on it. There was an app on the home screen called, ominously, TrackTarget, but there was very little else, and no photos or videos at all. That left the contacts list, which was remarkably short. The owner of the phone was labelled simply as 'me', with a phone number and the unhelpfully vague email address k95734@wigwam.net.

Wes started copying down the details of the other contacts into his notepad. Some of them were similarly cryptic, while others had actual names and fully formed email addresses. What he didn't expect to find at the end of the list was the name of someone he not only already knew, but worked with: Marcus Watkins.

9

At the kitchen sink, Alex flung her hair back over one shoulder and splashed water on her face. Then she washed both hands thoroughly, getting the soap in between the fingers and under the nails. Only after drying her face and hands did she allow herself to peek past the edge of the blind and confirm that yes, the drive was empty. She went through to the lounge, sat in the armchair, picked up her phone and rang Tom. While the tone purred in her ear she stared at the recently vacated sofa. There was disinfectant in the kitchen. Better still: there were matches.

Click. 'Hello?'

'Tom? It's Alex. I need your help.'

'What's wrong?'

'It's Wes, he …' Her voiced cracked.

'What's happened?'

'I – I don't know. I haven't been able to text him, and he hasn't come home, and there were these two men who came round and said he was mixed up in something, and I don't think I believe that they're … '

'Wait-wait-wait. He hasn't come home?'

'No.'

'Okay, I'm coming round. I'll be there in ten minutes.'

'Thank you,' she said with an exhausted gratitude, and hung up.

She could have phoned one of her girlfriends – maybe Svetlana, who was always good in a crisis – but no, this was about Wes, and that made Tom the right man for the job. Her relationship with him had always been a funny thing. If she had met him independently of Wes, she might never have warmed to him. His overconfidence, his posh way of speaking in spite of lower middle class origins, his endless string of sexual conquests – these things might easily have blinded her to his better qualities. But Tom had been a wonderful best man at their wedding. She had learned a lot from him about how to talk to Wes. And the thing that always brought her round in the end: he never took himself too seriously.

Like the time, a couple of months ago, when he had invited

them round for a fiery home-made curry. Tom had looked uncomfortable at the table, frowning and shifting position frequently. Finally, he had left the dining room, trying vainly to conceal his distress. After a few seconds' hesitation she followed him into the kitchen. What she hadn't known at the time was that he'd failed to wash his hands properly, and after a trip to the loo had managed to get chilli on his genitals. His efforts to discreetly deal with this 'itch' at the table had only compounded the problem.

'Are you all right?' she'd asked as she opened the kitchen door.

Tom stood there with an expression of beatific relief on his face, his trousers unzipped and his dick cooling in a family sized tub of yoghurt. They stared at each other, mortified. Alex pulled the door closed and retreated to the dining room.

Later, once Tom had disposed of the evidence and returned to his seat, Wes had written on his notepad:

Pudding?

'It was going to be yoghurt,' Tom replied, 'but there's been a bit of a cock-up.'

*

The doorbell sounded and she sprang up, but she paused in front of the door. The frosted glass showed a figure in a blue shirt. It *seemed* like him.

The bell rang again and a voice spoke, muffled but familiar. 'Let me in. It's Tom.'

She opened the door. Yes. Yes, it was. Behind him was his red Alfa Romeo, mounting the kerb, more abandoned than parked.

'Jesus,' he said. 'Are you okay?'

She shook her head. He came in, closing the door behind him, and drew her straight into a hug. She tensed, a reflex reaction to the encounter with the two men, but she relaxed into it. This was normal. She hugged Tom every time she saw him. This was nor-

57

mal. His phone buzzed and she sprang away from him as if electrocuted.

'Is it him?' she said.

'No,' he said as he read the message. 'It's a bollocking from Ursula.'

Ursula? Who was Ursula? Oh, for goodness' sake. Did the man never stop?

'Never mind.' He slid the phone back into his pocket. 'So, tell me everything.'

They sat in the lounge, Tom leaning forwards, elbows on knees, and she gave a summary of the evening's events. It helped to retell it, to sort out the facts from the feelings. By the end she felt much better prepared to start tackling the problem.

She took a deep breath and said, 'We should go to the office.'

'Agreed. I'll drive.'

They went outside to the Alfa. Alex paused with her fingers on the passenger door handle and said, 'Tom?' over the roof of the car. He was on the other side, about to get in.

'Yes?'

'I need you to be absolutely honest with me – is he mixed up in anything illegal?'

'No, of course not.' He paused, staring off into the distance, then added, 'Well, not since ...'

'The graffiti?'

'Ummm,' he said.

'What is it?' she said. 'What do you know?'

'It's all water under the bridge now. It can't have any relevance to –'

'Tell me.'

'Okay. There were these four kids at school. Horrible, vicious little tosspots. They made our life miserable.'

Wes had mentioned them before, but not his friend's involvement. Given how cocksure he was now, it was difficult to believe

58

Tom had ever been bullied.

'Well, we hatched this scheme – okay, *I* hatched this scheme – to punish them.'

'Go on.'

'We, uh … we learned how to pick locks, and then we broke into their houses, stole their prized possessions, and sold them on eBay.'

What came out of her was something between a laugh and a choke. 'You did what?'

'The money went to charity. We weren't just burglars, you understand. We were trying to make a statement. We managed three of the four houses – not a bad score, I feel – but we nearly got caught in the last one. After that we decided to pack it in.'

'And this stopped the bullying, did it?'

Tom toyed with the door handle. 'Not as such.'

'So what did?'

'Your husband was getting pretty good at Wing Chun by that point. One day they cornered us and he snapped and he … dealt with them. All of them. It was quite something to see.'

Teeth clenched against the onset of tears, she said, 'Why doesn't he *tell* me any of this?'

'He knows you'd disapprove.'

'And I do! What is it with boys and fighting?'

'He saved my bacon, Alex,' he said firmly. 'He didn't just wade in, unprovoked. He saved my bacon.'

'But –'

'They wanted us bleeding; they wanted broken bones. That's where it was heading until Wes stopped them.'

She supposed she couldn't argue with self-defence, or with protecting a friend. And again, it was too long ago, too trivial, for MI5 to be interested. She climbed into the car and Tom followed her lead. He started the engine and drove.

When he spoke again his voice was quieter. 'You know he was

expelled for it?'

'What?' More revelations. After three years together she shouldn't still be finding out these things about him. Important things.

'It didn't last long,' Tom said. 'His dad went into the headmaster's office the next day, and by the time he came out, Wes was reinstated.'

Wes's dad? The man always to be found in the corner of any room, hiding from the world behind a newspaper? Alex found him pleasant enough company, but he had never seemed very ... dynamic.

'What did he say?'

'To this day, I don't know.'

Alex shook her head, trying to get all these new facts to settle into a coherent view of this person she called her husband.

'Look, Alex, the reason he doesn't talk about this stuff is that he wants to forget the past. He wants people to take him for who he is now, not who he used to be.'

Wes had claimed she didn't appreciate how he felt about his past. And, yes, it was true, but that was only because he'd concealed half of it from her.

Tom said, 'If you'd asked him about any of this, he would have told you. You know that.'

'But he doesn't volunteer it, does he? He just stays silent and all these things remain conveniently hidden.'

'He wants to make the best impression. Every man does. Maybe him more than anyone.' Tom cleared his throat. 'You know he doesn't always feel ... worthy of you.'

'Stupid man.'

'Well, I can't deny that he can be the most awful fuckwit on occasion.'

'So, are there any more of these little episodes I should know about?'

'No.'

'Are you sure? No kidnapping or bomb-making?'

He stopped before the red traffic lights at the T-junction with the B3023, applied the handbrake and turned to her. 'Alex, I can assure you there's been nothing since. Nothing I'm aware of, any-way.'

She held his gaze, looking for the guilty twitch of the lips or dart of the eyes that would betray the existence of even deeper strata of mystery, just waiting to be unearthed.

'Alex, you are the wife of my best friend. I won't keep anything from you. I want this resolved as much as you do.'

It wasn't fair of her to challenge him like this, to doubt his honesty and intentions. It wasn't Tom that was the problem.

She shifted to face the traffic lights. 'We're green.'

He turned onto the dual carriageway. 'So what made you think your visitors might not be MI5?'

'I don't know. A hunch, I suppose. They just didn't seem right.'

'Have you met anyone from MI5 before?'

'Well, no.'

'Then how do you know what they look like?'

She needed support from him, not a grilling. She bit her lip, something he seemed to notice out of the corner of his eye.

'Look,' he said, 'I'm just playing devil's advocate here. We'll need to kick the tyres on our arguments and assumptions if we're going to get to the truth.'

'Okay.'

'So, if they weren't MI5, who might they be?'

'Debt collectors?'

'Not for the business. The accounts are sound, I can vouch for that.'

'A criminal gang, maybe?'

'The Strathurst Mafia?' he said drily.

'Tom, this isn't funny.'

'I agree. You get my point, though. Strathurst isn't exactly a hotbed of crime. And even if it was, how on earth would someone like Wes manage to piss off the wrong person?' Tom's brow creased into a frown. 'Hang on, why did they leave rather than waiting until Wes came home?'

'I don't know.' She hadn't given it much thought; at the time she'd been too eager to see the back of them. 'One of them looked at his phone just before they left, as if he might have just got a message.'

They glanced at each other.

'So,' she said, 'there might be more of them.'

Tom opened his mouth, but said nothing. He indicated and turned into the business park. Wes's Mini stood alone among the buildings, stranded in an oasis of light cast by a street lamp. They parked next to it, got out and looked in through the windows, tested the door handles. The car was locked, and there was nothing visible inside except for an empty bag of crisps and a plastic windscreen scraper.

It was already obvious from the darkness that nobody was in the J+H office. Tom unlocked the outer door and badged in.

'Security will have locked up around seven,' he said, 'so he must have left before then.'

There were no signs of anything out of the ordinary, except that Wes's computer had gone into hibernation rather than being switched fully off. Tom woke it up, typed in Wes's password – they really didn't keep secrets from each other – and searched for any hint of what might have happened. 'This is all just standard work stuff,' he muttered.

Meanwhile Alex checked the desk drawers – which rolled out on their runners with a hollow, mournful sound – but she found only stationery, half a packet of chocolate digestives and a couple of flyers for their dance classes. She watched Tom look under the desks and root through the wastepaper bins while she held onto

the back of Wes's chair. It was horrible, raking over all this ...
stuff. In the space of an hour and a half she had gone from
annoyance at her husband to seriously wondering whether he
might be gone forever. She started to shake again.

Tom checked the reception, the toilet, the upstairs landing
that led to the other offices. If there was any evidence of what
had happened, it eluded him.

He glanced at his watch. 'Security might still be here. I'll go
and ask if they've seen anything. They might have CCTV of –'

'No.' She grabbed his arm. 'If he is involved in something ...'

He looked past her and his eyes made a series of tiny, rapid
movements. 'You're sure?'

'Yes. I just want to go home.'

'Okay.'

When they got back, Wes would be there, sitting on the sofa
with a G&T, wondering what all the fuss was about. That was
the way these things happened. But as soon as she turned the key
in the lock and opened the door, her hopes died – the house was
still. It was now nine o'clock.

Tom put on the kettle and made tea. When he brought the
mugs through to the lounge, Alex made her confession.

'We may have ... sort of had an argument this morning. I'm
not sure.'

She realised she was being vague, but he responded with: 'I
know that feeling.'

'You do?'

'A couple of weeks ago I managed to write all over an external
hard drive that Wes had been using as a backup device. He'd mentioned it, but I just sort of forgot. I offered to pay for one of those
data recovery firms to get the information he needed from it – you
know they can "undelete" things you thought were lost – but he
said it was probably quicker to just re-do the work. Anyway, hours
later he came back with an apology for being so ratty. The thing is,

he hadn't been ratty at all – at worst he'd been briefly annoyed. It was like he'd had an argument, but he'd forgotten to involve me. I think his mind races ahead of him. Anyone else would just say something, but because it takes him so much longer, he keeps on playing things out in his mind until he reaches some kind of conclusion.'

'I tell him not to bottle things up like that.'

'Quite.'

Perhaps Wes had been giving more thought to the idea of kids than she'd been aware. Perhaps he'd already reached his conclusion, and decided to run as far away from responsibility as he could. Perhaps he'd paid the two men to provide a plausible excuse for his disappearance. And perhaps she was grasping at ideas, no matter how ridiculous, in an attempt to make sense of this.

'Does he know them?' she said out loud.

'What, the two MI5 bods?'

No. No, she could not start thinking like this. 'Never mind.'

Tom said, 'You're not thinking that he's done some kind of dramatic, run-away-from-home thing, are you?'

She looked down at her feet.

'He wouldn't do that,' Tom said. 'Trust me.'

'But you just told me how good he is at concealing his feelings from you.'

'No,' he said, 'not about something like that. There are limits. Anyway, you were going to tell me about this argument.'

'It was a bit of a big deal,' she said, 'about maybe having a child.'

Tom's face softened. 'You guys would make great parents.'

The tears came without warning. 'That's what I was trying to tell the stupid sod!'

She had seen the news often enough to know how this tended to end. The recovery of a body after months of misplaced hope.

'Alex …' Tom knelt in front of the chair and held her hands. 'Wes has been missing for a few hours, that's all.'

'But he might already be –'

'We're not even going to think about that. Look at me. I would walk to the ends of the earth for that man. We will find him.'

Such confidence. How did he do it?

But her amazement was short-lived. It was a bluff. He was trying to convince himself as much as her. This was Tom's way: to push through, oblivious to all obstacles, oblivious even to the facts. Great, if it worked. But she also saw that she could rely on him completely. She saw what Wes had seen all these years: his determination, his unshakeable loyalty.

'I believe you,' she said, not because she did, but because she had to.

10

KEIRAN knew there was no chance the cop would catch Henning – he'd obviously been at the doughnuts – but at this point anything that made Henning's life more difficult was worth having.

'Are you all right?' The man with the scarf was approaching. He was a few years older than Keiran, his clothes tailored, hair and beard immaculately trimmed. He looked like a banker.

Keiran stood, pain throbbing at the back of his head – an echo of Henning's jackhammer pounding. 'Is it any of your fucking business?'

The man backed away, hands held up in front of him. 'Whoa! Okay, whatever.'

Normally Keiran would have followed him – shown him that, yes, he was 'all right' – but he didn't need any more complications. He let the man and his woman scurry off, staring after them until they were out of eyeshot. He tested his ribs. Tender, but not cracked or broken. The greatest pain was the back of his skull and the muscles going down into his neck and shoulders. After Henning's assault, half his back was in danger of locking up.

The shop windows surrounding him were dark, betraying their true nature, their emptiness. During the day, these pedestrianised shopping streets were among his least favourite places – a funnel for directing sheep-like consumers to the next shiny, pointless, must-have object. Here, mankind was at his most distracted and defenceless, furthest away from the state of vigilance that any living creature must cultivate to survive. You could walk up behind any one of them, wrench the head to one side, snap the spine. Nobody would even notice until you were gone. And yet Henning had managed to jump *him*. It wouldn't have happened if all his attention hadn't been on his bloody phone. Over-reliance on technology – society's big mistake, and now his too. He was lucky Henning didn't have the killer instinct. And luck should never have been a factor.

Before Henning had taken it, his phone had showed that Keiran was right on top of him. The GPS was accurate to around four metres, but Henning had come from further away than that, which meant … He checked the ground, turned over a paper cup with his foot, then tried the bin. There it was. Henning's phone was an expensive newer model, proof that you would abandon any of the trappings of civilisation when your life was at stake.

Grant was right; Keiran had underestimated his target. Grant was always bloody right. Henning might have been a freak, one of nature's dead ends, but he was no less dangerous for it. As if summoned, he looked up and there was his brother, striding towards him with his phone held out in front of him. He was still trying to track Henning.

Keiran held up Henning's phone between thumb and fore-

66

finger and said, 'He figured it out.'

'So where is he now?'

'Gone.'

'Again?'

There was nothing to gain from examining the phone, but that's what Keiran did. It gave his hands and eyes something to do. 'He left it in the bin as a decoy,' he said. 'It's fingerprint-locked. We can't get anything off it.'

'Then throw it back in.'

Keiran had a better idea. He rested it at forty-five degrees between the paving and a shop wall, and took a morsel of satisfaction in stamping it to destruction. He expected Grant to quote another disapproving bit of DA lore, but his brother remained silent. Of course: breaking the phone was consistent with their plan to cut Henning off from all forms of communication. He pretended not to notice Grant trying to catch his gaze. Screwing things up once was bad enough; twice looked like incompetence. Best not to volunteer any information about the second pummelling, or the loss of his own phone.

'Let's go back to the car,' Grant said.

Yes, a good bollocking should always happen in private.

As Grant drove them out of the centre of Strathurst in an ominous silence, Keiran said, 'I'm going to fucking kill that man.'

'That was the general idea.'

'Yeah, well it turns out it's not so easy. He's cleverer than we thought.'

'Cleverer than *you* thought. I haven't underestimated him.'

'Maybe you should have a crack at him, then.'

'Anger should fuel, not rule,' Grant recited.

'Oh, don't worry about that – there's plenty of fuel.'

Rumble of road, hum of engine. His brother's stony stoicism was an example to him, something he ought to emulate, but it

67

betrayed nothing of Grant's actual thoughts or feelings. He would be planning something, looking for a way to get them out of this mess.

'What are you thinking?' Keiran asked.

Grant paused for a moment. 'I'm thinking you should have finished the job.'

Given that he had to suck it up at some point, it might as well be now. Keiran felt his head begin to dip in shame but he pushed it back up, ignoring the clench of his neck muscles, so that it looked like a nod of acceptance. It *was* a nod of acceptance.

Grant said, 'I may not have prepared you for how difficult this would be.'

For a moment Keiran couldn't believe what he'd heard. Then, reviewing the exact words Grant had used – 'I may not have' – he saw that his brother was exploring possibilities, not confessing to a mistake. And, as usual, there was an implicit criticism: that Keiran was finding things difficult.

'The fact is,' Grant said, 'it's impossible to know how easy it is to kill somebody until you try it. In some people, the instinct for survival is higher than expected. When you kill Henning, your brothers will respect you all the more, seeing how hard it was.'

It was the last thing Keiran expected to hear, and he had to work hard to contain the gratitude that welled up inside him. His only physical reaction was to lift his chin. Grant was right. Once it was all over, he could turn this into an epic tale of triumph over a deadly foe: resourceful, highly intelligent, an expert in martial arts.

Yes. *Yes.*

'What are we doing here?' Keiran said.

They were back at his flat, Grant making the turn into the car park behind the tandoori.

'You're going to get some rest for the night.'

'But I need to phone –' He cut himself off. He needed to

phone Sean and Jamal and get them to stake out the Hennings' house, but without his mobile he could only do this from his land line. So, yes, going back to the flat did make sense.

'I'll phone the other two,' Grant said.

Maybe he should have put up some resistance, but he had already been seduced by the prospect of a soak in a hot bath and a chance to give his body a few hours of recovery.

Grant clapped him on the shoulder. 'You're still at the stage where you need the support of your DA brothers. Your job is to make sure you're in a fit state to take Henning down.'

'Okay. What are you going to do?'

'Ditch the car. Think. Report back to Brad.'

Brad. Shit. He'd forgotten all about Brad. Well, there was nothing he could do about that now. He opened the door and tried not to tumble straight out onto the pavement.

'And brother ...' Grant said, as Keiran was about to close the passenger door.

'Yeah?'

'You need to shift to a lower gear. Henning will go underground. We're playing the long game now.'

*

Keiran unbuttoned his shirt while the bath was running. The bandage was stained with two circles of red that expanded in size each time he unwound a circuit of the dressing. He peeled the gauze away, pulling at the crusted blood that glued it to his chest, then washed the wound at the sink. Certain positions of his right arm caused stabs of pain as his chest muscles tensed, but the holes were disappointingly small. He took two ibuprofen, then lowered himself into the hot bath with a groan that bordered on the orgasmic. He topped up the hot water as it cooled, and only left when the need to piss became pressing. There was no blood in his urine, but he would give a different report to Grant: 'Yeah, there was some blood. Not a problem – it'll clear up.'

By the start of the second vodka and orange, Keiran began to feel more relaxed, almost enough to distract him from the constant fucking smell of curry that wafted up from downstairs. He couldn't stay in this place much longer – it was in danger of putting him off Indian food altogether. He imagined Grant bursting in, catching him lounging on the sofa, compromising himself with alcohol. That would be just bloody perfect. It was, he decided, a risk worth taking. He microwaved a shepherd's pie ready meal, and replayed the events of the day in his head. He was gaining perspective, able now to think in an orderly manner: analysing, not just reacting.

Anger should fuel, not rule. Yes, he saw the wisdom of it. He fished his diary out from its hiding place behind the bookshelf, and flipped to Henning's blog post, which he had written out, word for word, so he would have a copy even once it was erased from the internet.

A source tells me of another dangerous cult besmirching our sceptred isle: Darwin's Army. This one treats as its central text the most unlikely of books – Darwin's Origin of Species – and welds it to, you guessed it, an apocalypse cult.

They reject all ideas not directly related to the survival of the fittest (themselves, naturally) eschewing religion, society, and traditional power structures in preparation for the impending Doom of Our Race. They're like the Hitler Youth with all the frivolity removed.

They meet up (presumably not in a church hall) to indulge their Nietzschean fantasies. The compulsion to test each other is irresistible, and they spend their time in endless games of chess and beating each other up á là Fight Club (and, in the case of sore losers, maybe the former followed by the latter).

So far they have demonstrated all the fiery ferocity and

paradigm-smashing terror of a half-finished tub of supermarket value ice cream. They have made no mark on the public consciousness and I can find no evidence that they have troubled the boys in blue. Perhaps they are still psyching themselves up to take action, like the unpopular kid being persuaded by his 'mates' to ring the doorbell at number 12 and run away. Perhaps they are so exhausted from testing their strength against each other that they are left physically incapable of breaking the law.

Like so many marginalised groups, I believe they are crying out to express themselves in song. 'Anarchy in the UK' was a rallying call for punks. 'Y.M.C.A.' became an unofficial anthem for gay men. Darwin's Army could adopt another classic for their purposes: Gloria Gaynor's 'I Will Survive'.

Keiran's perception of it wasn't any different now he'd actually faced the man. The idea of people across the internet laughing at these words still stirred a quiet rage in him. And with so much detail Henning must, surely, have got his information from an insider. Could it be Hans? Please, let it be Hans.

Henning had missed the point of their organisation spectacularly. It was nothing like National Socialism for two very simple reasons: it wasn't nationalist, and it wasn't socialist. DA had nothing to do with government, patriotism, ethnicity or a desire for social justice. It didn't matter whether you were Jewish or black, gypsy or gay. It mattered that you were better adapted to survive. Drawing a parallel with the Nazis was a cheap shot to get some laughs. And the reason no-one had heard of them was because they covered their tracks so well. Only a moron would interpret this as a failing. The problem was that Henning had such a huge following on the web. But being popular didn't make you correct. Or invulnerable. It didn't stop your wife from agreeing to shop you to two strangers at the first opportunity.

He closed the diary and slid it back into its hiding place. It would have been simpler to kidnap Alex Henning and get to her husband that way. But there was an ironic twist to their planning: having cut Henning off from all forms of communication, it would be impossible to tell him that they had his wife. No matter; there were subtler ways.

What would Alex Henning be like in bed? Not very good, he guessed. She was tall and gawky and pale. Certainly nothing like Amber, with her unbelievable hips, her skill and experience. And yet there was that note from Henning in the box on their coffee table: *I love you, I love you, I love you*. Something about it tugged at him, some vestigial emotion. He identified it as pity – pity that such flawed human beings could ever profess such a thing for each other. It was just chemicals at the end of the day, chemicals that tricked two people into reproducing. And the Hennings hadn't even managed that much. When DA had required Keiran to leave Slough and come here, he had agreed immediately; he had not allowed his attachment to Gemma to compromise him. This was the difference between him and Henning, between him and most people. Anything that kept you in one place was baggage.

Gemma. She always came to his mind with such astonishing clarity: her short, coppery hair and eyeliner; her laconic smile. He pictured her in her natural habitat – behind the bar, bantering with a punter while she pulled a pint, her Celtic tribal tattoo visible below the sleeve of a black T-shirt emblazoned with the name of a band. He had spoken to her many times, and never for long enough. The nature of her job was to spread herself thinly among a hundred people. He admired her from a shaded corner, hypnotised by ... what? Her brassy confidence, her ability to talk to any stranger.

And yet, in the face of violence, her confidence had been worth nothing. It was his fists, his aggression, that had neutralised the threat. She had shown appreciation, in her own small way. If he hadn't been required to leave town so quickly she might have shown more. He had often wondered what a life with Gemma would be like. But he already knew. It would become a compromise. Like all relationships, it would become a prison. He didn't really know Gemma any more than he knew Amber. His feelings towards her might have seemed different, but this was just another of nature's strategies to produce offspring. Once the Henning matter was over, he would go back to Slough, less to confront Gemma than to confront himself, to neutralise these feelings. If he was lucky it might involve sex, but even if it didn't, at least he would be free of her.

So, yes, he knew what love felt like, and he could see why people clung to it so fervently. But in the end it was a weakness, one ripe for exploitation. And in this respect, Alex Henning would serve them well. She was a gazelle in a world of lions. Her love for her husband would be his downfall.

11

IT was anger that tempted Wes to dispose of the phone somewhere awkward, by throwing it up onto a high roof, for example, or into the trough of a public urinal. Instead he tossed it into a public bin outside Little Dean School. It would seem to be discarded, but he wanted them to recover it – he wanted the ability to text or email them. Why, he didn't yet know, but it seemed like a good idea to keep his options open.

Marcus lived a couple of streets beyond, in a tiny house on the Hillfields estate, coddled by technology. Wes had been there once before with Tom, shortly after they hired him. Marcus, in a spirit of gratitude towards his new colleagues, had invited them round for pizza and shown off his Blu-ray collection.

'I know it's a bit old-school, having actual, physical discs,' he had said, 'but if you've got a perfect collection you've got to let people know, yeah?'

'What makes it perfect?' Tom asked.

'Take a closer look.'

Wes and Tom scanned the shelves, trying to discern some pattern. The selection was incredibly diverse. Maybe Wes had misjudged Marcus – he couldn't imagine his new colleague sitting down in front of *Casablanca* or *Dr Strangelove*. He'd had him pegged more as a *Transformers* kind of guy.

'Nope,' Tom said. 'You'll have to enlighten us.'

'These are the hundred highest-rated movies on imdb.com.'

Tom and Wes turned towards each other with perfect comic synchronisation. It was to become one of their standard reactions where Marcus was concerned.

'That's a popular vote, is it not?' Tom said.

'Yeah – millions of votes. And remember,' he said, as if he'd discussed this with them before, 'you only need a thousand votes to reach statistical significance.'

'But what about your own personal preference?'

Marcus paused for a moment, as if Tom had asked the question in Italian and he had to translate. 'These are the hundred best movies. What's the point in me spending years trawling through every film in the world when other people have done it for me?'

What do you make of Chaplin?

Wes pointed to Marcus's copy of *Modern Times*, a film Wes had found both hilarious and unexpectedly moving.

'Oh, yeah. It's great. A truly great movie.'

'What happens if something new comes onto the list and something else drops off the bottom?'

'I buy the new one and put the old one in storage. Or sell it. Obviously, I hang on to anything that might come back into the top one hundred.'

Obviously.

This had marked the beginning of their suspicion that Marcus was only visiting this planet. Now Wes longed for the time, a few short hours ago, when he only thought that Marcus was a bit of an oddball, rather than a suspect in a plot to kill him. He arrived at Marcus's front door and rang the bell. Through the translucent kitchen blind, he could see there was a light on somewhere downstairs. Marcus opened the door and blinked a couple of times, as if it was brighter outside than in.

'Hi, Wes. What're you doing round here?'

Wes raised his eyebrows and indicated the interior, ready to take a rapid step forwards and jam a foot in the door.

'Yeah, sure. Come in.'

Blimey, as easy as that. How deeply involved was he?

The warmth of the central heating made Wes aware how cold it was out on the streets. He wiped his feet on the mat and closed the door carefully behind him. Patience. No use startling him.

'So, what do you …'

Wes displayed the message he had written a couple of minutes ago on his notepad:

Tell me about the muscular guy with the hollow eyes and buzz cut.

Marcus frowned. 'I don't know who you're talking about.'

The universal response of the guilty. If he was innocent, he would have asked for a name or some additional detail. Wes had anticipated this. He flipped over the page to reveal another sentence:

It's very important that you tell me.

'I really don't know who you mean.'

Okay. That was fine. That was absolutely fine. Marcus just might need his memory jogged, that was all. Wes wrote:

Have you got any string?

'What?'

Wes pointed to the word 'string' for emphasis.

'Er … yeah, I think there's some in the kitchen. Why the hell do you need string?'

Wes shooed him through the door and into the kitchen diner, which was just large enough to accommodate a drop leaf table and two cheap wooden chairs. The sink was overflowing with unwashed plates, cutlery and utensils. Marcus opened a drawer and with a kind of bewildered obedience held out a tightly wrapped cylinder of string. Wes unwound a couple of metres, formed it into three large loops, pointed at it and nodded.

'Er … yeah, like: some string. I'm not with you, mate. Can you write it down?'

Wes tapped one of the chairs and Marcus dutifully sat.

'What's going on? You're acting a bit weird, Wes.'

Wes walked past him. Marcus began to rise, but a couple of fingers applied lightly to the shoulder persuaded him to stay put. Wes crouched down beside him and pointed through the kitchen and lounge towards the front door.

Marcus squinted. 'Riiight. Like, what am I looking for?'

While he was distracted, Wes lassoed him over the shoulders.

'Er … wh-wh-what are you doing?'

With a foot applied to the back of the chair, Wes pulled the string tight, so that it bit into Marcus's arms just below the bicep.

'Ow!'

He tied off with a reef knot.

Marcus let out a nervous laugh. 'This is a practical joke, right? Tom put you up to this.'

He struggled against the restraint and looked surprised when he couldn't break through it. Wes had learned how little it took to immobilise someone during a friend's stag do, when they had tied the betrothed to a lamp post while they nipped off to the pub for a quick half. It wasn't like Hollywood, where all you had to do was flex your muscles and even iron chains would fall apart.

Wes moved the other chair and table further back down the kitchen, so he could stand in front of Marcus. He flipped back to his original message:

Tell me about the muscular guy with the hollow eyes and buzz cut.

'Oh. Oh, I think I know who you mean.'

His acting was atrocious. Had he not learned anything from owning the world's best film collection? Wes nodded in a slow, patronising manner.

'He was just after some information, that's all. He wanted me to text him when you were alone in the office.'

Wes rested the pad against the table and wrote:

And you never asked why?

'Why would I? He was offering good money for a bit of information and I need to supplement my income. I mean, look at this place. If you paid me more I wouldn't ... not – not that you can, being a small business and all. It's just, you know ... how it is.'

It was a pathetic and damning answer, which meant it was probably the truth. If Marcus had wanted to deceive him, he would have prepared a less incriminating story; he wasn't stupid. Well ... he wasn't stupid from an intellectual point of view; in terms of dealing with his fellow human beings he was a cretin of the highest order.

'Wes, this is really digging in. I think you've cut off the blood supply to my arms.'

I need to know his name.

'He told me he was called Sam Whiley ...'

Wes started to write it down.

'... but I know it was a fake name.'

Marcus paused. Even in a situation like this, he couldn't resist looking pleased with himself. Wes glared at him and stabbed his notepad with his index finger.

'He paid me in cash,' Marcus blurted, 'and when he opened his wallet I saw the name on his library card.'

His library card? What sort of a murderer was this? Did he volunteer at Oxfam too? Wes pulled on his earlobe to show he was still expecting an answer.

'Keiran Lowry,' Marcus said, and spelled it out. 'At least that was the name on the card. And that's all I know about him. Honestly. Wes, what the hell is this all about?'

Tell me about Alex.

'Alex?' Marcus looked bewildered.

Wes nodded.

'What can I tell you about Alex that you don't already ...? Wait a minute. You don't think we're ... Look, no offence, mate, but she's a bit old for me, you know what I mean?'

Okay, no more pissing about. Wes span round to the sink and its pile of unwashed stuff, grabbed the first knife that came to hand and turned back round to hold it in front of Marcus's face. But it wasn't a knife. In his haste he'd picked up a garlic crusher. Seeing Marcus's Adam's apple rise and fall in a gulp of fear, he decided maybe it wasn't such a mistake after all. He flipped the utensil open, then closed it and squeezed hard, so that the tendons on his arm stood out.

'No, no, she's lovely ... I mean ... no, not in that way. I mean she's fine as a person, but we haven't ... there hasn't been ... look, you can ask her. Why would anything happen between us? Jesus Christ, Wes.'

Noticing how Marcus's eyes never left it, Wes kept hold of the garlic crusher in one hand as he wrote with the other:

How is she involved?

'Involved with what? What, like, with the other guy? She isn't. Is she?'

Wes could have pushed further, but it seemed clear that Marcus was telling the truth. In fact, that was his problem: words flew out of his mouth on autopilot. He simply didn't know how to shut the hangar doors.

'Wes,' he said, his voice rising in pitch, 'will you please put that thing down and tell me what the fuck is going on?'

That man tried to kill me.

The fear left Marcus's face, to be replaced by a pallor that looked like a sudden illness. 'You are kidding me.' He looked Wes in the eyes and whispered, 'You're not kidding me. Well, shit, Wes – y-you need to go to the police.'

Wes gave him a cheesy grin and nodded, to demonstrate that he might just have thought of that already.

'How was I – how was I supposed to know that … I'm sorry, mate, but how could I have …'

Wes tossed the garlic crusher back into the sink, wrote two words on his pad and stuffed it under Marcus's face.

You're fired.

'That's unfair dismissal!' Marcus said, before clamping his jaw shut.

Wes turned and headed for the front door.

'No, no, hang on. At least untie me before you …'

Wes paused to appreciate his last few moments of warmth before turning the handle.

'Wes? Wes!'

The last thing he heard before he closed the door was the stutter of the chair scraping across the kitchen floor and the thump of something heavy falling. He left the cul-de-sac at a stride. The man was simply astonishing. How could he not see what he was doing? How could he not ask the obvious questions? This was not a matter of hindsight; it was basic human curiosity.

The road ahead split into a T-junction. He stopped. Across the road stood the squat cuboid of the Tesco Extra, illuminated from within and pumping light out into the darkness. There were people inside, shopping even now. He saw, through a sliver of light, a lounge that no longer seemed his own. He saw something white and rectangular being offered and taken. He saw a second hand coming in to cover the first, radiating warmth and sincerity.

His instinct was to turn left, go straight home to Alex and question her. It was a stupid idea. Having lost Wes in the streets of Strathurst, they would try to pick him up wherever they could: his house, his office, the train station, the home of any friend or relative. Everything he now wanted, he wanted from Alex: answers, reassurance, a blazing argument about who she should and shouldn't be trusting. But what he wanted was no longer of any importance. It was what kept him alive that counted.

He turned right.

Saturday

12

THE embrace of fresh sheets, suffused with warmth. His wife beside him, naked and long-limbed. Bliss. When Wes had sneaked back in via the patio doors she had taken him straight up to bed, not for sex, but for the long, indulgent sleep he craved after his ordeal.

He rolled over. A man stood in the doorway, dressed in black, a balaclava concealing his face. Wes jerked back towards his wife. As he turned, she was already throwing a leg over his hips, pressing down on his chest with one hand, rising up to straddle him. A wicked half-smile curled her lips. With her free hand she stroked – he hadn't noticed it before – her swollen belly. Beyond her, the man started towards the bed. Wes wriggled and pushed with his hips, but she wouldn't budge. He reached up to gain some leverage. She snared his hands and pinned them against his sides, saying, 'Sorry, hon.'

'You bitch,' Wes said, as the black skull of the balaclava filled his vision.

Artex in curved patterns. A tatty orange lampshade with a corkscrew-shaped eco light bulb. A great mass of light pressing against thin curtains. He was lying flat on his back. The only things pressing down on him were the duvet and a colossal, inexplicable erection. He still couldn't move – nothing except his eyes, which he pushed to the extremes of their range, trying to see as much of his surroundings as he could. It was a single bed, and the furniture was unfamiliar. Everything was a shade of white except for the figure in the doorway – no, it was a navy blue dressing-gown, hanging from a hook on the back of the door. His dream mind withdrew, a spider retreating to the edge of its web, and he managed to move a couple of fingers, then stretch his legs. He turned his head left, then right. Definitely no-one in the room with him. Thank God. He spotted a dreamcatcher hung on the wall beside the window. Well, that had been sod all use.

He remembered now: he had arrived at the Swallowtail B&B late last night. The owner, a sixty-something woman with purple hair and a tie-dyed skirt, had just been going to bed, but happily gave him a room. In order to deny his pursuers a lead if they came here, he claimed to be a Lithuanian holidaymaker.

'What's your name, then, love?'

He wrote down the first thing that sounded plausible:

Vilmos Zsigmond.

Wasn't he a famous cinematographer?

'And where's your luggage?'

The advantage of having to write his answers was that it gave him a few extra seconds to make things up.

Let us say Ryanair have not impressed me.

She laughed. 'Yeah, that's happened to us, too. Whereabouts in Lithuania are you from, then?'

He racked his brains for the name of the capital. Was it Riga? Tallinn?

The capital.

'What's Vilnius like at this time of the year, then?'

Nice.

'Matthew and I went there a couple of years ago. Have they re-opened the –'

Bloody hell, this was like University Challenge. Birmingham. He should have said he was from Birmingham – at least he knew where it was. He cut her off with a huge yawn, prompting her to apologise for keeping him up. She showed him to his room,

82

provided him with an unused toothbrush and a tube of tooth-paste, and left him to get some rest. Standing alone next to the bed, his mind blank and spent, he realised that what he wanted more than anything was for this pleasant, motherly woman to come back and give him a hug.

His voice in the dream had been high-pitched and panicky. In previous dreams he had spoken like a mellifluous radio DJ or, once, with the voice of Sean Connery. The disappointment he always felt on waking was tempered by the memory of it. He had learned, before the dream left him, to savour the taste of speech in his mouth, like expensive chocolate.

He rose, found the bathroom and showered. Then he dressed in yesterday's clothes and followed the smell of frying bacon down to a breakfast room with a bay window overlooking the road. There were four tables, but only one place set. It was out of season, of course, but the B&B's location was not ideal from a business point of view – not in the heart of the town, nor out in the country.

'Full English, you said?' His hostess put a steaming plate of fried food on the table in front of him. 'That should perk you up a bit.'

His sifu, who took Wing Chun just a bit too seriously, would have disapproved. Wes attacked the plate as if the sausages and mushrooms and tomatoes would escape if he didn't stop them. It was the best cooked breakfast he could remember, and the reju-venating effect on his body was miraculous. As he finished, he looked up to see his host standing in the doorway, a tea towel twisted in her hands.

'Will you be spending another night, then?'

Despite the woman's propensity for awkward questions he felt looked after here. They might never find him in this quiet little B&B, off the beaten track. He shook his head. If he was a target, he must at least be a moving target.

'Oh, that's a shame,' she said.

But I will recommend you to my friends in Vilnius.

She brightened. 'Ačiū!'

For a moment it seemed she had sneezed, then he realised she was trying her Lithuanian on him. He faked delight, but he had made up his mind – for all her warmth and hospitality, it was time to go. He paid for his room and made his way into town.

The sun fought its way through a haze of cirrus. The new morning brought a little more clarity to his thoughts, but not a whole lot more hope. It was a distinct possibility that they would find and kill him, and that they would get away with it. Unless he wrote all of his evidence down. Then there was a chance that whoever found his body would discover enough to start a manhunt and bring them to justice. A shame he wouldn't be around to see it. Still, writing things down seemed like a good way to marshal his thoughts, so, wedging himself between a wall and a bottle bank, he got his notebook out.

The facts:

1. A man is trying to kill me

2. I have no idea why

3. His name is probably Keiran Lowry

4. He has at least one accomplice

5. They tracked me via my phone

6. My wife has spoken to them and may be involved

It was this last one that was the real punch in the guts, worse even than the first. He had, by necessity, been fiercely independent when he met her for that first awkward cup of coffee, that first real test after the safety of conversing via the internet. She had softened him by degrees, made him surrender the bluntness, the guardedness, he had used to get through his youth. If he were to live his life over, he would let her do it again. With Alex he had been able, for the first time, to step out from under the shadow of 'the issue', to live a life that approached normality.

Again: that image of her, shaking the man's hand. There could be all sorts of reasons – she might be involved, but they had lied to her about their motives; she might have been playing along with them to protect him; he might have mistaken her look of calm for one of glazed shock. Any one of these would have been a comfort, but wanting them to be true didn't make them so. His doubts were not so easy to dispel.

He had only one real option: to find out why this was happening and persuade them not to murder him after all. It sounded hopelessly naive when spelled out in his thoughts like this, but it was all he had.

He returned to his notepad.

Plan of action:
1. Find out if Alex is against me
2. Find out why I'm being targeted
3. Make them stop

*

He chose a barber he had never been to before – off the main drag, with plenty of mirrors so he had a good view around him while his hair was cut. As the hairdresser worked, Wes kept his eye on the nearest pair of sharp scissors. If one of his assailants came in he would be armed and stabbing away in seconds, sending hair trimmings in all directions, the barber's apron whirling like the cloak of some 1930s superhero.

At one point the hairdresser paused, and he knew she'd spotted the abrasions on the side of his head. She said nothing and continued her work with the clippers. This was one of the reasons for cutting down to a grade two – in any further fights, his opponent wouldn't be able to grab him by the hair. The other reason was disguise. Face to face it wouldn't fool anyone, but in a crowd it might make all the difference.

He had never been a handsome man. His eyes were that bit

too far apart, his complexion coarse, eyebrows unruly as a hedgerow. What had Alex ever seen in him? And now, in the mirror, he was even worse: he had a convict's face. For the first time in his life he looked worse than his passport photo. The hairdresser looked a little doubtful about the result too, but Wes reassured her with a nod, paid and left.

At the library he took up residence at a PC in a secluded corner. By tilting back on the chair he could get a view of the entrance, but with the ability to lean forwards again so his face was hidden by a shelf of German poetry. First priority: email Alex and demand an explanation. But when he tried to access his main email, he found the account had been suspended. He tried his backup account. No luck there, either. With a mounting sense of outrage he also discovered that his entire blog and personal website had been erased, along with the J+H website and his Facebook and Twitter accounts. How had they managed this? They had separated him from his wife, compromised his phone, and erased his entire presence on the internet. They had made him a ghost.

The one thing he had, assuming he could trust Marcus's information, was a name. He searched the internet, but none of the resulting sites, articles or photos seemed to match the profile of the man who was after him. He was not the tonsured vet approaching retirement; he was not the children's entertainer in the stripy pantaloons. He tried typing 'Keiran Lowry' and 'Strathurst' into an online phone book, and it gave him an address and a telephone number. Was that him? Could it be that simple? Of course, he wasn't supposed to have the man's real name. For that, at least, Marcus had proved useful.

So, what next? He had to assume anybody he contacted might be in on it. Marcus had already betrayed him. Potentially Alex too. At this stage, perhaps he should even be suspecting … no. Not Tom, surely. They had grown up together. Wes had been witness to Tom's transformation in college from acne-ridden mess of insecurity to charm assassin. That particularly dull Maths lesson where Tom had revealed his new-found insights was as vivid in his memory as the day it happened. 'You are what you pretend to be,' Tom had said. 'If I pretend to be confident, even though I don't feel it, people treat me with more respect and I become more confident. If I pretend to be a sex god ... well, you get the idea.' It was unthinkable that someone who had shared such a huge chunk of his life could betray him. Wasn't this what they wanted – the feeling that he was alone, friendless, cut off? And if Alex was innocent too, she would be just as terrified by all this as he was.

He created a new email account under a false name and spent the next half hour composing an email, making sure it would send just the right message to Alex, while appearing innocuous to anyone that might intercept it. Then he wrote a much longer, less cryptic message on paper and stashed it in a pocket.

It was time to move on – he couldn't spend too long in any one place – but before leaving, he went onto TripAdvisor, created a new account, and wrote a glowing review for the Swallowtail B&B.

*

His next destination was the Chapel of Saint Francis de Sale – a tiny historical building adrift in a sea of new-build houses. He pushed open the gate in the stone wall surrounding the little garden and went in through the only door – a full-length glass panel with a modern lock: the only incongruous part of an otherwise historic building. It was a single, vaulted space, no bigger than a living room, built in the fourteenth century and able to seat a dozen, maybe sixteen at a pinch, though it had always been empty when he and Alex had visited. He slid his handwritten note under one of the pews, wedging it in the gap where the metal base met the wooden plinth.

The way they had silenced him was still foremost in his mind, and as he headed back towards the town centre, he was thinking of all the ways this plan might not work. Since worst-case scenarios seemed to be transpiring with an alarming regularity, he wondered whether the government was behind this. That would be the deepest of shit. They would have the power to stop access to his bank account, removing his ability to buy food or pay for shelter. He would end up living in a forest somewhere, harvesting blackberries and sleeping under a bivouac made from soggy bracken. As a test, he tried a cash machine at the edge of the High Street and was delighted when it let him withdraw £200.

It probably wasn't the government. What reason would they have? He wasn't a political agitator, a terror suspect. Okay, he had written a couple of critical blog posts about politicians – he recalled with particular fondness his headline 'MP buys sex toy collection on expenses; taxpayer gets shafted' – but they were no worse than what you could read anywhere else.

He bought a warm, waterproof coat in neutral grey and a box of paper clips. He considered buying a knife, or something that could be used as a club, but decided he was better off travelling light and relying on his bare hands. So far, they had at least been sporting enough to try and kill him discreetly. If they moved on to firearms there wasn't much he could buy that would help. M&S weren't big on Kevlar body armour.

He set off for the eastern edge of town, heading for the address written on his notepad, the address on Ashfield Road that claimed to be Keiran Lowry's flat. It was the lion's den, to be sure, but he would have to take risks. And he could not think of a better place to look for more information.

13

ALEX put the cordless phone face down on the coffee table, next to her mobile – two useless electronic lumps. So that was that, another dead end. It had been painful ringing Wes's parents. She'd pretended everything was fine, choosing her words carefully so they wouldn't arouse suspicion or fear. It wasn't easy sounding casual when all she felt was doubt and dread. Their replies made it obvious that they hadn't heard from Wes since yesterday.

'Can't you try someone else?' Tom said.

She shook her head. 'No reply from Marcus yet? A text, maybe?'

He checked his phone. 'No. He usually has a lie-in at the weekend, so we might get something later.'

She handed him the breakfast bowls. Even though she'd opted for an unusually small bowl of muesli, half of it remained untouched. 'Go to the sink and wash these up.'

'Yes, milady.'

'And while you're at it, take a look at the silver car just to the right of the lamp post.'

He froze in the act of receiving the bowls, then headed out to the kitchen as instructed.

Tom had stayed the night in the spare bedroom. Neither of them had discussed the matter, she simply made up the bed and he had slept in it. But even with Tom in the next room, the night throbbed with a terrible quiet. Wes had never been a noisy sleeper, but … there was silence and there was silence. She had risen at two in the morning, unable to sleep, and padded down to the kitchen in her pyjamas. Tom, also insomniac, had joined her. They ate toast together in the lounge and it seemed to do them good – when they returned to their beds they managed to get some sleep.

Having dealt with the breakfast stuff, Tom came back in from the kitchen. 'You think they're watching the house?'

'I know everyone's car in this street; that isn't one of them.'

'Is there anything you don't notice? It could just be someone visiting.'

'At 8:30 in the morning? Someone whose car just happens to have tinted windows?'

'No, I agree. It does look a little suspect.' Tom sat down on the sofa. Normally he would sprawl – he was an ostentatious sloucher – but today he perched on the edge like a man about to be called to the witness stand. 'So what do we do now?'

'We might have to report him to the police as missing.'

'Don't we have to wait twenty-four hours? I was still with him at five o'clock yesterday, so it's only been –' he checked his wrist-watch, a big, flashy chrome thing '– about sixteen so far.'

'Is that all?' she said, appalled at how much anxiety could be crammed into just a few hours.

Tom had already tried to connect the number on the business card to a name or address on the internet, but had come up with nothing. They were left only with the non-option of searching for Wes, being followed, and possibly leading them straight to him.

'You could check your email again,' he said.

So, he was also running out of ideas too. Why would Wes use email instead of texting?

She had long ago set her mobile up so she had to manually check for new emails – it was one less distraction in a life already far too full of them. She closed her eyes for a few seconds and offered up something akin to a prayer, though since she had no religious belief she wondered what she was actually praying to. The internet? Silicon? Snapping her eyes back open, she picked up the phone and tapped with determination.

One new message. She scanned the words, but it wasn't from … no, wait.

'Oh,' she said.

Tom sat up. 'What is it?'

'It's him.' The relief was unreal, dizzying.

He sat down beside her and read. 'Is this the right message?'

'Yes, yes. Read the whole thing.'

From: countdragula@freemail.com
To: alex_henning@wigwam.net
Subject: Missing you

Alex,

I'm sorry I missed you when I was in Strathurst the other week. It would have been wonderful to meet up.

I had a great time, but got soaked with muddy water by a passing car after coming out of Frank's house. Trust me to stand next to a puddle!

We must meet up again soon. Hope everything's okay with you and Wes.

Love,
Em

Tom said, 'Erm, Alex …'

She shook her head. 'It's from him. It's a coded message.'

'Really?'

'Yes. It's from Count Dragula. That's a reference to a fancy dress party we went to last year. He went as Dracula, but didn't have time to get a costume, so he used one of my black wrap-around skirts as a cloak, and because he looked so camp, I called him Count Dragula. He's also signed off as Em.'

'Meaning?'

'Well, M is an upside-down W, isn't it.'

She scanned the message again, trying to tease some more meaning out of it. Her husband was there, in the spaces between the words.

'He tells me to trust you.'

'How the hell do you get that?'

She pointed. '"Trust me to stand next to a puddle."'

'You'll have to explain that one to me.'

'He says "trust" and … you do know that he sometimes refers to you as Puddle?'

'No. Why?'

'Erm … It's just a …' How to say this tactfully?

'Come on. Out with it.'

'It's because your relationships tend to be shallow and a bit mucky.'

'Cheeky bastard! We definitely have to find your husband. I want words with him.'

'He's telling us to go to the Chapel of Saint Francis de Sale.'

'W-what? You're way ahead of me, here.'

'He refers to Frank's house. That's what we call the Chapel of Saint Francis de Sale, because it's so small.'

'This is that tiny thing in the middle of the housing estate?'

'That's the one.'

'If he's there, we'll be leading them straight to him.'

'He wouldn't be that stupid. Clearly he thinks they're monitoring my email. He's going to be careful. The reason he hasn't been home is because he knows they're watching us.'

'What if you're wrong?'

He was kicking the tyres again. No. She knew this much about her husband. And this was an opportunity to do something, rather than sitting on her arse.

'If I'm wrong we hole up in the church with him, barricade the door and phone 999.'

It wouldn't come to that. It had better not.

As they reached the end of the road, Alex saw, out of the corner of her eye, the door of the silver car open.

'They're getting out,' she muttered.

'Just carry on,' Tom said, with no movement of his lips. 'We didn't notice a thing.'

She swallowed and resisted the temptation to walk faster. At the end of Castle Street they stopped to have a mock discussion and get another look at the two men in their peripheral vision.

'One's dark-skinned, the other one's bald,' Alex said. 'They aren't the two that came to the house yesterday.'

Tom's eyes widened, just a fraction. 'So, that's four of them, at least.'

The bald one diverted into a corner shop; the dark-skinned man leaned against one of the trees that grew out of the cracked tarmac of the pavement and showed a sudden interest in his phone.

In a slightly louder voice, Alex said, 'What else can I do but pray for his return?'

'Come on, then.'

As she expected, the chapel was empty. There was nowhere to hide – the pews were simple planks of wood, the lectern not wide enough to conceal a person. Disappointment and relief warred in her. So why had he mentioned this place? It was special for both of them, but for acoustic, rather than religious, reasons. Alex would stand next to the lectern and sing unselfconsciously while Wes snapped his fingers or clapped his thighs as percussion. The chapel resonated like nowhere else she knew, flattering even her modest voice. Tom let the door close behind him, giving them a little privacy.

'Where are they?' she said.

'They've stopped a good way back.'

'He must have left something here – a clue, a message.'

They searched the place. At the back was a table with various leaflets and an information board describing service times and the chapel's history and restoration. Alex flicked through the paperwork while Tom checked the lectern. She found nothing out of the ordinary and stared at the board to see if he had written anything on it, or arranged things in some specific order, something clever, something cryptic …

'I've got it,' Tom said.

She whirled round to see him lying on the floor. He was detaching several sheets of paper from the underside of one of the pews – handwritten pages from Wes's notebook. She took them straight out of his hands and sat down to go through them. Tom read over her shoulder.

Alex,

A man tried to kill me at work on Friday night. He has an accomplice. You know what they look like because I saw you speak to them on Friday, in our lounge. You never pull the curtains properly.

There are two possibilities: (a) you are part of this conspiracy; (b) you aren't.

If (a) is true:

Well, I'm screwed, aren't I? Why you would want this, I have no idea. I can only apologise for whatever it is I've done.

If (b) is true:

I'm sorry for doubting you.

I need to find out why this is happening. I hope you'll understand that I have to stay away until I know I can trust you. I need you to do everything you can to keep us both safe.

Don't trust Marcus: he acted as their lookout, but I think he was being naive rather than malicious.

Don't trust the police: they weren't interested in my problem, and have other reasons to want to talk to me.

Do trust Tom.

These people are very ruthless and they're using technology to their advantage. Assume that your email and phone are being monitored. Assume you're being watched at all times. They tracked me via my mobile and have trashed my email, websites, and all other forms of communication. They have taken away my voice.

I'm sorry you're involved with this. Don't do anything to endanger yourself. I love you.

W

It was a match lit in darkness; it flared, it glowed, it went out.

'He doesn't trust me,' she said. 'Why doesn't he trust me?'

'It's not you. I mean, look: tracking him via his mobile … and Marcus involved too. You'd be paranoid under those circumstances.' He frowned and his jaw set. 'I always thought there was something suspicious about that little arsehole.'

But she already knew the real reason. 'It's my fault.'

'Oh, Alex. Don't be ridiculous.'

'I had to give them the impression that I was on their side, so I shook hands with … I shook hands with a man who tried to kill my husband. How was I supposed to know Wes was watching? I was just trying to get them to go away.'

It made her wonder whether this hand of hers would make other betrayals.

'It's a misunderstanding, that's all,' Tom said. 'You need to reply to his email and tell him.'

'But they're monitoring me.'

'Then we have to send it from somewhere else.'

'But he has no reason to believe me. If I really was betraying him, that's exactly what I'd say – that it was a misunderstanding.'

Tom had no answer to this.

'And what's this bit about the police wanting to talk to him?' She fixed him with a look of accusation.

'I know nothing about any problems with the police.'

'Then how is he in trouble with the law?'

'I don't know. I'm sorry – that's the truth.'

Answers. She needed answers.

'Have you got any paper?' she said. 'I'm going to leave a reply.'

'You can't. We have to assume they'll search the place as soon as we've gone.'

The air went out of her lungs. Her shoulders slumped. 'So what are we supposed to do?'

'I, uh …'

'I'm not going to just sit around and wait.'

'I agree.'

'Well?' Where was his cocky confidence now? She needed him to suggest something. Anything.

'We have to, er …' He paced about. 'They'll expect us to stop praying at some point, and then …'

'Go home?' she said.

'I suppose.'

'We're just going to have to put the kettle on and have a brain-storm.'

It was hardly a plan of action; it was so inadequate, so … feeble.

'Yes,' he said, 'only they may have bugged the house. They may be installing microphones or cameras right now.'

'Tom …' she pleaded.

Already he was cultivating the same pessimism she had seen in Wes's note. And she saw that it was a necessity. It wasn't that Wes was being too paranoid; it was that she wasn't being paranoid enough. But how could any of them live like this, suspicious of everything and everyone, fearful that a single instance of mis-placed trust would be punished with disaster?

How? Because there was no other option.

14

THE Ashfield Road flat was located at the end of a row of shops, above the Shiva Tandoori. It was a tired place: window frames of parched wood; a concrete staircase, bordered by a rusted railing which reached up the side of the shop and disappeared around the back; a plastic 'Flat 3' sign attached to the wall, almost unreadable from years of weathering. Wes observed it from the safety of a bus stop fifty metres down the road, his hood pulled up and hands thrust into his pockets. The bus stop's advertising board was his cover – if Lowry were to emerge and look in this direction, all he would see was a gigantic picture of a woman's face, her skin perfected by the action of an 'entropy reversal elixir'. Or Photoshop, as it was otherwise known.

Ideally, Lowry would come bouncing down the stairs and sod off somewhere, leaving the place unoccupied. At a minimum he could do Wes the courtesy of appearing at the window. But after twenty minutes of watching, Wes had seen no more than when he'd arrived. In front of him was a potential gold mine, and here he was, standing in the cold, ignoring buses like a moron. Enough of this hanging around; fortune favours the bold. He crossed the road and walked up the stairs to the back of the flat. A green door, devoid of glass. Green means go, right? He knocked twice – a hollow sound, thin wood – and retreated back down the stairs, close enough to hear if the door opened, but far enough away for a good head start.

He gave it a minute. There were a dozen reasons for someone to be inside but not to answer the door: they were in the shower, the TV was turned up loud, they were having a lie-in after a long night's murdering. None of these thoughts were helpful; none of them were getting him any useful information. Wes padded back up the steps. From his pocket he took two of the paper clips, which he had fashioned into a makeshift tensioner and rake. He adjusted them, inserted the tensioner into the lock and applied gentle pressure, then put the rake in and stroked the lock pins from back to front. He was in full view of a row of houses, but there was no other way to do this. He closed his eyes as he teased the mechanism, concentrating on the tiny vibrations of the paper clip.

He was rusty. The last time he'd done this was when he and Tom had broken into Dean Benford's house – their fourth and final act of burglary. By this time, they had become quite proficient at picking locks. They had practised for hours on desk drawers, padlocks, patio doors. The idea was to go up to Dean's room, nick his prized porn collection – which he had boasted about incessantly at school – and slope out. The beauty of it was that Dean could never tell his parents that anything was missing. What Wes and Tom hadn't banked on, in their naivety, was an alarm system. With the beep of the pre-alarm sounding in their ears, they had panicked and run. The stakes had seemed high at the time – a serious talking to if they were caught, maybe even trouble with the police. Shock, horror.

The cylinder released with a soft click. Not so rusty after all. He turned the lock the rest of the way, removed his tools and pushed at the door, managing to open it enough to step inside without any squeaking of hinges. He checked above his head for alarm sensors or cameras. There were only cobwebs. Beyond there was a short corridor with magnolia walls and a well-worn carpet the colour of fungus. Immediately to his left was a recessed coat rack, followed by a door opening into the bathroom. Ahead were two more doors, both ajar, one half-hidden by the corner of the corridor as it turned to the left. Directly ahead of him was the lounge. As he advanced he saw the front window looking out onto the street, a sofa, a TV. Once he reached the door – with a quick glance to the left to see that the corridor ended in an open closet – he peered round it. No-one here. He realised, as he walked in, that the room also opened out behind him into a kitchen area. He retreated from the lounge and peered into the other room. As expected: the bedroom. A punch-bag hung from the ceiling like a dismembered torso.

He could stop tiptoeing now – the flat was empty. He shut the outside door and identified three emergency hiding places: the space on the far side of the double bed; in the bath, with the shower curtain pulled; and behind the counter that marked the edge of the kitchen area. The illicit lover's hideout of choice – the bedroom wardrobe – proved far too small because it was stuffed full of monochrome clothing, not a colour in sight. The wire hooks of the hangars looked just like a row of question marks.

At the bottom of the wardrobe was a bulging rucksack. He loosened the fasteners to reveal tins of soup, bottled water, a portable stove, first aid kit and compass. A keen camper? A survival nut? He put everything back as it was, and closed the wardrobe door. The rest of the room was remarkably sparse. The bed was a double, but with just a single pillow. In the bedside drawer he found only a box of tissues and, strangely, an unopened bag of salted peanuts.

The lounge gave him little more. Beneath the TV was an Xbox and some games, mostly military shooters. A modest bookshelf housed a few well-thumbed titles, all non-fiction, and with a bias towards fitness, survival in the wild, and the collapse of society. Some incongruously academic titles sat among the books: a history of Sparta and a copy of Darwin's *The Origin of Species* – the only paperback on the shelf with an uncreased spine. On a small table beside the sofa was a laptop, plugged into a wall socket. He sat down and opened the lid. It sprang to life from hibernation in a couple of seconds, presenting him with a standard login screen. He tried a few passwords – 'Keiran', 'Lowry', 'Klowry', 'password', 'murderousshitbag' – before accepting that it wasn't going to let him in. He closed the lid.

The kitchen gave him an idea about Lowry's diet – mostly healthy, with lots of protein. The bathroom medicine cabinet failed to yield tubs full of powerful drugs to combat mental imbalance.

He went through the rooms a second time, searching more deeply, opening containers in the kitchen, lifting the mattress off the bed, wondering whether there was anything to find in a flat so devoid of the trappings of life. In Wes's house there were messages written on every spare bit of paper, cards still on show from his birthday a month ago, certificates from Wing Chun and dance classes. Here, there was nothing extraneous or out of place, very little to give any real insight into its occupant. It was a hotel room before the guest arrived, a prisoner's cell before inspection.

In the gap between the bookshelf and the wall – the gap dictated by the skirting board – he hit the jackpot: a compact black book held shut with an integrated elastic band. A diary – he knew it immediately.

The act of opening it was accompanied by an unexpected sound: a key sliding home in a lock, a door opening. It took him a moment to realise that the sound wasn't caused by his opening the book; that, yes, someone was coming in through the only exit; and, yes, Wes should be moving, right now. He went straight for the nearest of his hiding places: the counter that separated the kitchen area from the lounge. He pattered across the carpet, placing his feet more gingerly once he reached the harder lino, and crammed himself behind the kitchen units.

Shit, shit, shit.

Shoes on tiles. Lowry – he assumed it was Lowry – had gone into the bathroom. Wes reached up and slid a kitchen knife out of the block on the counter. If he made a run for the outside door now, he might get past Lowry before he came out of the bathroom, but he would certainly be noticed.

The hiss of water running into the sink. Was it worth the risk?

He could wait until he came further in: the bedroom or the lounge. Or until he left entirely. Yes – just leave; that would be ideal. But hoping for such good luck was idiotic. If one thing was going to kill him, it was hesitation. He began to emerge from his hiding place when he heard the flow of water stop. He was paralysed, stranded between the desire to remain concealed and the decision to make a run for it.

Steps again, moving from tile to carpet, towards him. The moment had passed. Wes ducked back behind the units and breathed through his mouth, fulfilling a sudden craving for oxygen while trying to make as little noise as possible. Hearing him moving away from the kitchen and towards the lounge area, Wes risked a look round the edge of the cabinet, aware that even this small movement caused the stiff, waterproof fabric of his new coat to make a sound. It was Lowry all right, topless and concentrating on his phone. So, he'd retrieved it from the bin. He slumped onto the sofa and uttered a heartfelt, 'Shit.'

Wes had missed a trick with the laptop. He should have stolen it and left immediately, then he could have worked on cracking the security at his leisure. Bollocks. Too late now. He had to concentrate on getting himself out. All it would take was for Lowry to decide that he fancied a cup of tea and he would be fighting for his life again.

One long breath and he broke cover. He had to run towards the sofa before he could reverse and head out of the lounge door. Lowry's head snapped round and Wes threw the knife straight at his face. Lowry's arms came up defensively, and he threw himself back onto the sofa. The blade passed over his head and clattered off the far wall. Wes was already swinging round the door frame, hooking his fingers over the handle and pulling the door shut behind him. Three strides down the corridor and he was opening the outside door, pulling that shut too and turning hard left onto the raised concrete walkway. At the steps, he decided it would be faster to jump onto the rail and slide down rather than negotiate the steps – it had worked for James Bond in *Octopussy*. But he still had too much sideways momentum, and after sliding a metre he lost his balance and toppled off. There was maybe three metres of empty air before he hit the pavement. If he broke his legs now … but he managed to land on his feet, knees bent, and absorb the impact.

He stumbled underneath the cover of the concrete staircase and heard the thud of shoes above him as Lowry ran down towards the main road. Wes bolted in the opposite direction, past the row of cars parked at the back of the shops. He turned left at a T-junction in the direction of the park and the edge of town, glancing over one shoulder as he did. No sign of Lowry. The noise of the traffic must have covered his footsteps.

It probably wasn't necessary to leave Strathurst entirely, but his legs refused to listen to reason. They didn't stop until the houses gave way to woods. Then he turned off, sliding between the trunks and the foliage, putting a good hundred metres between himself and the road. A tree stump gave him a place to sit, and he spent a couple of minutes panting hard and watching in the direction of town for any sign of movement.

Finally, convinced he had not been followed, he removed his prize from his pocket and opened it. Yes, it was a diary. Maybe this was even better than the laptop. He flicked through the pages to the last entry, and there he found the reason they were trying to kill him. Lowry described it as a word for word transcript of a post from Wes's blog. He read it all the way through. It was, he had to confess, a pretty good piece. Only one maddening little detail: he hadn't written it.

15

'WHAT have you got?' Keiran said, joining Sean and Jamal at the street corner.

'They're in there.' Sean nodded towards the tiny chapel, just visible through a cluster of trees. His arms were folded, head tilted back, a bouncer at the door of a nightclub.

'Both of them?'

'Yeah.'

'They've spotted you?'

'No, no, no,' Jamal interjected. 'We made sure of that.'

'And you haven't been any nearer than this?'

Jamal shook his head. 'We came round the other side, so that when they leave they'll be walking away from us.'

It was a tiny place, closer to a doll's house than a church. Here was the future of Christianity in a nutshell: a place of worship with space for less than a dozen. Maybe that had been Judas's beef at the last supper – not enough bloody room.

When Keiran had asked for information on the Hennings and Tom Jolliffe, he'd been astonished by the detail provided. The cell-like nature of DA hid from him any idea of its size, but it appeared to be much larger and more powerful than he'd thought. There had been no mention, though, that Alex Henning had any kind of religious faith. Something from her childhood, perhaps, that had only surfaced once her husband disappeared.

'Anything else to report?' he said.

'Nothing,' Sean said.

'Quiet as a mouse,' Jamal added. So eager to please.

Sean grinned. 'Perhaps they're fucking in there. You know what he's like.'

'With her?' Jamal said with a delighted contempt.

'Why not? She might be needing some comfort, now her husband has disappeared.'

Jamal chuckled.

'Children!' Keiran said, instantly silencing the pair of them.

Sean resumed his look of seriousness. Jamal looked injured and came out with: 'I was only messing around.'

Their wounded pride was of no interest to him. Keiran was already back to thinking about the two people in the chapel. Hadn't they twigged that sweeping the town for Henning would be more effective than prayer? He and Grant certainly had. But that was the curse of faith – to ignore an obvious course of action in favour of an appeal to superstition.

'They're coming out,' Sean said.

'Follow them,' Keiran said, once it was clear that Henning wasn't with them. 'Keep me up to date on where they're going.'

Sean nodded and the two of them left. Keiran walked into the chapel. He searched the place for any reason, other than prayer, that they might have come here. He climbed onto the stone lectern to reach the sill of the one and only stained glass window, checked the underside of the pews. His hope of a lucky find withered and the contortions opened the wounds in his chest. The pain had started again while he and Grant had been search- ing the town for Henning this morning, and now he could also feel the stickiness seeping through the dressing. He would have to go home and deal with it – yet more time he wasn't combing Strathurst for his target.

He'd already made a bad impression on Grant that morning. His body's desire for extra healing time had caused him to wake late, and before he did anything else he'd had to trace his phone via GPS from his laptop. He had found it in a public bin – clearly the only hiding place Henning's limited brain could con- ceive – smeared with chip grease and curry sauce, but still working. On checking it, he discovered that Grant had already made his way into town from Bordon and left him a voicemail: 'Where are you? Do you think that answering your phone under

104

these circumstances is optional?' Keiran called him back, saying he'd left the phone at home while popping out to the shops to buy some fresh gauze and bandaging for his chest. Grant wasn't mollified, but at least he stopped asking questions. His brother also hadn't mentioned the result of his report back to Brad last night. Was Grant protecting him? Or had he got a roasting over Keiran's failure? It would explain his irritability.

On entering the flat, Keiran stripped off his sweater and T-shirt, and went into the bathroom. He used a pair of scissors to take the bandage off, ran some water and started to bathe the wound. In his jeans pocket, his phone vibrated. Bugger. He turned off the tap and dried his hands. His entire body ached, and he wanted to sit. He went through to the lounge while he read the text from Grant.

Checked High and Broad St, plus Albion Hotel. Where are you now?

He thudded down on the sofa. 'Shit.' He could say he was at the eastern edge of town, in the Stockbank area – he could get there faster than Grant if he left now. His finger hovered over the touchscreen.

There was a rustle from the kitchen area. Not another rat, surely. He glanced over and there was Henning, running towards him, throwing something that spun end over end, glinting in the light. Keiran fell back flat on the sofa and the knife missed his head by the span of a hand.

He sprang back and launched himself into a run, yanking open the doors Henning pulled shut behind him. Within seconds he had gone down the concrete steps and was standing on the pavement, in front of the shops, looking one way then the other, his fists clenched. Where the fuck had he gone? Keiran could check the shops on either side, or grab a passer-by and demand to know if they had seen someone running in this direc-tion. But no – it wasn't the DA way. Everything had to be invisible, untraceable.

Of course: Henning had gone the other way, out the back. But how had he got down the steps so quickly? A blasphemous thought slipped into his mind – maybe Henning was just faster, better adapted, destined to win. Henning's hair had been much shorter, presumably a feeble attempt at disguise, but there was a secondary effect too. It made him look more like Keiran and Grant, more like a Survivor. It was the inverse of the story of Samson – cutting your hair off gave you strength.

People were staring at him. He was topless and bleeding. There was nothing to be gained here. He went back up to the flat, and searched, room by room, trying to find evidence of anything Henning had taken. Nothing seemed to be missing, and Keiran was confident the laptop was secure. He must have interrupted Henning before he had the chance to steal anything. So how had he got in? All of the windows were secure and the door showed no sign of being forced. He must have picked the lock; it had never been the most convincing piece of hardware. Keiran woke up the laptop, performed a quick web search, then dialled a number on his mobile.

'Hello. I need my lock changed … Today … I don't care, I need it changed today. I'll pay you an extra hundred quid, cash in hand … The best thing you've got … Five o'clock. Okay.'

He gave them his name and address and ended the call. Later, he would have to make another excuse to leave Grant and come home. More black marks on his scoresheet. And paying for the new lock meant he wouldn't be able to afford a night with Amber. Looked like he'd be relying on Madame Thumb and her four lovely daughters for a while. He needed this Henning shit to be over. He needed to go back to Slough and get another job, get some cash back in his wallet.

Another question came to him, something more fundamental: how did Henning know where he lived? Keiran had followed DA protocol diligently. There was nothing on the phone Henning had taken except for their common contact, Marcus, and he had been fed a false name that he accepted without question, the same way he'd accepted Keiran's money. There was no lead for Henning to follow. Unless someone had told him. Of course – the traitor in DA, the person who had fed him the information for his article in the first place. And the opportunity to root around his flat would come while Keiran was known to be elsewhere – say, at an empty chapel across the other side of town.

And now that he thought about it, Sean's tough guy posturing and Jamal's dicking around did not make them the most convincing fit for DA. Okay, so they were supposed to be novices, but their double act could be a misdirection from their real motives. It was a useful thought; he would hold it in reserve. Even if it turned out to be untrue, it could serve as a useful distraction for his DA superiors. And if it was true, what a triumph that would be – to deal with Henning *and* reveal the traitors who had caused the problem in the first place.

Until it was decided, one way or the other, he must work with more reliable sources of information. Using the app on his mobile, he checked the intercept on Alex Henning's email account. She had only received one message, from a friend she'd failed to meet up with. He did the same with Tom's email and found nothing more than a couple of penis enlargement offers, which – judging by his list of sexual conquests – the jammy bastard wouldn't be needing.

Why didn't Henning take the laptop? Why didn't he take anything at all? If Sean and Jamal had contacted Henning right after telling Keiran about the chapel, he should have had plenty of time to search the place and … He crossed the lounge in three swift paces and slid his fingers down the back of the bookshelf. He lifted it at one end, pivoting it away from the wall, sending paperbacks flopping onto the carpet.

'Shit!' he yelled at the top of his voice. 'Fucking shit!'

He ran his hand through the stubble of his hair. For a moment he had no idea what to do, no idea at all. Did DA know about the existence of his diary? Was this an internal hatchet job? Was it just bad luck that Henning had found it? He strode into the bedroom and attacked the punch-bag. He imagined Henning's smug face in front of him, or Sean's, or Jamal's, and pounded away, ignoring the pain in his chest.

Writing on paper was supposed to be more secure than using anything digital. He had always been careful not to record anything sensitive about DA in the diary – not enough for them to send someone after him. Still, it would not look good if they found it. Please, let it be Henning acting alone.

He gave himself a good minute to take the edge off his fury, then gave the punch-bag a fraternal pat as he left the room. Best thirty quid he ever spent. As he headed back to the bathroom, a pattern of knocks sounded from the front door: one loud, three rapid and light, another loud: Grant.

Keiran's head dropped. Not now, please, not now. But, yes: now. There was no getting round it. He jabbed at his chest, encouraging more blood to seep from his wounds. It was a good kind of pain, a purposeful kind of pain. He opened the door.

'Brother,' Grant said.

'Come in.' He closed the door behind him and gestured to his chest. 'This needed cleaning up again.'

'I see.'

Keiran turned away, went back into the lounge. 'I'm fed up with it. Why can't it just heal?'

He should confess to the theft of his diary. Which, of course, would mean confessing to its existence in the first place. That would be the action of a true Survivor – to own his mistakes, to overcome them.

'I have to ask you a question,' Grant said.

'Yeah?'

'How seriously are you taking this?'

Keiran turned round. 'As seriously as it can be taken. Having visible spots of blood on my clothes is not going to help me when I start asking round B&Bs for Henning.'

'You're looking tired,' Grant said.

'I ran back here. I wanted to take as little time out as possible. The more hours we're out on the streets, the more chance we have of finding him. Which brings me to a question, brother: why aren't *you* still out there? One of us is better than none.'

Grant smiled, that irritating lift of the lips that suggested he knew more than he was letting on. 'He's probably not even in town.'

'He is,' Keiran assured him.

'You've got evidence for that?'

'No, but it stands to reason. His wife will keep him close.' Later, when this was proved to be true, Keiran would seem like a shrewd judge of character.

'Love?' Grant said.

'Yeah: that.'

Grant looked past him into the lounge with a slight tightening of the eyes. 'What happened to your bookshelf?'

'Hmm?' And here was the opportunity to tell his brother about the diary. Get it out of the way, be shouted at, maybe cast some doubt on Sean and Jamal. Then move on, unburdened.

'Your bookshelf is at an angle.' Grant said.

'Yeah. I was lifting it. I needed something heavy ... to test whether the wounds reopened.'

Who was to say that keeping a diary wasn't the best way of purging his feelings? Just because his other DA brothers didn't write didn't mean they were free of the same bursts of enfeebling emotion. They would change their minds if they could be shown how useful writing was as a means of bringing clarity, perspective, self-knowledge. He had no proof that they knew anything about the diary, but it would do no harm to prepare his defence in advance – the words that would make his confession more acceptable to them. If it came to that.

'I'll get the bandage,' Grant said, and went off to the bathroom.

Keiran called after him. 'It just doesn't want to stop bleeding.'

'We'll tie it thicker, tighter.'

16

CONTRARY to the belief espoused by policemen and grandmothers everywhere, a cup of tea did not solve all ills. It did not bring Alex's husband slipping in through the patio doors; it did not make the silver car at the front of the house vanish; it did not remove from her mind the suspicion that there was a listening device behind the Waterhouse print, on the underside of the sofa, in the lamp shade. When Alex dunked her chocolate Hobnob for too long and half of it slithered into the tea, she lost her temper.

'I am not just sitting here: I need to *do* something!'

Even this outburst was carefully vetted. She had agreed with Tom on their way back from the chapel that they must say nothing their enemies might find useful. Tom ran his hands through his hair. The locks tightened across his scalp, then sprang back into place as he released them. He seemed as frustrated as she was. He was also, she had to remind herself, an outsider doing his best to help, without first-hand knowledge of events. He hadn't been there, hadn't listened to their robot conversation, hadn't been compelled to shake hands with the man who …

Wait a minute. She dragged the vacuum cleaner out from the cupboard under the stairs, jammed the plug into a power socket, switched it on and started to push it across the carpet.

Tom came over and said in a low voice, 'Good idea, but this'll

110

only work once.'

'I know. Listen, when they were here and I shook hands with Groves, I noticed he had this tiny tattoo on the inside of his wrist.'

'I'll get a pen and paper; you can draw it.' He turned towards the coffee table.

'No.' She caught him by the sleeve. 'What if they slipped a camera in here?'

He bit his lip.

'I'll show you with my hands,' she said. 'Here, take this.'

She passed the handle of the vacuum cleaner to him and he took over cleaning the carpet, crashing into the coffee table and the armchair in quick succession. Either he was working on the principle that more noise would make it harder for them to hear, or he had never manoeuvred one of these things in his life. Without needing to discuss it, they came together, as if by chance, their bodies forming a shield.

'It was just three lines in a sort of square C-shape.' She formed her hands into the shape, traced its outline rapidly with one finger.

'A gang tattoo?' he suggested.

'Still going with your Strathurst Mafia theory?'

It probably wasn't much help. The tattoo could be anything: the first letter of a lover's name, a religious symbol, even the hallucination of a mind eager to find some kind of meaning in an otherwise incomprehensible situation. She discussed this with Tom. He was certain she would never have imagined it, and his sympathetic ear helped shore up her confidence.

'And there was another thing,' she said. 'The taller one, Groves, said something strange.'

'Which was?'

'Something about lack of choice, but he said it as if it were a good thing ... I've got it: "There is one path and one choice."'

'Religious nutters?'

111

'Possibly.' At the time she'd been too busy dealing with her fear – and too eager for them to get out of her house – to register how weird this phrase was. 'It shut Kavanagh up immediately. It was like flicking a switch, and from then on Groves did all the talking.'

'So what prompted him to say it?'

'I can't remember. I said something and Kavanagh started to get angry and then Groves took over.'

'This is good. The more details you remember, the more we've got to go on,' said Tom thoughtfully, driving the vacuum cleaner straight into the TV stand.

'Okay, that's enough of that,' she said, pulling the plug out of the wall.

In the absence of a better course of action, they decided to have lunch. They made sandwiches and ate them in a thoughtful silence. Once they had finished, she took the plates through to the sink and faffed ineffectually for a few moments, trying not to look directly at the silver car outside. From the lounge she heard Tom talking on the phone. When he appeared in the kitchen doorway she raised her eyebrows.

'We're going to Aunt Monica's,' he said. 'I've decided you need a bit of TLC.'

'Erm … Tom, I –'

'No complaining. It'll do you good. And you know how much she enjoys your company.'

Who the hell was Aunt Monica?

'Okay,' she said. 'Let me just wash these up first.'

She turned the tap on full, so that the water thundered into the sink.

'She has internet?' she mumbled.

'Yes, exactly.'

'They'll follow us.'

'I know.'

'They might suspect we're up to something.'

'If you look tearful every time we leave the house, they'll just think you've gone to pieces and you're looking for emotional support.'

She bristled. 'I have not gone to pieces, thank you very much.'

'Well, *I* know that.'

*

They arrived at a row of bungalows nestling behind a barrier of box hedge. Tom led them through a gap in the greenery and knocked on the door of number three. It was opened by a small woman who wore her hair in a bob, dyed with henna, the roots just beginning to show her natural grey.

'Lovely to see you, Tom. And this is … ?'

'Wes's wife, Alex.'

'Ah, I've heard so much about you. All of it complimentary, I might add.'

Alex smiled, but her concentration was on the silver car pulling up on the street behind her.

'Come in, come in.'

Aunt Monica closed the door firmly; invited them into a bright, plant-filled lounge; plied them with tea and a slice of home-made chocolate cake. She seemed both younger and older than her sixty-five years. Her mouth was downturned, yet always seemed to be smiling. She was devoted to traditional arts and craft, including macramé, calligraphy and home baking, but she was also admirably open-minded.

'Have you ever listened to any Grandmaster Flash?' she said.

'No,' Tom said. 'Not my cuppa, really.'

'Nor mine, I suspect, but you have to give these things a go, don't you? I've been watching him out on Youtube. Very clever what he can do with a pair of record decks. I'd never appreciated before how much skill it took.'

'And how many Twitter followers do you have now?'

'Nearly two thousand. That's the power of cake recipes!'

They continued to chat for fifteen minutes or so before Tom dropped the question. 'Do you mind if Alex uses your computer? She's been having a bit of trouble with hers.'

Aunt Monica blinked a couple of times. 'Be my guest.'

'As long as you're sure it's no bother,' Alex said.

'Of course not. I'm sure you can drive it better than I can.'

The laptop was on a table, next to a window that overlooked a closeted, well-tended garden. While Alex worked, Tom assumed responsibility for the bulk of the conversation. She kept one ear on the small talk and dipped in whenever she could, trying to appear relaxed and chatty while her fingers carried on with business.

She created a new webmail account and replied to Wes. They might be able to track *her* account on *her* laptop but this, surely, was safe.

From: countessdragula@freemail.com
To: countdragula@freemail.com
Subject: Missing you

Wes,
I got your note from the chapel.

I realise how bad the conversation in our lounge must have looked, but I assure you I'm not in on this. I love you, I miss you, and I will do anything to have you back. Tell me what you need and I'll do it.

Tom is helping me. I'm emailing from his Aunt Monica's. I wish you would trust me the way you trust him.

When you saw me speaking to those two men, I was trying to fool them into believing that I would help them. They claimed to be from MI5, but I'm not convinced. I have given them nothing, but you're right: they're watching me. A silver car with tinted windows is stationed out the front of our house. Whenever we walk anywhere, two men (not the two you saw) get out and follow. I don't think they know that we know.

I'm going to find out why this has happened. I will send you any information I gather.

Stay safe.
I love you,
Alex

How forceful she sounded, how certain. The temptation to tell him to run as far away as possible – while she and Tom got to the bottom of things – was strong, but she recognised the futility of it. Wes would already be engaged in an obsessive, single-minded quest of his own, and there was nothing she could do to dissuade him. She hit 'Send'.

Googling for the phrase 'There is one path and one choice' yielded millions of results, so she enclosed the words in double quotes to make it search only for the complete phrase. She tried to hide her surprise from Tom and Aunt Monica – just one result, from about a year ago:

The Perils of an Investigative Journalist

A sinister visitation last night at Truth Towers. From the start, the man who rang my bell looked a pretty poor prospect for a stimulating evening's conversation, but being the open and accommodating soul that I am, I felt compelled to invite him in and hear what he had to say. It amounted to this: 'Stop what you're doing or we'll hurt you.'

I'm no stranger to this sort of thing. I've endured all sorts of threats and abuse over the years, from being yelled at in the street to receiving a phone call from a man threatening to separate me from my genitalia with the aid of a pair of scissors. I explained to my visitor that I didn't know what he was talking about, and this is the truth: I'm running any number of investigations at once, so it can be difficult to know which is the subject of the conversation when a thug fails to be specific with his threats.

He looked very angry, and I have to confess I was so convinced he was about to do me violence that for several seconds I failed to make a cynical quip. In order to calm himself, he muttered: 'There is one path and one choice'. Religious mania? Evidence of a mind unhinged by the relentless hectoring of the tabloids? Alas, I will never know – after a restatement of his threat he was out of the door and gone. I had no desire to invite him back for a fuller explanation.

Update: Four weeks have gone by, and nothing has come of it. I can only assume he was (and here I use the vernacular) 'avin' a larf. Either that, or I've run into a dead end on the investigation that so upset him (an all too frequent occurrence in my line of work). At any rate, your intrepid investigator escapes peril once more.

There were similarities with her own experience. No claims to be a figure of authority, though, and in her case at least there had been no overt threat. The website containing the article – www.standish.co.uk – was run by Fraser Standish, who had worked as an investigative journalist for the BBC and a couple of daily broadsheets before ending up at what he described as 'the arse end of the web; the place where truth crawls to die'. If the articles on his website were true, he had found hints of corruption, malfeasance and manipulation in half the world's major corporations and every British government going back to the Second World War. The site was peppered with alarm-bell phrases like 'what the government doesn't tell you' and 'a thorough cover-up has erased most of the evidence'.

And the comments section of each article – good grief. While there was some support for his theories, the major part amounted to a tidal wave of criticism, mockery and insults. Why had he let anyone comment at all? She found her answer in the About page: 'Free speech is the cornerstone of a civilised society, so I've allowed anyone to say anything they want on this website. Throw as much shit at me as you like. I've endured far worse than anything you buggers could type on a keyboard.' People seemed to have accepted this as a challenge. In all her years using the internet, she'd rarely seen such condensed vitriol. If the BBC website, with its carefully moderated comments, could be compared to surfing the sparkling waters off a Blue Flag beach, this was like wading across condom-strewn cobbles next to a sewage outlet.

An email address was given, plus an additional suggestion: 'If you don't trust normal communication channels, I'm in the Dog and Duck most evenings ... unless they've already got me. ;-)' It was that smiley – plus several other flashes of bitter, ironic humour – that gave her hope. If he had been completely po-faced about his investigations she might have written him off as one of the internet's innumerable nutcases.

Written him off? Who was she kidding? He was their one and only lead. She would meet up with him even if he was foaming at the mouth.

She found the Dog and Duck from the link Standish provided – it was in a village about fifty miles west of Strathurst. She panned across the map to find another nearby pub, the Half Moon, and wrote Standish an email:

From: countessdragula@freemail.com
To: fraser@standish.co.uk
Subject: Need to meet you

Mr. Standish,

I read your article 'The Perils of an Investigative Journalist'. I have also been visited by men similar to the one you describe, and who used the phrase 'There is only one path and one choice'. I'd like to meet you and discuss it.

Rather than the Dog and Duck, I propose the Half Moon at 12:30 tomorrow. I'll wear a black beret and I'll be bringing a friend.

I hope to see you there,
The Countess

There was no way they could meet Standish and not arouse suspicion – they would have to give their tails the slip. They would be on the run, like Wes. She was acting unilaterally, and perhaps she should have consulted Tom first. Would he really stick with her, no matter what she decided to do?

These constant doubts had to be dispensed with. Boldness, certainty: that's what she needed. She bit her lip and sent the email. Then she wrote down all the information she needed – email and web addresses, directions to the Half Moon. Periodically, she checked for replies to either of her messages, but the inbox remained stubbornly empty. There was nothing more to be done. She returned to the sofa, accepting another cup of tea and slice of cake to prolong the visit. It was comfortable here, but in the end they had to go. She checked her email once more, in vain, before leaving. They would just have to go on spec. Before closing the lid of the laptop, she deleted the web browser's history and cache – if someone were to come snooping they wouldn't find any evidence of what she'd been doing.

Alex used the toilet before they left, and overheard a conversation through the door.

'I hope one day you'll explain what this visit was all about,' Aunt Monica said. Her tone was one of curiosity, rather than annoyance or judgement.

'Um ... yes,' Tom replied.

'Ah, good,' she said with triumph. 'That's a promise to visit again soon, then?'

'Yes, yes, of course.'

'And I wouldn't complain if you brought Alex again. She's delightful.'

Really? She was delightful? It was impossible to reconcile Aunt Monica's words with the way she felt – assaulted by a clanking fear and hollowed by loss.

As they left, she hugged their host for rather too long. When they released each other, the older woman tilted her head to one side and said, 'Good luck, my dear.'

17

WES chose a seat near the front of the bus, noting the position of the door control in case he needed to lean over the driver and operate it. He wedged himself into the seat sideways and looked towards the back. The passengers were of two sorts: young and absorbed in their phones, or old and staring out of the window. Neither group seemed to harbour any murderous intent. This constant vigilance was exhausting Wes, and exhaustion would make him vulnerable. At Petersfield, he waited for two other passengers to get off, then slipped through the doors just before they closed. None of the remaining passengers even glanced at him.

He ate a hot, purifying green curry in a Thai restaurant, then went shopping for fresh clothes and a small rucksack. A disguise might have been good too, but the practicality of it put him off – he was not going to go all fancy dress and get fake glasses or a wig. Better just to keep a low profile and be ready to run at the drop of a hat. A hat – yes, of course. He decided on a baseball cap, small enough to shove into the rucksack but useful for concealing his face with just a tilt of the head.

His apprehension at buying a new phone was strong but probably unfounded: he saw no way they could track a newly registered device. He took some pleasure from buying the cheapest smartphone the salesman would sell him, resisting his efforts to steer Wes towards something that would 'make a much better impression on your friends and colleagues'. He bought it outright on a pay-as-you-go basis with £10 of credit rather than a contract, compounding the salesman's disappointment.

Finally he booked into a cheap chain hotel at the edge of town. He tried to pay with cash, hoping to retain anonymity – or at least to give a false name that wouldn't commit him to chatting about Baltic countries he'd never visited – but they insisted on ID. Could he be tracked via his credit card spending? How paranoid should he be? There was comfort, in a way, that the hotel receptionist gave him no choice. He relented, handing over his credit card and a note:

Please don't give my name out. My girlfriend's ex insists on ignoring the restraining order.

The man behind the counter assured him they would be discreet.

He scouted the entire site – he was sure that no-one had ever paid more attention to the hotel's fire escape routes – and his room, when he got to it, was so gloriously bland that he fell in love with it immediately. If not exactly a needle in a haystack, it was at least a needle in a pile of needles.

As soon as he set up the new phone with his countdragula

email address, a message from Alex came through. One sentence in particular grabbed him:

I love you, I miss you, and I will do anything to have you back.

Her words made him think she was rooting for him, made him yearn for her in a powerful, almost physical, sense and twenty-four hours ago he would have taken her at her word. But now an ugly, animal instinct clawed at his trust. Being separated so forcibly was like an amputation.

It was not until he had showered and dressed in new clothes that he allowed himself to settle down on the hotel room bed and concentrate on the diary. Wes took care over every word, trying to draw inferences and extract clues wherever he could. The entries represented a chaos of unconnected thoughts, and great chunks of time were missing, weeks when he wrote nothing at all. It would, he realised, only ever fully make sense to Lowry himself.

It began in crisis:

Now is a good time to start a new diary. Everything changed tonight. I have to sort my thoughts out but God where do I start?

So Chris has come back. Only now he's called Grant. Like that's a surprise. Bummer to be called Christian if you've come to hate everything about Christianity. I can see why he didn't tell mum where he was going when he left. But why didn't he tell me? It was like I was part of the problem. Hard to admit but maybe I was back then. Mum still had a hold on me.

He tells me our entire childhoods were bullshit. We were brought up in a cult. Yeah I figured that one out for myself. But what he says next blows my mind. The obsession mum and dad had with sacrifice is the exact opposite of the way the world really is. Everyone has to be in it for themselves. Nothing else makes sense.

It sounds too simple. I want to argue with him but before I can say anything he tells me that I'll want to argue with him. I was indoctrinated. I'm in the habit of making sacrifices for other people. I need to de-program myself. Free myself.

I thought I had.

He tells me his life is honest and self-sufficient. He's hard as fucking nails now. Completely confident about what he says. I still want to argue with him but I can't find a way to win any arguments. Doesn't that basically mean he's right?

Since leaving mum I've been out in the wilderness. I've been trying to make a new life for myself. Get rid of my shitty childhood and start again. Hasn't been easy.

And now Grant comes here and everything he says seems to make sense.

Shortly after this, Grant had introduced his brother to Darwin's Army, and had him camping out on Dartmoor to test his survival skills. Lowry had failed to identify DA as another cult, instead embracing it as the solution to all the problems of his childhood.

As the pages turned, Wes pieced together a picture of Lowry's past. His parents belonged to a fringe Christian cult called the Last People. They were very strict, eschewed almost all pleasures and took a masochistic delight in the sacrifices they could make for other people. The brothers were closeted from the rest of the world. They were home-schooled, their friends carefully vetted, and their lives micromanaged into an expression of their parents' faith. Teenage rebellion had kicked in hard, both of them leaving home and never speaking to their mother again. By this time things were falling apart anyway – their father had died, possibly in an accident, and their mother had become deranged and incoherent.

This Grant was the other man who had spoken to Alex in his lounge; Wes felt sure of it. Every time he found a hint of conflict between the brothers he noted it down, hoarding the stuff like ammunition.

Why won't G tell me about dad's death? It's the third time I've asked him.

'It's the past. It's history.' That's what he says. But it's my history! I have a right to know. DA says you have to break with the past. But to do that I have to know what the past is. I wish I'd been there to see it for myself. It might explain why mum went off the rails. It might explain why both of them refuse to speak about dad.

~~One day he's going to tell me.~~ One day I'm going to make him tell me.

Their immediate superior in DA was called Brad, a name that matched one of the contacts Wes had copied down from Lowry's phone. DA 'brothers' at their own level were also mentioned, but Lowry was careful never to give anyone's surname. In fact, the more he read, the more he realised how careful Lowry had been to avoid giving anything useful away. The diary was meant to be of emotional value to the writer, not factual value to anyone who happened to read it. To compound this dearth of information, Lowry himself knew nothing at all about DA above Brad. Cells were kept separate from each other so that if one was compromised the whole would carry on unhindered, even in the face of the most thorough interrogation. Classic terrorist hierarchy.

Wes saw Lowry's twisted logic as it developed. It was a logic based on false premises, but not without its own internal consistency, and in the echo chamber of Darwin's Army it was constantly reinforced. Wes himself was prone to pessimism, but the diary presented whole new vistas of bleakness. Peppered throughout were Lowry's visions of how the world might be after The Collapse – the coming disaster for which DA were preparing. Scenarios ranged from anarchy caused by financial meltdown to World War Three with a full nuclear exchange. It appalled him, in part because he found some of Lowry's reasoning alarmingly plausible. At his worst he reached a Biblical fervour. People cavorted while the world burned. There's not enough food, not enough oil, not enough water. There's too much consumption, too many people. He repeated these things to himself over and over, almost as if by repeating them he could make them true. Lowry described arguments he had with people over these issues. They thought the world would carry on as it was, indefinitely. But he knew better. And history was on his side.

Emotional purging was a recurring feature of the diary:

Some people are going to be better at DA because of the way they were brought up. That's just a fact.

Hans had a much better childhood than me. Lots of sports. A pushy dad. Everything he needed. And while he was winning the 400m in some athletics competition what was I doing? Delivering pamphlets about how we should give up all pleasure because that's what Jesus did. Spending Saturdays 'volunteering' at a charity shop.

Did Hans have to scavenge a toy car from a skip so he'd have something to play with? I think Daddy's pockets were a bit too deep for that. And when mum found out about the car she made me donate it to some other kid less fortunate than I was.

Only one tiny problem with that. There wasn't any fucking kid less fortunate than I was.

DA says you should feel nothing about your old life. Well I do. I wanted a proper childhood. Not a million duties to perform for some imaginary bloke my parents believed in. I wanted to have fun. I wanted opportunities. I wanted friends. But it's too late for any of that. My childhood is gone. A big chunk of my life was stolen from me and it was done by my own parents.

You shouldn't feel anything about your past? Well I feel bitter. There's no point pretending I don't. I feel bitter.

But it wasn't all doom and suffering. Comic relief came right on cue:

Watched '2012' and 'The Day After Tomorrow' last night. Nothing practical in either of them. Five hours completely wasted. That's the last time I listen to Hans.

Wes couldn't help himself: he doubled up on the bed, prey to the convulsions that overtook him. It lasted so long that the muscles in his abdomen began to ache. He had to take a break from the diary, use toilet paper from the en suite to dry his eyes.

I said seven whole words to Gemma this evening. 'Orange and lemonade' 'Same again' and my feeble attempt at wit 'The usual.' I screwed up my bar approach the fourth time and got served by a bloke instead.

What is wrong with me? Love is a weakness. A serious bug in our evolutionary software. We must procreate to continue the human race but all the ancillary garbage (as G calls it) is a genetic mistake.

I know all this. None of it changes the way I feel.

The fact is I shouldn't want her the way I do. It would be acceptable to have sex with her. I wouldn't mind having sex with her at all. But I know it wouldn't be enough. That would make her just like Amber or Kristal. She's more than that.

She clouds my mind. I must be stronger than this.

There were a few entries on other topics – Wes tried not to skim them – before Gemma was mentioned again:

Following Gemma home at the end of her shift without being spotted has been a good test of my DA skills. Yesterday it was something more. I'm sure I've seen the guy before. Maybe even at the bar. I couldn't hear what he was saying to her but it wasn't anything good. I carried on walking towards them. Like I was just another pedestrian.

When I came alongside them he said 'Move along mate'.

I punched him in the face and the knife fell onto the pavement. And that was it. My brothers would have been impressed. Strike first, strike hard. One punch and he was on the ground. He was screaming and his nose was bleeding.

Gemma stared at me for two seconds then turned and ran. I don't blame her.

I wanted to talk to her about it tonight but the words sounded stupid in my head so they never came out. I just ordered my drink. As I was turning away she said 'You forgot your peanuts' and handed me a bag for free. It might seem like nothing but it isn't. I know what she's saying.

Christ. And Wes thought he had problems talking to women.

After a few more entries he reached the article he was supposed to have written. It had been cleverly constructed, capturing his tone well and reusing phrases from some of his other blog entries. But it offered him no more than when he'd first read it. The rest of the diary's pages were blank. He stood up and chucked it onto the bed. He wanted facts, clues, leads, not all this emotional detritus. He knew a lot more about Keiran Lowry, true, but nothing about how to stop him. He paced the room. The laptop, that's what he needed. But having caught him once, Keiran would know what he was after. He might already have wiped all the useful data off it. He might not even leave the flat without it now. The opportunity had passed; Wes had ballsed up.

Regret was not going to get him anywhere. He could only deal with what he had, and right now that meant lying back down on the bed and reading the entire diary again. So be it.

The critical line almost passed him by. It was shortly after Keiran had moved to Strathurst for his Ascension – or Wes's murder, as it might be less euphemistically phrased.

Brad came here to bollock us. I'm convinced of it. That's ex-army for you. He doesn't think we've done enough prep for the Ascension? Fuck off. Then he started going on about how our survival skills had never been that great. Where did that come from? He just enjoys saying this shit. G tried not to show any emotion but I could tell he was as pissed off as I was.

After the meeting G said 'Screw the diet' and we went to the chippy next door. I had a deep-fried Mars bar with my fish and chips. After all the healthy eating … fuck me. The sugar rush. If Brad thinks we need a test of our survival skills this would do brilliantly.

Brad came 'here', and they had met next door to a fish and chip shop, specifically one that sold deep-fried Mars bars. Hardly an x marks the spot, but it was something.

He finished the diary for the second time, and perhaps it was inevitable that thoughts of his wife would rush in to fill the void. More than anything else, he yearned for the sound of her. At times she would fill their house with song, anything from old folk classics to pop hits to a warbling, comical attempt at opera. He would phone her sometimes just to hear her voice, and she would pour herself into his ear, into his head, as if she were taking up residence there.

She was probably innocent. It was probably unfair to suspect her.

Probably, probably.

It was an agonising state to be in, doubting a woman's love.

Keiran knew it too, in his own way – it shone through the pages of his diary like daylight through the thinnest of curtains. That man needed love more than anyone. And it was this thought that prompted Wes to sit at the desk, tear a couple of pages out of his notebook, and start to write. Keiran's emotional detritus might be useful after all.

Sunday

18

NAKED, and digging a finger into the corner of one eye, Keiran shuffled down the corridor to the bathroom. Another night's sleep like that and he would be back to normal. The note on the doormat brought him to a halt: two sheets of lined paper, white against mud brown, covered with words handwritten in pencil. Obvious who it was from. At least the new lock had kept him out this time. Proof, too, that he was the sort of person to post a note of disapproval rather then spraying lighter fluid through the letterbox and tossing in a match.

He scooped up the sheets, abandoning his shower for the time being.

Keiran,

In case you haven't already noticed, I've managed to get hold of your diary. It's an interesting read. I felt quite moved at times by the terrible upbringing you had to endure. Then I remembered you're trying to kill me, and I didn't feel so sympathetic.

Here's the crazy thing: I never wrote that post on my blog. Someone has set you up. It's time for you to ask yourself some serious questions. Were you shown the web page by someone else? Did you click on a link that took you to a fake site, designed to look like mine?

I knew nothing about your organisation before all this kicked off. I don't know much more now. What I do know is that you are a product of your past, and your reaction against your parents has led you straight from one cult into another. This individualist mentality of Darwin's Army is crazy. Coming together is what human society is all about. Collaboration, friendship and closeness are fundamental to us. They're why we're so successful as a species. Without it, there would be none of the video games or TV shows you enjoy. It's what prompts your chums to meet up rather than camping out on Dartmoor forever. It's what you long for in Gemma. Love is the solution, not the problem.

It might do you good to ask Gemma out on a date, but here's a helpful hint for you: women don't usually want to go out with murderers.

You're an intelligent guy, I can tell that, but you're being misled by some very dangerous people. Now, engage your brain and stop trying to kill me.

Wes

It wasn't me that did it! How predictable. It was a confused mixture of taunt, boast and begging letter. It was the scatter-gun approach of a person with a poor sense of their own argument: chuck a bunch of doubts and questions in your opponent's direction and expect it to stall them. Keiran didn't need to spend any time thinking these things through. His knowledge was firm because it wasn't a case of what he believed, it was a case of what was undeniable. Naturally, Henning was approaching all this from the perspective of a Refuser; it was inevitable that he would spout the same tired arguments. It was *he* who had been misled, not Keiran. He was a victim of argumentum ad populum: whatever the greatest number of people believed must be the truth.

His claim that Keiran was duped into going to the wrong website was an insult to his intelligence. He had checked the web address – www.inabsurdia.co.uk – and he had been there on many occasions. This was Henning's feeble attempt to wriggle out of responsibility. There was some truth in the idea that people had to collaborate to achieve things, but what Henning had missed is that they only did this out of self-interest. This is what everyone missed. They thought the world was one big happy family, all getting along together. It was a veneer, a façade. People chose the happy delusion because they found the alternative distasteful. And 'love is the solution'? Give it a rest. Only if the question was 'what will stop me from becoming all I can be?' His mention of Gemma showed that he knew the most effective place to strike. Yeah, he was a dangerous opponent all right.

Keiran started to crumple the pages, then stopped himself. No: he should burn them, destroy them forever. No: better still, he would keep them. There might be something in there that was useful to him: some clue that might reveal Henning's intentions, something that wasn't obvious. He went back to the bedroom, folded the pieces of paper and tucked them into his wallet.

*

He arranged to meet Sean and Jamal on Castle Street – round the corner from the Hennings' house, so they wouldn't notice the changeover. The passenger window slid down as he approached.

'So, what's been going on?' he said.

'Not a thing,' Sean said.

Of course not. He was tempted to ask them if they'd both had a good night's sleep, but no, he didn't want them to know how little he thought of them. At least not yet.

'Fine,' Keiran said. 'Get out, then.'

'What?'

'I'm taking the car.'

They both stared at him gormlessly.

'What's the problem?' Keiran said. 'It's not yours, is it?'

He saw that it was. What amateurs. Well, if it was traced back to them, that was their problem. They knew the rules: if they got into trouble, DA would cut them off with no more regret than trimming a fingernail.

'Come on,' he said, 'your brother needs it.'

'Can't you … use your own car?' Sean's forehead was wrinkled, his hands caressing the steering wheel.

'If they've been watching you, they'll make their move now you've gone. I need to get back there now.' He snapped his fingers, jerked a thumb over one shoulder.

Sean and Jamal climbed out, stunned and obedient.

'Check out the train station,' Keiran said, 'and if you see anything …' he held his hand up to ear in imitation of a phone call.

He watched them walk away. Seconds later, Grant appeared – punctual, as always – and joined him in the passenger seat. Keiran started the car, dropped the handbrake and hit the accelerator. It was poky for a hatchback – 2.0 litre engine, bucket seats. Shame he was only driving it two hundred metres.

'Nice car,' Grant said.

'Yeah, I suppose.'

He slowed as he turned into the Hennings' street and parked at the side of the road.

'How's the chest?' Grant said.

'Good as new.'

Grant reach out to give it a prod. Keiran blocked him.

'And I'd like to keep it that way.'

Grant smiled and lowered his finger. 'So, why are we taking over from Sean and Jamal? What's the plan?'

If only there were something as solid as a plan.

'That's up to Henning,' Keiran said.

'He could have skipped town as early as Friday night. He could be in another country by now.'

'No,' he said firmly, 'he's still around.'

'You really think he wants to stay close to his wife? Even with his survival at stake?'

'Yes,' Keiran said with conviction. 'You're thinking like a Survivor. Either of us would be long gone, but Henning is afflicted by love. Sooner or later he'll make contact with her.'

Grant nodded slowly.

'We just have to wait.' Yeah, unfortunately that's what it came down to – more bloody waiting.

'Even a predator requires patience,' Grant said.

'I know.'

'There will be a time to strike.'

'Grant, I know.'

They fell into silence and Keiran's thoughts turned inwards. Alex had left her house only twice yesterday: once to pray at the chapel for her husband's safe return, and once to visit the person they had identified as Tom's aunt. Both had surprised him. The information provided by DA had made no mention of Tom's aunt and her importance in their lives. Keiran had anticipated Alex running to her friends or parents, but she had done neither. Apart from the hour and a half visit to the old woman, Tom seemed to be providing all the support she needed. They had been stuck together like glue since her husband had gone missing. Suspiciously so. Sean's speculation about them might not have been so stupid after all.

To all outward appearances, the Hennings were a close couple, but maybe there were cracks in their relationship that DA hadn't uncovered. Perhaps it had already run its course. Keiran toyed with an idea: that he was doing her a favour by killing her husband. She would be shocked in the short term, but would ultimately become stronger as a result. And then she would have the opportunity to start a relationship with a man who wasn't so compromised, so clearly one of nature's failed experiments. Tom wasn't a good catch either. Too soft, too lazy. She might choose Keiran himself if she was made to realise how he had freed her. Like all animals, she would be unable to deny her admiration of him as the stronger mate, the alpha male. She would give herself to him. They would have rough, dirty sex. He wouldn't even have to pay for it. He saw her legs wrapped around his waist, her head thrown back, exposing her long, white neck to him.

Well, that was unexpected. He put his hands into his lap to conceal his erection.

'I reckon she might be up to something,' he said abruptly.

'The Henning woman? What makes you think that?'

'Well ... why his aunt? It doesn't make sense.' Something had been tugging at the line of his thoughts. It was there, somewhere below the surface. He just had to reel it in.

'Why not? We don't know about all of her relationships. You could be reading too much into this.'

'What would they stand to gain by going there?'

'You tell me.'

'Apart from those two calls they made yesterday morning to try and find out where her husband was, how many phone calls have they made? How many emails have they sent? Zero. They've gone silent. But then they go to someone else's house – someone who must have their own computer that we aren't monitoring – and then they come back. And it all seems like a happy little visit for some emotional support. Maybe because it's supposed to.'

'You think she knows more than she's letting on?'

'She's clever. Like her husband.'

Grant examined his fingernails. 'We could go back in there and beat it out of her.'

He turned to face Keiran, and there was a fervour in his eyes, a challenge. Did Grant think this would be a useful thing to do, or was it just sport to him? Trying to kill a man with years of martial arts experience in a fair fight was one thing; beating the shit out of a woman with no self-defence skills seemed ... different. It was, however, perfectly in line with DA thinking: he was stronger, and if he needed something from her, he should take it.

'We could kidnap her,' Grant said, 'take her to the safe house, interrogate her. Also, if Henning is still around and he sees us, she would act as bait.'

But there was no guarantee she knew anything. It was a theory, nothing more.

Keiran stared at the house. His brother's suggestions felt wrong. Was this just a vestige of his old life as a Christian, before he had matured, before his eyes were opened? What did she mean to him, after all? Nothing. Despite his fantasy, the chance that she would ever give herself to him was remote.

'Your call, brother,' Grant said, 'but ... be decisive.'

Keiran was facing away from Grant. He saw a dark street, a man lying on the pavement, holding his bloodied nose, a knife skittering to a stop near the kerb. He saw Gemma's face, distorted by fear. Why had he done it? The mugger was also acting out of self-interest, just trying to take what he wanted.

So, what was the right course of action? No, no – what was the *best* course of action? One thing he knew for certain: if they lost an opportunity due to his hesitation he would never hear the end of it. Grant would tell Brad, and soon everyone else would know. He imagined Hans mocking him. He imagined his reputation wrecked, a setback so severe he might never be given another chance at Ascension.

The door opened. Alex and Tom stepped out onto the porch.

He felt Grant stiffen beside him. 'The street's clear. You could get her now, bundle her into the back. I'll take care of the floppy-haired toff.'

'No,' Keiran said. 'It's better if we let her lead us to him.'

'That's what you think, is it?'

'If we beat her up and she knows nothing, we blow our story about being MI5, she goes to the police, everything gets more complicated.'

'If you say so, brother.'

He turned to Grant. 'What was that you were saying about patience?'

They locked eyes for several seconds. Here it came – the accusation of weakness, of failing to act. Grant started chuckling, but gave no indication whether he was coming round to Keiran's way of thinking or whether he had been bluffing all along. He really could be an arsehole sometimes.

They watched Tom reverse his Alfa off the pavement, then drive towards the end of the road. Keiran put his phone on the dashboard and started the app to track Tom's mobile. He waited until the car had disappeared from view, then twisted the key in the ignition.

19

THEY sat in silence while Tom drove them to the big Tesco on Harvest Road. Alex exchanged a glance with him occasionally, but there was nothing to say. Everything had been worked out; they just had to go through with it. He parked near the entrance, just before the disabled spaces began. They locked the car and as they approached the store, the doors slid open for them. She tried to see it as a welcome, an intimation of how easy and effortless this was all going to be.

'They've parked a few spaces away from us,' Tom muttered as Alex picked up a basket.

'Have they got out?'

'Not yet.'

They walked through the supermarket, stopping to look at bags of noodles and pasta so they could cast a furtive glance back in the direction of the entrance.

'Here will do,' Tom said. 'Hand it over.'

Alex looked down at her phone and the excuses came flooding

back in: she would be abandoning all contact with her friends; she wouldn't be able to make an emergency call; it was *expensive*. Surely there was another way.

'Come on,' Tom said. 'They could be in here at any moment.'

The fact was, if she kept the phone they could use it to hunt her down. Why was she even questioning the need to get rid of it? She placed the phone in Tom's hand, on top of his own. He slid both of them to the far back of the shelf and rearranged the tins of soup to conceal them. Right. It was done. She grasped Tom's fingers and they marched towards the back of the shop. She dumped her basket and they continued out of the exit on the other side, following the road round until the side of a furniture shop concealed the supermarket from view.

'Slower,' Tom said. 'Fast movement catches the eye.'

'I am going slowly.'

'You're practically jogging.'

They turned into the Mazda dealership. Tom surveyed the cars on the forecourt and latched onto an MX-5 in stormy blue. Alex saw a salesman hovering at the edge of the showroom and gave him a nod and a big smile. He didn't need any more encouragement to start walking over.

'This is the one,' Tom said.

She stroked the wing of the car. Too much? No, she decided, noticing the salesman's eyes were lit up like headlights.

'Yes, you're right, darling,' she said, 'it is nice.'

Tom fixed the car with a look of desire so convincing that she wondered whether he was acting after all. The salesman slid between the parked cars as if he himself was on wheels, and said, 'Have you driven a two-seater before, sir?'

Tom turned to him and said in a confessional tone, 'I've never had the chance. But we've come into a bit of money recently, haven't we, darling –'

Alex nodded.

137

'– and I thought maybe it was time to splash out on something.'

'Well, you've come to the right place.'

'Excellent,' Tom said. 'I don't suppose it would be possible for us to take it for a quick spin around the block?'

*

'Any sign of them?' Alex said, as they drove south, out of Strathurst and into the country.

Tom glanced in the rear-view mirror. 'Nope, nothing.' He turned onto a tree-lined road and punched the accelerator. 'Well, that was easy enough, wasn't it, darling?'

'Yes, it was, darling.' A brief laugh escaped her lips. Then, 'You're sure they can't follow us some other way?'

'I can't be certain of anything any more. They could be tracking us through my boxer shorts.'

'Don't. It's not funny.'

Cresting a tiny stone bridge that crossed a stream, Alex became weightless for a second and braced instinctively against the armrest. She tensed further as he took a sharp bend, the tyres beginning to protest against the tarmac. She frowned at him, but he was concentrating on the road.

'So, this chap you found on the internet,' he said. 'I don't want to be a downer here, but he sounds like he might be a bit … cracked. I think we should retain a healthy scepticism when we meet him. We can't afford to go down the conspiracy theory rabbit hole when we could be doing something more effective for Wes.'

'More effective like what?'

He shrugged. 'I don't know at the moment.'

'That's why we're doing this, isn't it? Because it's all we've got to go on.'

'Yes, I agree. I just hope he's worth leaving Strathurst for, that's all.'

'You think this is a bad idea?'

'Not necessarily,' Tom said. 'I'm just worried about being away for too long, in case Wes contacts us again and needs us to do something.'

'Why didn't you say so before?'

'It only just occurred to me. I'm not used to all this cloak and dagger stuff either.'

Alex bit her nails – something she'd never done before, but which now seemed perfectly natural. 'Doesn't this thing go any faster?'

*

Tom parked in Basingstoke, on a residential road flanked by terraced houses.

'Are you sure he's going to be in?' Alex said.

'It's before twelve on a Sunday. He'll be in.'

Alex tried not to think of this as a test of her confidence in him. He rested a sheet of paper on the steering wheel and wrote:

Apologies for the delay in returning your wonderful vehicle – there's been a family emergency. We'll be in touch.

Tom knocked on the door of number twelve. It took a couple of minutes, but eventually a man in a dressing-gown appeared at the door, hair wild and eyes bleary.

'Tom?' he said. 'What are you doing here so early?'

Tom dangled the car keys in front of his face. 'Hi, old chap. How do you fancy driving a sports car?'

*

Continuing by train, they arrived at the Half Moon at 12:30. With its dark wood and open fires, it was doing its best to look like a traditional pub, but its wipe-clean tables and crowds of noisy punters wrecked whatever character it might otherwise have had. The place was permeated by the aroma of roast lamb from the Sunday carvery and swarmed with flocks of children, fleeing and alighting.

Alex recognised Standish from the picture on his website: he was the one in the corner, bent over a laptop, a half-drained pint on the table in front of him. His age was difficult to guess. His face was smooth and ruddy-cheeked, but his hair – which reminded her of a breaking wave – was iron grey.

He glanced up at Alex. 'Ah, you must be the Countess,' he said in a voice that suggested his entire educational history at once: Eton and Oxbridge.

'Alex Henning,' she said, taking off the black beret and reaching out to shake.

'Fraser Standish, at your service.'

He bowed his head and took her hand the way a knight took a damsel's. For a moment she thought he was going to kiss it. Out of the corner of her eye she saw Tom shift his feet. Yes, he was right – they'd have to be careful with this one. As they sat, Standish took a sip from his pint and winced.

'I do hope this is going to be worth it,' he said. 'I've never been keen on the beer in this establishment.'

'We're after some information,' Tom said.

'I'd prefer to hear it from the lady, if you don't mind.' He turned to Alex and fixed her with a winning smile. 'She's the reason you're here, isn't she?'

Tom folded his arms.

'No need to be so protective.' Standish lounged back in his chair. 'After all, you're not in a relationship with her.'

'How do you know that?' Alex said, wary but impressed.

'I've always been a good observer of people.'

'Modest too,' Tom said.

'I'm a man of scrupulous honesty, that's all,' Standish drawled.

'That's interesting,' Tom said, 'because you seem to have a bit of a reputation as a conspiracy theorist.'

'I don't deal with conspiracy theories, I deal with conspiracies.'

140

'There's a difference?'

'Of course there is,' Standish said, with some heat.

This was not the way the conversation was supposed to go. Alex butted in. 'Look, what Tom is trying to say is that you have to see things from our point of view, Mr Standish.' How could you tactfully suggest that someone might not be reliable? 'Your website paints you as a person with, um … somewhat fringe beliefs, and we need to be sure that –'

'Copernicus,' Standish said, 'was thought to have fringe beliefs when he suggested that the earth orbits the Sun. Fringe beliefs, that is, until he was proven right.'

'But having an alternative belief doesn't mean it's right,' Alex said.

'That I grant you.'

'Good, so we're basically in agreement,' she said, but given his guarded expression, this was obviously wishful thinking.

'The only reason you should believe anything,' he said, 'is evidence.'

'Which is presumably what you believe your website contains,' Tom said.

'Yes, I do believe that, *Tom*, otherwise I wouldn't have bothered to write it.'

'Then why are there so many people on your own website denouncing you?'

'Because the consensus is against me.'

Tom hitched one leg over the other. 'The Consensus? I'm sorry, you're going to have to fill me in – I haven't seen Star Trek in a long time.'

'Oh, aren't you the clever one? So you'd rather believe ten idiots than one person with all the facts?'

'But, once again, how do we know you're giving us the facts?'

'By questioning my claims and seeing what convinces you and what doesn't. So, let's do that, shall we? Give me an example of something on my website you don't find convincing.'

Tom glanced at Alex for backup, which was pretty rich given that he was the one who was causing the argument.

'Look,' she said, 'let's get back on track. We're only really here about the one article.'

'In other words, you can't refute anything.'

Neither of them had anything to say to that.

'Dear Lord above.' Standish rolled his eyes. 'How can you make a fair judgement on whether I'm right or not by *skimming* my website? Don't tell me you went straight to the comments section and sided with those arseholes who insist on dragging me into the gutter.'

'We didn't have time,' Alex said. 'We've got things to do that are just a little bit more urgent than –'

'Please don't tell me you're the sort of people who get their so-called knowledge from Wikipedia without checking at least one independent source. This is exactly what I mean by the consensus – it's the smug and unthinking certainty of the masses, who, by sheer volume and the mutual reinforcement of their beliefs, *must* be correct. When the world was less connected, people would come up with their own ideas in isolation, and those ideas got tested – and either reinforced or disproved – whenever they came up with a conflicting theory. Now everyone happily conforms without having to do any thinking of their own. And the question you have to ask yourself is: who is controlling the consensus? Because that person rules the world.'

For the space of five heartbeats none of them spoke. Then Tom uncrossed his legs and said, 'The man's clearly nuts. Come on, Alex, we're not going to find any way of helping Wes here.'

Alex opened her mouth to tell Tom that he wasn't in charge here, but before she could, Standish leaned forwards on the table.

'Wait a minute – you're Wes Henning's wife?'

'Yes,' she said.

'The author of *In Absurdia*?'

'That's right.'

'I read it every Sunday.'

'So you're a fan,' Tom said. 'Bully for you. But just because you like Wes's work doesn't mean –'

'Listen,' Standish interrupted, 'I owe you precisely nothing. Perhaps you should –'

'Stop it, the pair of you!' Alex hissed with as much force as she could without drawing the attention of the rest of the pub. To her surprise, they both shut up immediately. 'My husband's life,' she said in a low, urgent tone, 'is in danger and you two are trying to score points off each other like a pair of schoolboys. Now, I need *you* –' she rapped her knuckles on Tom's chest '– to be less antagonistic. And I need *you* –' she pointed at Standish '– to say whether you're going to help me or hang me out to dry.'

She saw Tom visibly deflate. He made several attempts to say something before looking down at the floor and muttering, 'I'm sorry, Alex.'

Standish said quietly, 'Someone is trying to kill your husband?'

'Yes.'

He downed the rest of his pint. 'Okay. Let's start over. I can be an insufferable arse, I'm well aware of that. In my line of work, the hide of a rhinoceros and a forceful manner are often a necessity.' He closed the lid of his laptop. 'Come with me.'

*

When Standish – 'Call me Fraser' – had described his place as 'not exactly palatial' he hadn't been kidding. It was a messy, one bedroom flat with peeling wallpaper, and the carpet couldn't have seen a vacuum cleaner in years. Standish plonked the laptop down on a huge desk littered with papers. Lined up against the wall were a series of whisky bottles.

'To show there's no hard feelings, join me in a drink,' he said.

143

'I've got Aberlour, Ardbeg, Auchentoshan, Balvenie, Blair Athol, Bruichladdich, Caol Ila, Cragganmore, Dalwhinnie, Glendronach, Glenfarclas, Glenfiddich, Glenlivet, Glenkinchie –' He paused, narrowed his eyes, and swapped the positions of the Glenlivet and Glenkinchie bottles '– Lagavulin, Laphroaig, Oban and Talisker.'

It reminded Alex of the shipping forecast on Radio 4, and was equally impenetrable.

Tom stared at the line of bottles, his mouth ajar. 'You've got Talisker 18?'

Without another word, Standish opened the bottle, poured a dram and handed it to Tom.

'And for the lady?'

'Uh, no, I … you couldn't whip up a cup of tea, could you?'

'Nothing would give me more pleasure. I've got English breakfast, Earl Grey, lapsang souchong –'

'English breakfast will be fine.'

'You have to understand,' he said, 'that for any journalist worth his salt, tea and whisky constitute two of the major food groups.'

He found a couple of wooden chairs – one of which was splattered with dried paint, although the flat showed no evidence of ever having been decorated – and once he had returned with her tea, he asked Alex to tell the whole story of Wes's disappearance. His former flippancy was gone; now he was all business.

'So,' he said, once she had finished, 'you want to know who I was investigating at the time Mr "one path and one choice" visited me?'

'Exactly.'

He had already started flicking through a diary. 'Lucky for you I keep a record of everything.'

'The tattoo,' Tom reminded her.

She grabbed a pencil off the desk and drew it in the margin of the nearest sheet of paper:

⊏

'Does this mean anything to you?'

Standish regarded it for a moment. 'Wait just one second.' He returned to the diary and found what he was looking for.

'Try it this way,' he said, and rotated the sheet of paper through ninety degrees:

Π

'Did it not occur to you,' he said, 'that it might be the Pe logo?'

She frowned at him. 'The electronics giant?'

Standish nodded. The company made both Wes's phone and hers. Is that how they'd been able to track him?

'Do they also own wigwam.net?'

'I believe so. They have dozens of subsidiaries.'

So, she'd been right to create a different email account for the purpose of contacting Wes. Paranoia paid.

'What else do you know about the company?' Standish prompted.

'Well, I remember the TV adverts from a few years ago, where they encouraged people to pronounce it "pay", and had all those plays on words: "Pe as you go", "Pe phone".'

'Do you know why they're called Pe?'

She shook her head.

'The company was started by a Russian billionaire, Piotr Dolokhov. If you write his name down in Cyrillic, the first –'

'It's a Russian letter P,' she said.

'Exactly. Which tells you what?'

'He must have a bit of an ego,' she guessed. 'He could have chosen a company name that didn't remind English people of the word "pee", but he stuck with it because he wanted his own first initial on every product they made.'

His lips crinkled into a smile. 'You're definitely Wes Henning's wife. And why do I know so much about the company?'

'You used to work for them?'

'Christ, no! I was investigating them for corporate malfeasance. And I was doing that,' he tapped the diary, 'around the time our enigmatic thug came to visit.'

Alex reminded herself to breathe.

Standish said, 'I do know someone who used to work for them, though. Since leaving she's had reasons – fairly peculiar reasons, admittedly – to gain access to their computer systems in a ... not entirely legal manner.'

'Anything,' she exhaled. 'Anything that might help us.'

'There's one condition on my putting you in contact with her,' Standish said.

Ah, here it came – the bargaining. 'And what would that be?'

'If there's a story in this – a proper, newsworthy story – toss me a bone, would you?'

'I don't mean to be, uh ... disrespectful, but if a multinational corporation is trying to kill my husband, don't you think we should go to the biggest news organisation we can find?'

'No offence taken. If this really is that big, I'll sell the story as an exclusive to a friend at one of the big papers – yes, I do still have some connections in the trade. I can push for a good price and we can split the money fifty-fifty. As you should have gathered from my website, my purpose is not self-glorification but dissemination of the truth.'

He trusted them, she realised with some amazement. He was willing to help them out based on nothing more than a promise and a handshake. He really was old-school.

'Okay,' Alex said, 'it's a deal.'

Standish phoned his contact and exchanged a few words.

'She says to come over as soon as you like,' he said after ending

146

the call. He wrote down the name, address and phone number of the contact. She was in Bristol.

Alex said, 'I know this has been brief, but we'd, uh … like to get going as soon as possible.'

'I understand completely.'

They put their coats on and prepared to leave.

'Thanks for the whisky,' Tom said.

'Good, isn't it?' he said, in the manner of someone sharing a secret. Then, more seriously, 'You know, I don't want to make you any promises: this may not lead to anything.'

'We know,' Alex said.

'You'll like Tina. She's a little nuts, though.'

'*She's* a little nuts?' Tom said.

Alex was prepared to intervene again, but Standish laughed – a dirty, whisky-sodden laugh. 'I don't mean it as a criticism. As Montaigne said: "Once conform, once do what others do because they do it, and a kind of lethargy steals over all the finer senses of the soul." Most people feel a ridiculous urge to conform, but not Tina. She's definitely one of a kind.'

'In what way?' Alex said. This was not setting her mind at rest.

'You'll see,' he said. 'Now, find your husband. And get me my juicy scoop while you're at it.'

20

WES caught the eye of the proprietress and pointed to his empty cup, laced with foam and chocolate residue.

'Another one? Large cappuccino, was it?'

He nodded. Why not? It would keep his thoughts sharp, might even give him enough of an edge to save his life some time later today. You never knew. And besides, it was really good coffee.

Earlier that morning, back in Strathurst, he had faced Lowry's new lock – two rows of buttons and no keyhole whatsoever – and accepted for certain that the laptop would not be his. It wasn't really a surprise; Wes would have done the same. Breaking in through a window was also a non-starter: the only window big enough was at the front, and that would require him to obtain a ladder and climb up above the tandoori, in full view of the street. Instead he had settled for posting his handwritten message through the letterbox and retreating to Petersfield.

The contents of Keiran's diary had haunted last night's dreams in ways he couldn't articulate or properly remember. There had certainly been a lot to digest from last night's reading. What he now knew about Keiran had come through the slow accumulation of impressions rather than any orderly presentation of facts, but, ironically, the article Wes was supposed to have written provided a great summary of Darwin's Army. It hinted at how they had shaped Keiran's thinking.

Wes's dad, always a quiet man, had given him a piece of advice when he was young that had always stuck with him: 'If you don't think for yourself, someone else will do it for you.' As a child, struggling through school and all its demands on his mind, this had seemed a comforting thought. But adolescence had seen him return to it and reconsider, to see the warning implicit in it. Keiran should have had a father like his.

Wes used his new phone and the café's Wi-Fi to search on 'Darwin's Army', but it yielded nothing of any relevance. He found himself narrowing his eyes every time he used the phone, suspicious that it might choose to betray him at any moment. He knew this was impossible but, as he was discovering, logic and rational thinking stood no chance against the visceral power of fear.

If Wes could prove that he had never written the article, would Keiran stop trying to kill him? Perhaps, he thought with dark humour, Darwin's Army might end up offering him a written apology. He imagined it landing on his doormat one morning while he was eating breakfast – a pleasant surprise, like a tax rebate. But how could Wes even prove his innocence any more? His website had been deleted. Even if he could sit Keiran down – perhaps tied to a chair, like Marcus – and reason with him, he would only be able to offer his backup as proof, and Keiran would assume it had been doctored.

So who had written it? Who had gone to the trouble of mimicking his style so accurately? Was it just Keiran being manipulated by the rest of DA, as part of this initiation, perhaps, with Wes the regrettable price of his success? And why? For fuck's sake why? Keiran was trying to kill him for a non-reason. There were layers above him in the organisation, and Wes had to go higher if he was going to get an explanation. Only then could he start formulating a plan to end this.

He took the bus back to Strathurst in time for 11:30 and the opening of Charlie's Fish Bar. He showed his standard message to the young woman who was serving:

I'm Wes Henning.
I'm unable to speak
but I'm not deaf.

'Ah, okay, cool.' She tugged at one earlobe. 'Um … so, what can I get you?'

He flipped the page over.

Do you sell deep-fried Mars bars?

'Oh, yeah. Yeah, we do.'

In her eagerness to please her poor, mute customer, she turned aside, stripped the Mars bar of its wrapper and battered it in preparation for the deep fat fryer. Out of her range of vision, Wes tried to indicate with his hands that he didn't actually want one, but it was already too late. These misunderstandings did tend to happen.

'There we go,' she said and dropped it into the oil, where it sizzled for a few seconds. 'Anything else?'

He shook his head.

'Healthy lunch, then, eh?'

He did his comical shrug, which made her laugh.

'Nothing wrong with having one every once in a while, though, is there? I mean, you never know – you might be dead tomorrow.'

If Wes could have laughed out loud, he would.

Once the chocolate bar was cooked, she put it in a paper bag and said goodbye as he left. Outside, he surveyed the location and tried to make it match up with Keiran's description: 'the chippy next door'. On one side there was a bookmakers, on the other a bathroom fixtures shop. He might have used the phrase 'next door' figuratively rather than literally, but none of the other shops in this row – a Chinese takeaway, newsagent, hairdressers and pharmacy – seemed likely as a secret meeting place. Absent-mindedly, he bit into the Mars bar. It wasn't as bad as he expected. Not as crispy or as hot, either; just a sort of warm, sweet mush.

He visited all of the other fish and chip shops in Strathurst: The Lighthouse, Cod Almighty, The Fish Hut and Lord of the Fries. None except the last sold deep-fried Mars bars. He was so caught up in thinking about Keiran that he fell into exactly the same trap again: another Mars bar was being sacrificed to the hot oil before he had the chance to stop it.

'Anything else?'

He sighed.

Chips and curry sauce.

The deterioration of his diet in the last few days would have given Alex a fit. He didn't feel any the worse for it, though. It seemed that the body of a man on the run could process any amount of calories.

Although the chippy was located in a row of shops that looked like all the rest, there was, at the end, a door of the kind that led to an upstairs office: maybe an accountant or solicitor. No company name was given. Next to all the bright shop signage, most people wouldn't even have noticed it. This looked ideal, and was the only place that fitted the description in Keiran's diary. The door was made from uPVC and the lock was modern. He would try picking it tonight, after the chippy had closed at eleven o'clock and the place was quiet.

Once he had finished his chips, he retreated to a coffee shop and used their Wi-Fi to install an anti-theft app on his phone. From a nearby hardware store he acquired a roll of duct tape, and from a Barnardo's he bought a paperback of Dostoevsky's *Crime and Punishment* – a book he had long intended to read, and which seemed darkly appropriate. If not now, then when? He might never get another chance. Returning to the row of shops, he scouted out the surrounding area for a suitable vantage point, eventually deciding to retreat across the road to a bench inside the grounds of the Sacred Heart Roman Catholic church. Would they mind him lurking here, possibly for a long period of time? He would pretend to be simple, but docile and unobjectionable, relying on their Christian tolerance to let him stay. It was the ideal location. He could only just see the row of shops through the foliage, and would be all but invisible from there. He settled down and pulled the baseball cap over his eyes.

The day was grey, windless, dead. He fidgeted on the bench, not finding a comfortable position. He didn't feel like starting his book. He was nervy, ready to act; if only there was some kind of action to take. All that coffee hadn't been such a good idea after all. He waited for half an hour, then glanced at his phone. Somehow the half an hour had only been fifteen minutes. A soldier's life was probably something like this – endless periods of waiting, punctuated by bursts of intense physical activity that could end in death. It was no surprise that so many of them ended up suffering from PTSD.

At 1:15 a service in the church ended and a couple of dozen

people – most of them in their seventies, at least – made their way towards the car park. Many of them glanced towards him, but none questioned his right to be there. He was not one of their flock, that was the impression he got, but that didn't seem to be a problem for them.

As they passed by, he caught a snatch of conversation – a man with a walking stick saying, '… not a patch on Father Robinson. Yes, I know he left years ago, but even so …'

And yet the man was still here, and Wes guessed that he probably attended church every Sunday, in spite of his grumbling. What was it that made people become part of these groups? Upbringing? Habit? A need for answers? Wes didn't remember much about the Bible from school apart from the famous bit in 1 Corinthians 13 about faith, hope and love. As a kind of thought experiment, he imagined how he might apply the verse to his situation, as if he were a member of this congregation, as if he thought like them. So, faith … He had to have faith in his plans; hope that they would work; and … love for his enemy, Keiran? Up to and including turning the other cheek? Well, two out of three was still more than he'd expected.

Keiran's contempt for these people would be boundless, and yet … a group who met to share their commitment to a set of beliefs, who recited a litany to reinforce it, who took instructions from a hierarchy – there were obvious parallels, even if one was committed to acts of kindness and the other to murder. For these churchgoers, coming together was a central part of their belief. Keiran didn't seem aware of how bizarre it was that he belonged to a group championing individuality and self-reliance above all else, and yet they still met up regularly.

The churchgoers met in an attempt to reach out, he supposed: to God, but also to each other. Communion, communication, community. Wes appreciated why they did this. He had long since established Sunday as his own day for reaching out to oth-

152

ers. On Sunday he would conscientiously write a new article for the blog and compose the weekly email for his parents and in-laws that kept them abreast of what was going on in his and Alex's world. They all appreciated him taking the effort. His in-laws had initially been awkward with this silent young man their daughter was bringing to family gatherings, but after a few email exchanges they had become more comfortable with him. It was typical of the topsy-turvy nature of his life: the further he was away from them, the easier it was to communicate.

This writing habit was so ingrained now that there were complaints from his blog readers if he failed to post, or from his relatives if he failed to email. Both would be disappointed today.

21

THEY sat in silence for half an hour before Keiran felt compelled to act. It had seemed like the right decision not to go blundering into the supermarket after them, but now a tension spread across his shoulders, a growing suspicion that something was wrong. He turned to face Grant, who raised his eyebrows in an expression that seemed to say 'are you finally going to do something?'

'Right,' Keiran said, 'we're going to check up on them.'

He left the car and Grant followed him through the sliding doors of the supermarket.

'You take this side, I'll take that one,' Keiran said.

They traversed the edges of the store like the x- and y-axes on a graph. Any blind spots behind the shelves that one of them couldn't see would be covered by the other. They made two sweeps each, returning to the entrance once they had finished, and confirming what Keiran already suspected.

'Fuckers,' he spat. 'How long have they known?'

'Impossible to tell,' Grant said calmly.

Keiran went back out to the car park and stopped next to the Alfa. It would feel good to get the tyre iron from the boot of Sean's car and smash all of their windows. People would stand there, stunned, and they would be gone long before the police arrived. No: someone would memorise their number plate, give the police a description of them.

'Are you not enjoying this, brother?' Grant said from some-where behind him.

Keiran remained facing away. Best way to hide the fury. A memory pinged into his mind, an echo from another life. A model of a red Lamborghini retrieved from a skip – scuffed and dented, but serviceable. He hid it from Mum and Dad, but revealed it to Grant, like a stolen ruby. And then, within minutes, his mother inexplicably knew about it, and the car was gone. In the hours that followed, his parents had remained impassive while Keiran cried to the point of asphyxia. Grant, meanwhile, said nothing. He just smiled and smiled and smiled.

Maybe Keiran could make a decent case for Grant's sadistic streak being against DA principles, but complaining would not make a good impression. He'd done too much of that already. Making sure no-one was nearby, he got his keys out of his pocket, stabbed them into the wing of the car and ran it the full length of Tom's Alfa. The red paint came off in curls, revealing bare metal underneath.

'Is this helping us?' Grant said.

Did his brother really not experience frustration any more? He seemed to have expunged it from his life.

'Why shouldn't I?' he replied.

Where was Grant's support, his encouragement? Maybe he had turned a corner and this was the start of DA letting him go. Maybe they had already decided that the attempt on Henning's life had become too messy. An alarming scenario unfolded in his mind: the involvement of the police, the complete lack of support

154

from his DA brothers. Arrest. Prison. And in jail his frustration, as ever, would spill over. He would tell the other inmates about DA and how they had betrayed him. In the laundry room one day he would find himself alone with one of the other prisoners, bright-eyed and wordless. There would be an accident.

The sort of end he had imagined for himself was very different: a farmstead, fortified with corrugated steel and barbed wire, some time long after the Collapse. He would be old, but wiry and strong. He would have had a good, long life. It would take a gang of younger men to kill him, many of them destined not to survive the encounter. His last stand would be epic, heroic, and his blood would live on through his sons. He would leave behind his partner – a tough, lean woman with only a Celtic tattoo on her arm to remind her of the old world.

Once, this had seemed like a vision, a prophecy. Now he struggled with how much it resembled a scene from a bad movie.

'If you've finished daydreaming, we'll be needing a plan,' Grant said, 'You know, some kind of way forwards. If you've got one.'

Lurching out of his past, red and shiny, Keiran felt it again – that threat of asphyxia. He turned to face his brother.

'This is much harder than your Ascension,' he said. 'You have to admit that.'

Grant raised an eyebrow.

'The guy invited you into his nice, quiet house and you saw to it. Simple.'

'This would have been simple too if you'd killed Henning in his office lobby, like we planned.'

'Yeah, but it turns out he's a fucking expert in Kung Fu.'

'We already knew that before we started.'

'Yes, but …'

'But you didn't realise what that meant.' A rare hint of contempt edged Grant's voice. 'And my target was trained by DA, remember – more dangerous than Henning will ever be. Don't tell me it was easy.'

'So how come it was over so quickly. How come no-one heard?'

'I was efficient.'

'So this guy just rolls over and dies? He's trying to escape from DA, knows all about our methods, you're squaring off for a fair fight with him, and it's over in seconds?'

'Whether you want to believe it or not, it's the truth, brother.'

If Grant could push buttons, so could he. 'So how come I won our last fight?'

They had been matched up twice at DA meetings. The score was one all.

Keiran said, 'Don't tell me you let me win out of brotherly love?'

'Oh, please. I wouldn't be doing you any favours by letting you win.'

'So I'm good enough to beat you, but this guy of yours – who's a hot-shot arse kicker – is dead before he can even cry out for help?'

'Look, are we going to keep raking over the past, or we are going to find a way forwards with Henning?'

Keiran saw the rise and fall of Grant's chest, the clenching of the jaw, and he felt an immense unburdening, something close to joy. 'Don't worry, I've got a plan for Henning,' he said.

It was exactly what Grant did so often to him – get him worked up, then start talking shop again and see how quickly he could vent the emotions and get back to business. Grant managed it in the time it took them to walk back to the car, unlock it, and get in.

'I have to arrange a meeting with Brad for tomorrow,' Grant said. He could have crowed, used it as a way to win the argument, but he said it with a measured calm. Another demonstration of his superior control.

Keiran had always known it might come to this, but he didn't expect to feel such a rush of fear. He wanted to say, 'Give me one more day.' But no. It would sound desperate, pathetic. In spite of their arguing, Grant had shown him some leniency over the Henning affair. There would be no such quarter from Brad.

'We've lost the target and both of the secondaries,' Grant said. 'I have no choice.'

Was that regret in his voice, even sympathy? Or was he anticipating reprisals from Brad for failing to mentor Keiran effectively? Maybe, despite their arguing, they were still bound together as tightly as ever.

*

Keiran parked the car outside the Hennings' house. He killed the engine and turned to Grant.

'We've been careful, right?'

Grant was expressionless once more.

'I mean, we planned everything, we thought everything through, and we've still been given the slip.'

'Correct.'

'How did Alex and Tom know where to go?'

'We're not party to that information.'

'They wouldn't leave unless they knew where he was, which means that Henning has been in contact with them and arranged to meet up. We know it's not through email or by phone, so he must have been back to the house.'

'But Sean and Jamal have been watching the place.'

'That's what they were supposed to be doing, yes.'

Grant's eyes narrowed. 'You think they've been slacking?'

There would be no better time than this. Keiran offered him the whole thing: 'Possibly, but it could be worse than that. They might have told him when the coast was clear. They might even be the ones who gave Henning the information about DA in the first place.'

The air between them seemed to grow denser. 'Brother, this is a serious accusation you're making.'

'I'm not saying it's true, but it would explain a lot. I don't think we should be relying on them any more.'

'That's your call.'

The doubt was planted. It might buy him some time.

'So, what are we doing here?' Grant said.

Keiran got the glass cutting kit from the boot of Sean's car – at least he had stocked up properly – and handed Grant one of two pairs of latex gloves. 'We're breaking in.'

'You're sure about this?'

'Why not? Because it's illegal?' He tried to keep the sneer out of his voice.

'No,' Grant said, 'because it may limit our options in the future.'

'And it may expand them. Yeah, I'm sure about it.'

He went round to the back of the house. When he had met with Alex Henning, the key had been in the patio door, on the inside. It still was now. Perfect. He clamped the suction cup against the window, near the edge, about two feet up from the ground.

'Cover me,' he said and Grant shielded him from the watching windows of the neighbouring houses.

A quick circle, application of the cutting fluid to the score mark, a deeper circle, repeated tapping to propagate the crack … the process was time-consuming and loud, but the neighbours would put the noise down to a couple of tradesmen at work rather than breaking and entering. The first piece of glass was sucked inwards by the vacuum of the double glazing, coming away in a near perfect circle, with a little debris showering down into the gap. He repeated the cutting process for the inner pane, making a slightly smaller circle. Once he was done, there were two neat holes. He reached in and down to undo the deadlock, then up to twist the main key. He pushed the door and it rumbled aside.

'So, give me your plan,' Grant said.

'We search the place. Find anything useful we can.'

'You realise we won't be able to go back to Alex Henning and persuade her to give us the location of her husband?'

'Yes, we will.'

Grant frowned.

'We tell her that we're trying to get to her husband before a third party does.'

'The third party that trashed her house?'

'Exactly.'

The movement of his brother's lips – almost a smile – told Keiran that Grant hadn't written him off quite yet. He strode through into the lounge.

There was a satisfying symmetry to this: Henning had been through his place, and now he would go through Henning's. He would find things every bit as private, as intimate, as comprom-ising. He wanted to empty the kitchen drawers of cutlery. He wanted to lever the bookshelf away from the wall and let it crash onto the sofa, scattering volumes of false words over the floor. But there was no benefit in alerting the neighbours. He worked quietly, but that didn't mean he couldn't turn their house upside down. He pulled the books off the shelves and left them on the carpet. He took handfuls of stuff out of drawers, sifting through and then discarding. He removed clothes from wardrobes, food from cupboards, and let everything fall where it would.

He allowed himself a few minutes to enjoy this quiet but thor-ough violation, then he got to work, submerging himself in the details of Wes Henning's life, discerning as much as he could about his patterns of behaviour.

And that was a problem, because the more he looked, the more he saw the evidence of Wes and Alex's happiness. There was the framed photo of their wedding, Alex in an impossibly long white dress and Wes in suit and tie, pointing to a whiteboard with the words 'I do!' written in magic marker. There was the certificate from a dance class proclaiming 'Best Waltz: Wes and Alex Henning'. There was the half-finished box of condoms – a pack of eighteen, no less – in the bedside drawer. If someone had told him about these things, second-hand, he would have treated them as mere information, facts to be squirrelled away for potential later use. Seeing them for himself was another matter. He didn't know why. Dancing was pointless and idiotic; he could get good sex any time he could afford it; marriage was a bizarre, archaic institution that had mystified him even as a kid. He would feel no regret wrecking lives like these.

He carried on searching, half-hearted now, for several minutes, but his attention was wandering. What would it be like to have a supportive partner, a house of his own, money in his pocket? Maybe it really was better to live a life of happy delusion than to accept the relentless, exhausting challenge of the Truth. Henning's handwritten note was even now nestled against his thigh, leaching its poison into his skin. What would Gemma think of his way of life? Had she really been so dazzled by his strength? He was assuming that she thought the way he did. And, of course, she didn't, because she wasn't a member of DA. If he were to stand any chance at all of taking things further than a few snatched sentences in a noisy pub, he would have to fundamentally change who he was. When he joined DA he had accepted there would be sacrifices, but that was before he had met her.

Well, this was all very interesting, and it was good that he should challenge his assumptions, but in the end a relationship with her would be a temporary thing. It would become a burden. And yet still he thought about it regularly. Too often, in fact. It was a mystery why the question of her kept coming up when he had already answered it so many times, and so conclusively. The truth was that Ascension would be a far more permanent achievement. He had to be strong. She was a siren, luring him away from the true path for the fleeting pleasures of the flesh. Weaker men would give in at this point. But life was a test, and DA was its greatest expression. He would stand firm. As a distraction, he called to mind what Henning had written about them, prodding the coals of his anger.

When he met Grant on the landing, his doubts had been banished once again, leaving him with a small sense of triumph. Only their impending meeting with Brad cast a shadow over things. At least they could try to appease him with what they'd found here. There was a sheet of paper containing a list of single words, all but the last crossed-out, that were obviously computer passwords. There was Henning's driving license and passport, some utility bills, a piece of paper listing his bank account details. There was enough, in short, for them to assume his identity and convince his bank to cancel his credit and debit cards.

Yes. They would continue to cut him off from the things that sustained him, denying him options, manoeuvring him into a corner. Keiran would demonstrate to DA that he was tightening the noose, that his success was only a matter of time.

22

OUT of the train window Alex saw a series of rooms whisk past, glimpsing each for a fraction of a second – colours and patterns and shapes, curtains and desks and beds, each little box the stage on which a life was acted out. What sort of people were they? What was happening in their lives? Were they angry, frustrated, in love? It was bewildering, the size of the world. All these people she would never meet, never know.

It made her think. Could she ever really know Wes? He had

tried to impress on her how his upbringing had been, using a string of metaphors to make his point – he had felt stranded, ring-fenced, quarantined. And she'd said, 'Yes, of course.' But she had only ever known it in the abstract. Only now was she beginning to truly understand, now that she had cut her own mooring, now that even the umbilical of her phone was gone. Her only remaining support was from Tom, just as it had been when Wes was growing up. She would apologise to her husband when – yes, *when* – she saw him again. *I didn't know what you meant. How could I have known?*

It took them two hours to reach Tina's place – a tiny flat in a run-down part of Bristol. Alex pressed the button for flat 8 and stood back. Everything here was concrete and puddles. A movement caught her eye and she turned towards it, expecting a rat, but it was just a crumpled paper bag, tumbling end over end in the breeze.

'Hello?' came a voice from the speaker.

She leaned forward. 'It's, uh … Alex and Tom.'

'Come right up. First floor, second on the right.'

A buzz and the door unlocked. They went up an echoing staircase and the door to flat 8 opened in front of them. Tina could only have been a couple of inches above five feet, slim, with dark, cropped hair and a big smile.

Her first words to Alex were: 'God, I'd sell my parents to be your height. Come in.'

Tina's flat consisted of a central kitchen/lounge with doors off to a bathroom and bedroom – very small, very simple. Despite being so compact, it seemed to contain little apart from some well-worn furniture, an expansive coffee table and some cooking apparatus. There wasn't even a TV.

'So, how long have you known Fraser?' Tina said.

Tom consulted his watch. 'About four hours.'

'Oh, really? I've always thought of him as the sort of guy you need to get used to.'

'Yes, he probably is,' Tom said wryly.

'Let me guess – an argument?'

'Kind of.'

'He's the sort of person you *can* have arguments with, though, don't you think? It's quite refreshing. Did he ply you with whisky as a peace offering?' When she saw that this was the case, she grinned. 'Standard procedure. I keep telling him I don't like the stuff, but he won't listen. He treats it like medicine. Now, what can I get you to drink?'

*

Alex stared at her untouched cup of tea, an old DVD acting as a coaster. Tom had taken up the telling of the story when she had faltered, concluding with their meeting with Standish.

'Bloody hell,' Tina said, 'you've been through the wringer, haven't you?'

'We don't want your sympathy; we want your help,' Alex said, then added: 'I – I didn't mean that to sound …'

'No, no – I understand,' Tina said. 'Let's get to work.'

She produced a laptop from beside the sofa, opened the lid and logged in. The computer had seen better days – the case was cracked and the cap for the J key was missing.

'So, we need to have a poke around Pe's servers for your husband's name. This could take a while, I'm afraid.'

To fill the silence – she needed to fill the silence – Alex made herself say, 'What led you to quit working for Pe and starting hacking into their systems?'

Tina grimaced while continuing to type rapidly. 'You really wanna know?'

'Yes.'

'So, the short answer is that I'm looking for evidence of a molecular assembler.'

163

Alex looked at Tom and imagined that her expression must have looked very much like his. Oh, God. Not another one.

Tina said, 'Yeah, I know how that sounds, but ... well, okay, let me explain.' She stopped typing for a moment while she collected her thoughts. 'The way I see it is like this: the world is full of doors you're not supposed to go through. But how are you supposed to know what the world is really like unless you do? They're just there to keep you in line, to stop you from asking the difficult questions.'

'And you've been through these ... doors?'

'Yes. And I'll tell you what's through there: a whole other world. A place where things are different.'

Tom chipped in: 'Is this place ruled by a talking lion, by any chance?'

Tina rolled her eyes. 'I was being metaphorical.'

'Well, thank Aslan for that.'

'One day,' she said, ignoring his flippancy, 'I went through one of those doors. I was unhappy at work, I'd just split up with my boyfriend, and I read this article on the internet about a guy who had decided to give up money completely and live in a cave. What a nutjob, I thought. But I read the whole article and by the end, I wasn't so sure.

'He called himself Diogenes, after a Greek philosopher. People mocked him, as you'd expect, but he always had a good answer to all the criticism. I read more about him and became kind of a bit obsessed. People went on pilgrimages to see him, and I thought, why not – it could be interesting. I booked some time off work and made the journey. He was in Devon, the middle of nowhere, and you had to rough it while you stayed there. That was pretty hard for me at first, but everyone who was there just sort of mucked in. It was a real community. And the stuff that Diogenes said just blew my mind.'

'What did he say?' Alex asked. If nothing else, it was an interesting story and a distraction from her own troubles.

'He said that money is an organism.'

'An organism,' she said flatly.

'Not a physical organism, obviously, but a kind of virtual one. In fact, it's the dominant organism on Earth – a parasite that uses human beings to multiply. Just think of all the problems money causes: corruption, debt, jealousy, poverty, war. And yet we let it. We are its slaves.'

'But you can't live without money.'

'Which is exactly how it maintains its control over us, because the alternative is unthinkable. Diogenes thought the unthinkable.'

'But …' Alex spread her hands helplessly. Could Tina not see the furniture, the walls of her flat? Did she not eat?

'No, you're right. I haven't reached the level of purity Diogenes did. But he's an example to us, and the more we push ourselves away from a dependence on money, the better things will get. He devised a ranking scheme – here, look.'

She opened a file on the laptop and turned the screen so they could see:

Level 0: Complete renunciation of money. No cash or bank accounts. No debt or credit.

Level 1: Freedom from debt to any person or institution. Preference for non-monetary solutions and use of money only as a necessity.

Level 2: Freedom from debt to any person or institution. Credit. Use of money for necessities and luxuries.

Level 3: Debt and credit. Use of money for necessities and luxuries.

Level 4: Addiction to money. Compulsive spending. Making money for its own sake rather than as a means to an end.

'Gamblers and investment bankers are at level 4. Diogenes was a 0. I'm at level 1, with maybe a few slips to level 2 every once in a while. And you know what? My life's better for doing it.'

Alex identified herself and Wes as being at level 3. In that distant, mythical future where the mortgage was paid off, they might rise to level 2. Anything beyond that was back in the realm of the talking lion.

'I think I heard about this chap,' Tom said. 'Didn't he die a couple of years ago?'

Tina's hands left the keyboard for the first time. 'He did.'

'How old was he?'

'Forty-five.'

'And he died of malnutrition?'

'No. No, that's bullshit. That's propaganda put about by people who have a vested interest in portraying him as a madman. He was examined in hospital and the official cause of death was pulmonary oedema due to an undiagnosed heart condition.'

Tom nodded acceptance, but she hadn't finished.

'I don't understand why people feel the need to undermine him like that. I mean, what's it to them if we want to live differently? It's because they're afraid we've got a point, because we could upset the status quo. First they ignore you, then they laugh at you, then they fight you, then you win.'

Tom said, 'I was only saying what I'd heard.'

'Sure. And I'm fine with people thinking I'm a fruitcake. But people who twist the facts ... How are we going to get anywhere if we don't even accept the facts?'

'So what do you do now he's gone?' Alex said.

'After he died, everyone went their own way and had their own ideas about how to go forward with his theories. There have been a lot of arguments about it. Like you say: finding a way to give up money is bloody hard. But I think I've discovered how it might happen. Sooner or later someone is going to make a molecular assembler: a machine that can construct any object from raw mat-

166

ter, including food, houses, machines, electronics … anything.'

Tom's mouth hung open, his head moving fractionally from side to side.

'Look,' Tina said, 'I know it sounds bizarre, but think about it. We already have 3D printing, where you can make things – with moving parts – using a desktop machine and some software. We have self-assembling items. And we have the beginnings of nano-technology, where simple objects are engineered at the atomic level. At some point a full molecular assembler is going to be invented. It may not happen this year, this decade, but it will happen eventually.'

Tom managed to find some words. 'It could take centuries.'

'Look how fast computers developed.'

'It might not even be possible.'

'We know it's possible. Nature does it all the time. Think about it: a baby is a human being synthesized in a molecular assembler (its mother's womb) from raw material (the food its mother eats) using a software blueprint (DNA).'

Tom said, 'This all sounds a bit, uh …'

He gave Alex that look. Yes, of course Tina was nuts, but Alex couldn't say it. Something had clicked. She and Tina were look-ing for the same thing. Birth. An impossible birth. She shrank back into the armchair and let the others carry on talking. She didn't feel so good.

Tom said, 'So how does your hacking come into this?'

'The crucial thing about a molecular assembler is that it can also make a copy of itself. And once the cat's out of the bag: boom! Every community could have one, and where's the need for money when you can make anything on demand? The prob-lem is that it will be so disruptive to society that it'll be kept out of the hands of the masses. We won't even be told it exists. The authorities will want to keep their power over us. So I've made it my mission to keep watching out for it. If it's invented in my lifetime it must be outed, stolen, duplicated and given to the people. Just think about it: no more hunger, no more poverty, no more want. You may think this all sounds far-fetched, but the stakes are about as high as they get. Somebody's got to do this.'

It was clear to Alex that Fraser and Tina meant well, but were their weird beliefs and unorthodox thinking just a distraction from getting Wes back? Was Alex's search as hopeless, as forlorn, as Tina's? After all the pretence at fortitude, all the grasping at hope, she could feel herself crashing – a plummet in mood that seemed chemical, inevitable.

'So you think Pe are going to be first to make one?' Tom said.

'No idea, which is why I keep tabs on so many other big companies. But Pe do have a research lab in the States that specialises in nanotechnology, so they're worth ...' She broke off as her gaze fell on Alex. 'Are you okay? Are you cold?'

'I ...' She wasn't sure.

Tina went to a cupboard and produced a blanket. The shivering wasn't from being cold, exactly, but Alex accepted it with gratitude and wrapped herself up, like a survivor from some natural disaster.

*

As evening approached, Tom went out to get them all a Chinese takeaway, leaving Alex alone with Tina, who was – bizarre theories notwithstanding – perfectly pleasant company.

'I hope you find your husband,' she said. 'He sounds lovely.'

Alex wasn't aware of having said much about him. Maybe she should. Maybe in his absence it was her duty to keep him alive and vital and present. 'I hate it when he goes quiet,' she said.

Tina frowned. 'I thought you said he was ...'

Alex didn't explain. How could she? But after a moment Tina nodded in understanding.

'He has to stop hiding things ... or letting things stay hidden.'

Tina knew when to just sit and listen.

'I love him,' Alex said. Realising how incoherent she must sound, she added, 'I don't know what I'm saying.'

Tina sat down beside her and hugged her wordlessly. It was the sort of thing Joanne would have done. She'd have been no use on this journey, though, given that she'd have to tow along the eighteen month old twins. And now, just when Alex was feeling at her most lost and alone – a hug from this crazy girl. She let Tina pull her close, rub her back. There were no platitudes, no 'it'll be all right'. Good.

Tom returned, tearing the lids off half a dozen plastic trays and slapping the contents onto the plates Tina provided. Alex ate automatically, like a calorie processing machine.

Tina carried on typing into the evening. Was this going to yield any kind of fruit? The fact that she liked Tina was no guarantee of her effectiveness as a hacker. She had only the word of a man she'd met for the first time this morning that Tina knew her onions. There might not even be anything to find. Was there an entire underground of these people, convinced and convincing, but utterly delusional? She was reminded of the artilleryman in HG Wells' *The War of the Worlds*, filled with optimism at rebuilding England under the Martians when it was obvious that all hope was gone.

'We should find somewhere to stay,' Tom said as the time approached ten o'clock.

'I can put you up for the night,' Tina said, 'as long as you don't mind blowing up the inflatable mattress.'

'Are you sure?' Alex said. 'We don't want to impose.'

'Don't be silly, I'd be happy to –' A glance at the laptop made her break off mid-sentence. 'Hang on a moment … So, I've found a reference to your husband on a Pe marketing database.' She continued to type. 'Pe keep a lot of details on their customers. This is all standard … Wait a minute. Oh, hello. What the hell are you?'

169

'What?' Alex said. 'What is it?'

'There's a link from your husband's profile to a high security file.'

'Can you get into it?'

'With my access rights? I'm already there. It's a bunch of people's names, eight in all. The file's called "Dubai A-list", whatever that means. It's also marked "Strictly Confidential" and "Restricted Access".' Tina swivelled the laptop so they could see.

'Dubai?' Alex said. 'He's never even been to Dubai. Scroll down.'

'That's all there is.'

'But what use is …?'

'No, you don't understand: this is it.' She beamed at them. 'This is your lead. We need to speak to Clive Goddard. He's head honcho of Data Mining at Pe. He'll be able to find out why this file was generated and what data it was based on.'

And so the trail of breadcrumbs continued. Hope and frustration, once again. Why could it not have been something conclusive? Alex pictured meetings with strings of businessmen in dark suits, each more serious and less helpful than the last; she saw a staircase she was required to climb, a staircase with no end in sight. But what else could she do? Stop in despair?

Tom put his arm across her shoulder. 'It's good news. We've got a way forwards.'

'Yes,' Alex said.

'You'll need me to come with you,' Tina said. 'Clive's a bit … funny.'

Tom rolled his eyes. 'How did I know you were going to say that?'

'What's funny about him?' Alex said.

'He's a genius, but in that slightly odd way that some people are. Don't get me wrong, he's a lovely guy, but he needs to be handled the right way. We can go tomorrow.'

'Don't you have to go to work?'

'Pff. I'll pull a sickie. It's not exactly a dream job.'

Why would she do that? What was in it for her? But there was no point questioning such an offer; Alex just decided to be grateful for it. The kindness of strangers.

'Wait,' Tom said. 'You have a job? But doesn't that mean –'

Tina pointed a finger at him. 'Don't start.'

Tom tried to hide a smile by zipping his lips.

'I have to tell Wes about this,' Alex said. 'Can I borrow the laptop?'

'Sure.' Tina passed it over.

Alex logged into her webmail and sent a message:

From: countessdragula@freemail.com
To: countdragula@freemail.com
Subject: Urgent information

Wes,

Tom and I are now free of the people who've been watching us. We're on the run and we've been doing some digging. Too much to explain here, but we think Pe – the electronics giant – might be involved.

We don't know how much credence to give this at the moment, but couldn't pass up the opportunity to tell you.

Will keep you up to date.

All my love,
Alex

The laptop packaged up her email and sent it wirelessly to the router. From there, it was forwarded through the telephone network to a data centre in Hounslow, then routed through a maze of servers until it reached the one that hosted Wes's webmail. The computer analysed the message, found the words 'urgent', 'free', 'credit' and 'opportunity', and decided that this was an unwanted sales message. Rather than put the email in his inbox, the server helpfully squirrelled it away in Wes's spam folder.

Monday

23

CLIVE started the day the way he started every Monday: sat in his office, with the lights off and a cup of steaming Italian roast in front of him, espresso strength but mug-sized – an antidote to the two bottles of Shiraz he'd put away last night. This was his thinking time. Or at least that's what he told his colleagues. In reality it was the last phase of a transformation that started at home with affirmations muttered in front of the bathroom mirror: 'I am powerful. Men respect me. Women desire me. I am in control.' It was the office equivalent of donning his superhero costume, ready for a week of problem solving, of arse kicking. All he had to do first was overcome the desire to throw himself under a bus.

No. He had managed to get through last week; it stood to reason that he could endure this one too. It was logic, pure and simple, though he heard it in the voice of his mother.

The fact was that he hated superheroes. In any Hollywood movie, the most intelligent person was always the villain. It was the villain who devised the clever plan, the new technology, the radical social change. And, naturally, they used it for evil. The hero was just some jock who came along and ruined it – a murderer who happened to be on the winning side. Punching and shooting people is good, the movies said; using your brain is evil. And yet this ludicrous, lunkhead heroism was exactly the face Clive had to present to the world.

A knock on the door. It opened before he could reply. Rob

came in, holding a plastic cup of coffee which he plonked on the desk before making himself at home in the guest chair. He didn't even bother to close the door. Clive stared at him: the tight designer jeans; the tanned skin; the short beard, little more than stubble, trimmed with millimetre precision. He had begun to think of Rob as an homme fatale.

'SP are pushing for us to start the T1 and T2 inference runs,' Rob said. 'Marketing expressed an interest too.'

Clive stared at Rob's coffee. It was the muck from the vending machine again. Clive's nausea was stirred by the froth of bubbles on its surface – glistening, evil clusters like frogspawn or spiders' eyes. Difficult to assume the mantle of a hero when you were unhinged by the sight of clustered holes or seeds or bubbles. Trypophobia was controversial in medical circles, but he could personally vouch for its existence. And it was only getting worse – maybe there was a stress-related component. He tore his eyes away, making sure his disgust remained hidden. The muscles around his eyes and mouth were under strict instructions not to move, like a row of soldiers before a drill sergeant. This had been a highly successful innovation for him – people saw him as thoughtful, aloof, demanding. But he had never been sure it worked on Rob.

'The T1 and T2?' Rob prompted.

Clive imagined pulling the two halves of his shirt apart to reveal an S symbol, then delivering a knockout punch to Rob's perfectly formed jaw.

'Make them wait,' he found himself saying, to a chorus of protest in his head.

'Really?' Rob said.

His surprise was gratifying.

'Yes.'

'Clive, you don't make Special Projects wait.'

'That's exactly what I'm doing. The algorithms haven't been optimised yet. They won't get the results they want.'

'Most of the optimisation has been done. It's probably enough.'

'Probably?' Clive said with contempt. 'There are two entire data sets that haven't been merged into Dubai yet.'

'Which two?'

'Online personality tests and the data from the mobile apps.'

'Oh, those. But they're not going to make a difference.'

'The bigger the data set …'

'The better the results,' Rob finished dutifully. 'Yeah, I know, but SP –'

'I won't cut corners. If they want workable results, tell them they'll have to wait.'

Rob leaned back in his chair. 'Well, since it's such an important decision, I think the news would be better coming from you.'

'I'll be delighted to tell them,' he said, and again the klaxons sounded. What the hell was he doing? But this was the cost of the disguise – no hesitation, no backing down. 'I'm not going to have my department blamed for anything going wrong in SP. To be honest, I don't know how you can say the data is good enough when we don't even know what they're doing with it.'

Rob shrugged.

'What *is* Jay going to use this for, Rob? A targeted marketing campaign? Creating a shortlist of brand ambassadors? Or will it be something bigger, more ambitious?'

'I dunno.'

'Exactly. But you must wonder what he's doing with our data. I mean, just out of basic scientific curiosity.'

It was pleasing that even through the wine-red throb of his headache he had the wit to ask such a double-edged question. If Rob claimed he had no interest, he would be admitting that he wasn't much of a scientist; if he said he was interested, he would be breaching SP's express instructions. And since it was pretty much a foregone conclusion that his office was bugged, Rob's only choice was how he wanted to condemn himself.

Rob shook his head. 'But knowing what they do would compromise our neutrality.'

The company line, as expected.

'Conversely,' Clive said, 'a more in-depth understanding of what they need would help us supply them with better data. We could hone our algorithms specifically for their purposes.'

There was no answer to this, and Rob knew it. Even if Clive couldn't match his colleague for deviousness and an ability to ingratiate himself with upper management, he could at least maintain his intellectual supremacy.

'So, what are you suggesting?' Rob said.

Clive feigned surprise. 'I'm not suggesting anything. It's purely hypothetical. I was just wondering whether you thought it was a benefit or a hindrance to be working in a vacuum.'

'Hmm.' Rob nodded for a few moments, as if pondering this, but he gave no answer. 'It's an interesting idea, Clive,' – *fence-sitter* – 'but I've got something more pressing to discuss.'

He reached over and nudged the door shut. As if that would give them privacy.

'It's about Giselle,' he said.

'Oh?'

'I've been looking at her profile,' Rob said. 'It's surprisingly low on extroversion, and remarkably high on stubbornness.'

'Her work is good, though. She's extremely thorough.'

'Yeah … maybe too thorough. It takes her forever to do anything.'

'But the quality is good.'

'Look,' Rob said, 'I guess what I'm saying is that her profile doesn't really match the job requirements.'

'Well … again, the data set might be too small to give an accurate picture.'

'No, no. It's a comprehensive data set. We've harvested stuff from her email and web traffic. We've done keyword searches on her phone audio. She's posting on social networks all the time. There's a lot of material and it's all been parsed.'

Giselle reminded Clive of his younger self – nervy and academic, but with great potential. The sort of employee who needed some nurturing. He had taken a risk when he hired her, throwing out the rulebook and going by instinct in the hope that he could shake up the department a bit, introduce someone who wouldn't just join the parade of yes-men. Someone unlike Rob. He should have known it would come back to bite him. His only defence for hiring her was to claim there was something wrong with the process – the AI routines for the inference runs, the algorithms used to construct the profile – but admitting that would undermine his entire professional credibility, all the way back to his postgraduate work.

Rob certainly knew how to riposte.

But Clive did still have *some* confidence in his work. Useful, accurate results *could* be gleaned, as long as things were done properly, as long as the results weren't treated like gospel. At Cambridge they had understood the value of academic rigour, caution, statistical significance. The problem with Rob and SP was that they wanted certainties. Certainties from incomplete data.

'So, what are you saying?' Clive said.

'Well, the sad fact is that she'll probably be ranked in the bottom 20% at the next appraisal, so we'll be getting rid of her anyway.'

The sad fact? Rob really was a world class shit. Was this his tactic – to remove all of the people who were sympathetic to Clive and then bag the top job for himself?

'I'm sorry. I know how fond you are of her. Not that I'm suggesting anything ... well, we both know that wouldn't happen.'

Clive sat back and folded his arms. How much did Rob know

about him? They were both supposed to be exempt from having entries in the database. They'd been told this by Jay, so Clive knew it was a bare-faced bloody lie. No, Clive knew he was being scrutinised every bit as thoroughly as his colleagues. Probably more so, given his level of seniority. His profile must be held on a separate database somewhere, and there could only be one person maintaining it. Clive had been diligent about poisoning any data they kept on him. He had seeded the internet with misinformation for Pe to scoop up and integrate into his profile. Just this weekend he had ordered a pair of dumb-bells from Amazon that he would never use, and posted a picture of Scarlett Johansson on Facebook with the comment 'Is there any sexier woman alive?'

Had Rob found a way to see through all this? And why hadn't Clive been asked to maintain a similar profile on Rob? At least then he might have been able to dig up some dirt on him.

'Well, I'd better be going,' Rob said.

He was about to lever himself out of the chair, but paused, in a poor imitation of someone who had just thought of something, and sat back down.

'You know,' he said, 'you've changed since I first started working here.'

'Oh, really? In what way?'

'You're a lot more … forceful.'

Clive conjured a frown. 'That's the way I am, Rob. Don't expect me to apologise for it.'

'But you weren't like that a couple of years ago.'

'A couple of years ago I was looking after a friend with lingering, terminal cancer, Rob. That tends to take the wind out of your sails. He was thirty-eight. Any other questions?'

Rob looked gratifyingly stricken. 'I'm … sorry. I …'

Clive felt no qualms over this carefully prepared fiction. In this place, you did what was necessary to survive.

'Look,' Rob said, 'I didn't realise. Forget I said anything. I'll, uh … I'll be getting on.'

Clive watched his retreat. The conniving little bastard would be straight off to add it to his profile. At least this time he had the decency to close the door. Clive collapsed into his seat, and as his back hit the leather, the breath whooshed out of him. How had he ended up here? He should be the head of a research lab, not a passenger in some ruthless, unstoppable corporate juggernaut. And yet what was the alternative? His work was his life, and it was so specialised that there were very few places he could really take it forwards. He should have stayed at Cambridge, but he had comprehensively burned his bridges by calling his faculty head an arrogant, self-absorbed old git. If he did quit Pe he would take a huge pay cut, and then, of course, there would be the cataclysm of his mother's disappointment.

Mother. It always came down to Mother. How absurdly Freudian. None of the myriad problems in their relationship would seem quite so bad if only he could come out to her, but that would mean excommunication, assuming the shame of it didn't kill her outright. But for all the pain she had caused him, he couldn't entirely blame her. He had run her through Dubai under a pseudonym and it predicted a personality he recognised all too well from countless conversations, sipping tea at the oak table in front of the Aga. She was a product of her environment, her experiences, her personality archetype. The same thing that made her so inflexible was also what had spurred her on to such success, and to foster it in her son. He could revile her more extreme opinions, but not her. Never her.

Another knock on his office door. Whoever it was at least waited for him to say, after a deep breath and a fortifying sigh, 'Come in.'

Giselle entered, tottering on high heels and holding a tablet. 'Morning, Clive. What's this I hear about you sticking it to SP?'

So the weasel had spilled the beans already. That didn't take long.

'I am not "sticking it to SP",' he said, 'I'm sticking *up* for the department. I'm giving us time to actually do the work properly, which is something you, of all people, should appreciate.'

She adjusted her glasses. 'I, uh … didn't mean to –'

'What is it with everyone in this place? The constant attacks, the constant undermining. Do SP have to put up with this?'

Her fingers curled round the top of the tablet. 'I'll come back later,' she said, and clattered out into the corridor.

Clive stared for several seconds at the door after she had closed it. Elbows on the desk, he put his head in his hands. Clarity came, as always, far too late. It should have been the other way round: he should have made Rob sod off, and he should have made time for Giselle. It was the cost of the disguise. The habits he had erected to protect himself intruded into every part of his life now, wrecking anything true or worthwhile or valuable. Perhaps eventually he would be consumed by the illusion of this person he wasn't. There would be nothing of the real Clive left, just a thick, gristly layer of machismo wrapped round a core of self-loathing.

24

Crime and Punishment was a strange book – part literary fiction, part crime novel, heavy on the psychology and philosophy. Wes had set himself a rule: he was allowed to look up at the row of shops only at the end of each paragraph. The lengths of the paragraphs – some stretching on for pages – meant he broke the rule frequently. Even with these interruptions, Dostoevsky's feverish prose wormed its way into his mind. Wes was Raskolnikov – skulking, hesitant, half-mad with stress. No, Keiran was

Raskolnikov – a man who believed he had found a justification for murder.

Wes half expected to be moved on from his bench, but few people paid attention to him. Those that did were treated to a big smile, and seemed happy to take this as proof of his harmlessness.

The lock of the door leading to the upstairs room had defeated him last night. He had retreated in frustration, shivering and dejected, to the White Horse Inn on Midhurst Road, having missed the last bus back to his base in Petersfield. Although they had stopped serving food, the barmaid took pity on him and arranged for a slice of microwaved lasagne to be brought to his room. In his eagerness for something hot to eat, he burned his tongue.

He had forced himself out of bed before seven o'clock and was sat on his freezing bench to watch the sun come up, weak and hazy and orange, over the footbridge that straddled the railway line. Dog walkers and early risers appeared, hands in armpits against the cold, breath fogging; light and life returning to the world. The sun climbed higher, burned through the mist, graced the town with its warmth.

When, after three hours, he looked up to see Keiran and Grant going through the door, his eyes wouldn't register for several seconds what he was seeing. But no, it was them. It was really them. His rucksack opened under fingers that quivered with cold and sudden adrenaline. He stowed the paperback and took out the duct tape and phone. He concealed the rucksack in a nearby bush; no point carrying excess baggage. A car pulled up and parked – a black, well-worn Mercedes estate. A bald man in a dark sweater and camo trousers, stocky as a rugby player, got out. He slammed the door and strode in after the others.

Wes crossed the road, ready to lower the concealing peak of the baseball cap and turn in another direction if any of them came back out unexpectedly. He cast a glance left and right, then laid down just behind the Merc, face up, like a mechanic, the phone and the roll of duct tape in his hands. Now, where to attach it? Taping it to the chassis wouldn't be secure enough. Too close to the exhaust pipe and the heat might cause it to malfunction. He opted for a bracket near – not too near – one of the wheels, and began tearing off strips of duct tape with his teeth and attaching them to the phone. It didn't tear very straight, and bits of tape stuck to his tongue and lips. Some scissors might have been a good idea.

'All right, mate?' came a voice from somewhere above him.

Shit. He tilted his head down towards the thin strip of light between the underside of the car and his own body, expecting to see two legs clad in camouflage. No, it was jeans. Had Keiran or Grant been wearing jeans? He didn't remember. He should be memorising this sort of thing. Leaving the phone and duct tape out of sight, Wes extricated himself from the underside of the car. The guy was reassuringly unfamiliar – tall, maybe late twenties, with a round face and spiky blonde hair. In one hand was a plastic carrier holding six takeaway coffee cups.

'Exhaust, is it?' he said cheerily.

Wes stood up and shook his head – no help required.

'I work at the garage round the corner. I'll give you an 'and.'

He started to crouch down, but Wes shook his head again, more vigorously this time.

The man frowned. 'Mate, I can't help you if you ain't gonna speak to me.'

Wes got his pad out and showed him the standard message about being mute.

'Oh. Oh, right. Well, look, I'm not gonna charge you or nothing. Just gonna have a quick look.'

Wes put a hand on his shoulder.

'What?'

Wes glanced back at the door. No time to write, or to invent

182

some plausible explanation. He set his face into best pissed-off frown, extending his arm and stabbing a finger off to the right.

'You do understand I'm offering you free help, here.'

Wes jabbed the finger again. There was no other option; it had to be done.

'All right, all right. I'm going.' As he left, he muttered to himself: 'Fuckin' 'ell. You try and do someone a good turn …'

Wes dived back under the car and finished his work. The phone dangled, but not enough, he hoped, for it to get caught in the wheels or suspension or work loose and get dragged along the road or … it would have to do. He scooped up the roll of duct tape and retreated to his bench.

He needn't have hurried. It was forty minutes before the bald man emerged and got back into his car. God, he looked like a bruiser. He drove off without any indication that he'd noticed Wes's tampering. The other two came out a couple of minutes later. Grant moved with assurance, but the slump of Keiran's shoulders suggested it hadn't been an easy meeting. Ahh, the poor lamb.

*

Retreating to the library in Petersfield, Wes settled at one of the public computers, brought up the website for the anti-theft app and checked the phone's location. He knew from an experiment he'd conducted earlier in the morning that the phone's GPS still worked even if it was underneath a car. The signals from the satellites must bounce off the road. After refreshing the web page a few times, he could see the progress of the bald man – the 'Brad' of Keiran's diary? – as he drove up the A3, then started clockwise on the M25. Once the location settled, Wes would hopefully have a fix on his house, although that did depend on him not stopping off at a Wetherspoon's for a bite to eat, or a DA meeting for a recreational punch-up. Stumbling into a room full of these psychos was definitely not part of the plan.

He opened another tab and checked his webmail. Nothing from Alex. No more heartfelt reassurances that she was innocent. What did this mean? He waited a few seconds and refreshed the page. Still nothing. He could see where this was heading. If he allowed himself, he would keep refreshing the page indefinitely. Each click would be a disappointment, part of a slow accumulation, driving him to madness. Instead he switched back to the map and watched the car's progress, pixel by pixel, mile by mile. After a few minutes staring at the screen, he realised this was no better than checking for emails from Alex. It was the same trap in a different form.

He went to the disabled toilet and practised siu nim tau in the cubicle. When he had first started Wing Chun he'd had little patience for these drills, but his sifu had insisted on them being performed regularly and with millimetre precision. Wes had gradually surrendered to their necessity. Now he found the movements calming and meditative. He heard Ant telling him that Wing Chun was about the middle path, that life itself was about the middle path. Not an easy thing to accept. Wes had always found it easy to fixate on things, trying to push for something to happen when it was clearly out of his hands, when all he could really do was wait. He sought patience in the rhythm of his movements. He would allow himself to go back and check his email and the car's progress every half an hour, but no more frequently than that.

The drill ended with a chain punch – three strikes in quick succession: left-right-left. Wes extended it to a hundred punches, as he often did, and imagined Keiran's face on the other end. He did this not out of anger, but to neutralise the spike of adrenaline he felt at the prospect of another fight with him. The calmer and looser you were, the better you fought. With Keiran, Wes felt like a novice again, trying to resolve the paradox of remaining relaxed

184

while being assaulted.

He passed the time by reading more of his novel. He went back to the loo to practise the other empty hand forms: chum kiu and biu jee. The latter contained the techniques designed to get out of a compromised position – the last-ditch attempt to avoid losing a fight. They were powerful, risky, and potentially lethal. He had never practised them with such diligence.

He also wanted to practice chi sau – wrist to wrist, foot to foot, relying on touch to find a way through his opponent's defence – but he needed a partner for that. Ant's party piece was to perform it blindfolded, and he still managed to best anyone in the class four times out of five. Wes longed for a focussed training session with Ant or his wife, Xiaoying, who was like an eel, slithering past Wes's arms to tap a palm on his chest, or knuckles against his jaw. But he would miss his class tonight. It was part of his routine, somewhere Keiran and Grant could find him. He continued to train alone.

*

The car stopped in Reading and stayed there for two of Wes's half-hourly checks, but just as he was deciding this was the man's house, it started moving again. Eventually it settled on a street in Enfield. He recorded both street names, and gave it two hours before he felt sure that this should be his destination.

He bought a street map of London and took the bus back into Strathurst, getting off at the bus stop just outside his business park. Seeing the blue J+H logo brought a pang of ... it could only be described as homesickness. It was Monday afternoon and he should be in there, designing websites, checking the comments on his latest blog post, drinking tea and exchanging sarcastic communications with Tom and Marcus. He could see that there was no-one there now. Beyond the tinted windows had the office been ransacked? He would not go in to find out.

Maybe he would never set foot in there again.

It was half past three, the car park still full. In the centre, his Mini stood patiently. Even if they were watching him now, he was relying on them not to murder him in such an exposed place. He strode across the tarmac, unlocked the car and got in, chucking his rucksack into the passenger footwell. He turned the key in the ignition, and only then did it occur to him that they might have wired it with explosives and scattered him across half of town. But no: there was nothing more than the cough of the engine coming to life. Putting his seat belt on, he pulled away, and from that point he spent longer looking in the rear-view mirror than out of the windscreen.

At first he was being followed by a blue Toyota, then a white van. But both turned off onto side roads, their suspicious driving the fabrication of an overactive mind. He crossed the A3 and turned left onto Longmoor Road, going west – away from the direction he would be taking later – then parked the car in a lay-by next to the woods. Taking the rucksack, he headed down the footpath. He was beginning to feel an affinity for trees, some atavistic impulse shared with his pre-human ancestors, who had used the concealing trunks and foliage for exactly the same purpose. He found a good spot – well off the path, but with a view of the car – and sat there for thirty minutes on a fallen trunk, surrounded by gently swaying oaks. He read some more of *Crime and Punishment*, looking up regularly to check the car or to see that the rustling he heard was only the sound of a squirrel nervously navigating the forest floor.

Satisfied that he hadn't been followed, he returned to the car and began a thorough search for tracking devices. He scoured the interior, including the glove compartment, the door pockets, under the mats. He checked the boot and the engine compartment, inch by inch, thorough and methodical. Nothing. Even when he had run out of places to search, the doubt would not leave him. But he needed the freedom of his own car. Buses and trains travelled on fixed routes at predictable times. Well, semi-predictable. If he continued to use them, he was conforming to a pattern they could exploit.

He put the street map on the passenger seat, and marked it up so he could navigate without the usual crutch of his phone's sat-nav or Alex's directions. God, what a blissful scenario that would be: to have her in the car next to him, missing the turnings because she was distracted by a flock of geese or an unusually shaped electricity pylon.

Did this person still exist? Had she ever? He had not seen her for three, nearly four, days and already she seemed to be retreating into myth. He was questioning whether everything they had said and done meant something different to him than it had to her. How could he tell which of his memories about her were real and which were fabrications, distortions, misunderstandings?

There were times he wished he'd never picked up that damned Dostoevsky.

25

EVER since Tina had told her about Clive, Alex had wondered what a Head of Data Mining actually did. As the curving, tree-lined drive opened up onto a sea of gravel and a magnificent thatched cottage straight out of a Jane Austen novel, she con-cluded the answer was: something important. The walls were flint, the window frames dark wood. It looked like it had origin-ally consisted of two separate buildings, but a short connecting piece – tiled rather than thatched – made it into a single house. She'd expected something more modern from a man who worked in computing. Perhaps this was his way of putting work behind him. It was idyllic and inviting. A warm glow emanated from within, a contrast to the grey-blue of the darkening sky.

Tina stopped the car – there was room to park four or five – and they got out. Alex was surprised they'd made it all this way in Tina's Astra, a vehicle so dilapidated that the former owner hadn't sold it, they had *given* it to her.

When they had stopped at the petrol station, Tina had stayed in the driver's seat and started sifting through her purse.

'Put that away.' Alex said. 'We'll get this. It's the least we can do for all your help.'

Tina had looked relieved. 'It's so expensive these days, isn't it?'

Comparing the rustic splendour of Clive's house to Tina's tiny flat, Alex wondered whether the two of them really could have any kind of connection.

Alex and Tom hung back while Tina rang the doorbell. The door – a slab of wood with no windows – opened little more than a crack and an owlish eye surveyed them. Then the door swung wider to reveal a short man, prematurely bald and dressed in the unironed shirt and tweed jacket of an absent-minded university professor.

'Hello, Clive.' Tina said.

Clive's lips hovered between a smile and a gape of surprise. 'Tina Derby! Good Lord. How long has it been?'

'A couple of years now. We're on our way to meet up with some people in Maldon, but we've got plenty of time and we were passing right by your door, so I thought I might …'

'Well, yes, of course. Come in.'

'These are my friends, Alex and Tom,' Tina said.

They shook hands and exchanged pleasantries. The inside of the house was as striking as the outside, full of beautiful objects and acres of polished wood. A glance down a corridor showed Alex a glimpse of Clive's study, where a laptop sat next to an antique escritoire.

'Come through to the lounge and take a seat,' Clive said.

'Would you like tea?'

Alex nodded, and so did the others. They settled into studded leather armchairs.

'Butter him up,' Alex whispered.

Tina nodded impatiently. 'I know, I know.'

Alex fidgeted, trying to feel like a guest rather than what she was – an intruder, here under false pretences. She had been on edge all day. Wes had not replied to her previous email, so she had sent another from Tina's laptop that morning:

From: countessdragula@freemail.com
To: countdragula@freemail.com
Subject: Where are you?

Wes,
Please, please, please reply. I need to know you're safe.
Love,
Alex

She felt the urge to write a longer message, but after several minutes dithering over the keyboard she accepted that these few words encapsulated everything she wanted to say. Right up until four o'clock, when they had left Tina's flat, she had kept checking in vain for a reply. This silence was a poison, slowly but steadily overwhelming her.

Clive emerged from the kitchen, set down a loaded tray, and poured tea into bone china cups that looked too decorative to be used as mere drinking vessels. The handle was so delicate that Alex struggled to get a grip with one hand, and the contents were too hot for her to use two. She put the cup back down on a side table, realising she didn't have to drink it immediately.

'It's so good to see one of the old guard again,' Clive said. 'It's not the same without you.'

'How are things?' Tina said.

'Oh, you know … so, so.'

'Still rattling round this old place?'

'Yes.' Somehow he managed to sip his tea without scalding his lips. 'One or two girlfriends since I last saw you, but none that felt the urge to stay. I think I'm quite difficult to live with, to be honest.'

'Really? I can think of people who are far worse.'

Clive set his cup down on its saucer. 'I always did like you, Tina.'

She grinned.

'So who are you working for now, then?' he said. 'You left rather abruptly, as I recall.'

'I'm doing some freelance security work at the moment. Penetration testing, that sort of stuff.'

Clive nodded.

'Are you still throwing your garden parties?' she said.

'Oh … uh, not for a while, actually. I really must get round to that again some time. You'd come along, I hope?'

'Of course. Is Nathan still working at Pe?'

'No. He left about six months after you did.'

'That's a shame. He was a lovely guy, wasn't he?'

'Mmm.'

'Actually,' Tina said, 'we're, er … sort of here to talk about work.'

Alex saw the fingers of Clive's right hand clutch the arm of his chair. She looked towards Tina, hoping to signal a warning, but she was busy gazing down into her cup, oblivious to the danger.

'You mean … Pe?' Clive said.

'The very same,' Tina said.

Clive gave an indulgent smile. 'You know I can't talk about that, Tina. Not to an ex-employee, and certainly not to your friends, here.'

'Of course, of course,' Tina said, nodding vigorously.

She fell into an awkward silence. Alex was scrambling for some way to bring them back to the easy chat of a few moments ago. Something about these parties of Clive's, or their impending, fictional holiday in Maldon. They had worked up some convincing details earlier in the day. But it was difficult to see how any of it could be made to seem natural; the conversation had moved on.

Tina said, 'It's just that it's quite important.'

No. This was all wrong. She couldn't just go blundering –

'Tina, I –'

'A matter of life and death, as it happens.'

'I ... beg your pardon?'

Alex closed her eyes slowly. Since Tina had already taken them down this road, there was nothing left to do but go for broke.

'Some men are trying to kill my husband,' she said.

'I ... well, I ... that would be a matter for the law, then. Nothing to do with me.'

'Our investigations have led us to believe your company might be involved.'

Clive's eyes rolled momentarily up towards the ceiling and its exposed roof beams. He laughed – a forced, humourless thing. 'What sort of conspiracy theory twaddle is that?'

Alex was going to tell him they had excellent reasons for believing it, but ... did they? A tattoo on a man's arm. The pet theories of a washed-up journalist. A vague list of names stolen from a private computer. These things only seemed convincing to her because she had nothing else to go on. Desperation had made her credulous. She could see that they were losing him, so she had no option but to play her ace, to try to shock a reaction out of him.

'What do you know about the A-list?' she said.

That did it. Clive sprang up from his chair. 'You have to go,' he said. 'You have to leave now. You have no right to come into

191

my house and make accusations like this. How dare you.'

They were onto something, then, but it seemed this would be as far as they got. Clive made ushering motions with both hands. All three of them remained seated. How had things deteriorated so quickly?

Clive took in a deep breath. 'I will not discuss company secrets with you,' he shouted, 'and I will not listen to your ridiculous, paranoid accusations. Now get out of my house, before I call the police.'

They stood slowly, like synchronised sleepwalkers.

'Mr Goddard,' Alex said, 'I'm so sorry. We've got off on the wrong foot here …'

'Go on: fuck off.'

The swear-word sounded awkward on his lips, as if it was the first time he'd used it, but there was no doubting his anger – he was visibly trembling. Alex appealed to Tom, who gave a tiny shake of the head. Even his charm had limits. Wordlessly, they backed out of the house and Clive slammed the door on them.

Tina turned to her and was shaking her head. 'Alex, I'm sorry, I didn't realise he was –'

'Get in the car,' she said.

Tina unlocked the Astra.

'Drive,' Alex said, wrenching open the rear door and throwing herself into the seat. 'Just drive.' She wanted to be away from Clive's house, away from the scene of this disaster. Once they were back on the road, she changed her mind. 'Pull over. Turn the engine off.'

Tina did as she was told and the engine ticked as it cooled. There was no other sound in the car. Alex felt like she had been climbing a cliff face and her rope had been cut. She was at the bottom of a ravine: bruised, stunned. And there was no way back up.

'What did you think you were doing?' she said to Tina's back.

'We agreed that you were going to win him over gradually, not dive straight in and tell him to grass up his company.'

'I did not dive straight in!'

'I think you've been spending too long with only computers for company.'

Tina twisted in her seat, trying to see behind. Her mouth was open in outrage. 'Well what would you have done? It gets awkward when you run out of things to say. Either you get to the point or you leave.'

'I thought you said you knew this man. You should have found *something* to talk about.'

Tina faced forwards again and said in a small voice, 'I did my best.'

'That was your best, was it? I'd hate to see what your worst is like. This is not a game, Tina.'

'I never said it was!'

'It may have escaped your notice, but my husband's life depends on what we do.'

'Look, Clive is …' Tina spluttered. 'I never gave any guarantee that I could …'

'Girls, girls,' Tom said, lowering his hands in a placatory gesture.

'Don't call me "girl"!' Tina yelled.

For half a minute, no-one said anything. The air in the car curdled.

Alex no longer recognised herself. She never shouted at anyone. It just wasn't in her nature.

When Tina spoke again her voice was calm, but clipped, wounded. 'Look, maybe you want to do this on your own.'

Alex became aware of the world beyond the car windows – the gloom that preceded night; the drizzle; the indistinct foliage, flat as a cardboard cut-out. Without even the headlights for illumination, everything was grey. Where was she? In a stranger's car, miles from home. And what had just happened? She had blown it. She hadn't briefed Tina properly. Everything had become confused. It wasn't Alex's rope that had been cut, but Wes's. She saw a vivid picture of him, arms flailing in panic, face upturned, as he plunged silently into the void. Though her fingers were outstretched, she had failed to catch him.

She fell forwards and felt the fuzz of synthetic fibre against her forehead as she made contact with the back of the driver's seat. She wanted to curl over fully, to cradle the emptiness she felt inside, but there was no room. She ground her face into the back of the seat. Her stomach contracted, a wrench like a hiccup. Then again, and again. She had been strong for so long. You could deny tears, but not forever. She howled and howled.

An arm across her shoulders. Two hands reaching backwards to find hers. For a time, her world consisted only of touch. She tried to say something. It might have been 'Why can't I just have him back?' She wasn't even sure herself. If they let go, something terrible would happen. The universe would tear open; she would be swallowed by the abyss. She knew this, beyond sense, beyond reason.

But they held fast, until the back of the seat was soaked with her tears, until, finally, there was quiet again.

When Alex felt able to speak, it was to say, 'Don't leave us, please.'

Tina's voice was hoarse. 'It's okay. I already decided not to.'

Alex pushed herself back up to sitting and accepted the handkerchief Tom offered, an item he always had at hand for moments of chivalrous opportunity. Outside the car, two rows of orange dots perforated the darkness. The street lights had come on.

*

They booked three separate rooms at a cheap chain hotel. Once again, Tina opened her purse and rummaged through it.

'Bit impractical, this "no money" policy of yours,' Tom said, handing over his credit card.

'If it was easy we'd all be free of money already, wouldn't we?'

They had been speaking like a double-act, trying – perhaps a little too hard – to lighten Alex's mood. It was good of them to try. Tom offered to foot the bill for whatever Alex wanted to eat, mentioning a promising French bistro they had passed on their way to the hotel. But she knew she wouldn't eat much, and they ended up at a tiny, slightly shabby Italian restaurant instead. Tom suggested they didn't talk any more about their plans for the time being.

Alex said, 'I don't want to stop you from coming up with ideas just because I'm ...' she made a vague gesture. 'It's just that I'm so tired. If you guys have got any thoughts, any kind of ... I'll just sit here and listen. And drink wine.'

She gazed down at the Montepulciano as she swirled it round in her glass and felt absurdly grateful for it. Wine was so lovely. It's not that she wanted to get drunk ... just a glass or two to help her sleep.

'Well,' Tom dabbed at his lips with a napkin, 'I've come up with a plan, girls – I mean, uhh ... ladies?'

Tina arched one eyebrow and pointed a warning finger at him.

'Women? Females? Oh, please, I'm running out of words, here. At least give me some credit – I haven't gone all hip-hop and tried to refer to you as bitches.'

Tina reached across the table and thumped him on the arm.

'I said I hadn't!'

'How about "friends"?' Alex said. Exhaustion had made her mawkish.

'Okay, then: friends,' Tom said, but he made it sound grand, like something from Shakespeare. 'The solution is simple. We go back to Clive's –'

Tina interrupted: 'You think he's going to let us back in?'

'Irrelevant,' he said. 'We go back to Clive's, force our way in, tie his hands, bring him out to the car and take him away. Then we treat him impeccably until he gives us the information we want.'

'You're suggesting we kidnap him?'

'Kidnap is such a … loaded word. Think of it more as a day trip.'

'A day trip against his will?'

'Why not? People with kids do it all the time.'

26

JAY'S phone vibrated against his thigh in a pattern of buzzes: two long, two short, two long. A priority alert, but it would have to wait until the end of the meeting. He returned his attention to the screen on the wall.

'So, as you can see from this upswing,' he indicated a point on the graph, 'Deneb and Vega are yielding fruit.'

Jay glanced at his audience. In the darkness Noonan was lounging again, something he did to project confidence. Smith and Thompson flanked him, basking in his glow. Noonan could break wind and they'd praise him for it. Gutiérrez was the interesting one, the unknown quantity. Without him Jay could have wrapped up in fifteen minutes. That had been the point in moving this meeting to the end of the day, just after the mammoth Business Efficiency get-together – to keep things short. It's what they would want.

'If we look at the consolidated reputation metric –' Jay tapped a key on the laptop '– you can see that we're already beginning to see more positive press.'

Gutiérrez was stroking his beard in consternation, the theatrical prelude to a question. Whenever you're ready, Miguel.

'Here are the budgets for Deneb and Vega,' Jay said. 'Compare that with the increase in company value, and you can see they're giving us a solid return on investment.'

'A moment, please,' Gutiérrez said.

And there it was. 'Yes?'

'How do we know that these increases in share price are due to SP's projects?'

'All other effects have been removed from the graph using statistics gathered from other departments. The process for doing this is … complex, to say the least.' So complex, in fact, that no-one had ever managed to get to the end of Jay's explanation before throwing in the towel.

'You believe it is possible to achieve this with any degree of reliability?'

'Oh, yes.'

'I would like to see the thinking behind this.'

'I'll send you a couple of white papers from Microsoft and Google. They're using similar methods.'

Noonan cut in: 'You don't need to worry, Miguel; Jay has an excellent track record at this sort of thing. Our methods may seem unorthodox at first, but you'll soon fit in.'

'Mr Noonan, with the greatest respect, I am here to do a job, not to "fit in". I was hired to help with the company's reputation and I cannot do that without understanding the business processes and the statistical methods used to present data.'

Jay watched Smith and Thompson try to conceal their surprise. Yes, Gutiérrez was definitely the interesting one. Someone with fire in their belly. Good.

Gutiérrez said, 'You will forgive me if I seem awkward, but it is my duty to question, to bring new things to light.'

'Of course.' Noonan's calm was admirable, but there was a hint of steel behind it.

'Okay,' Gutiérrez said, 'so let us assume for the moment that the statistics are accurate. There is something else that troubles me. Your measure of company reputation …'

'This slide?' Jay said, swiftly bringing it up.

'Yes, exactly. You have given the traditional press a 25% weighting while social media account for 75%. Why is this?'

'You're thinking traditional press should be given more?' Jay knew where this was going.

'Exactly. Why are we not courting good will among the major news organisations – the BBC, CNN, Wired? For example, the BBC recently described us as "beleaguered tech giant Pe".'

'A comment that will be forgotten in a few weeks.'

'This I doubt.'

'On the contrary, I guarantee it.'

'No-no-no. People see the BBC as an authority – something more reliable than a post on Twitter or a hack writing on some website they have never heard of.'

'No, they don't. That's entirely wrong. Joe Public perceives all sources of news as equally reliable.'

Gutiérrez snorted.

'It's irrational, I grant you,' Jay said, 'but that doesn't mean it isn't true. By and large, if something is printed on paper or appears on the internet, it will be treated as authoritative. Look at the newspapers. Everyone has heard the expression "don't believe everything you read in the papers". And yet, overwhelmingly, they do. The same is true for the web.'

'Ridiculous. Traditional news organisations will always be more reliable than social media.'

'Oh, I agree; they will. But reliability has nothing to do with it. It's what people read – what people want to believe – that counts. Where do you think news organisations pick up their stories in the first place? As an overworked journalist, how do you get the news up on your website fast enough that you don't lag behind everyone else? It would be nice to double-check every story for accuracy, but there just isn't time. Even if you get your story from an established source, like a wire service, *their* journalists are also overstretched and get most of their stories from web sources. You cannot overestimate the importance of millions of freelancers all covering their own area of interest, twenty-four hours a day. Social media and blogs are where news starts. It *is* the mainstream.'

'But, the reliability of –'

'People don't want reliability. They want news as fast as they can read it. That's what news is. That's what the word "news" means.'

Gutiérrez opened his mouth, closed it, folded his arms.

'We can't control the BBC or CNN,' Jay said, 'but we can have a reasonable influence in the online world. We can get stuff trending on social networks, and all of it has a trickle-down effect. This is part of what project Sirius is all about. Pe has a long history of engaging brand advocates to help manage the company's reputation. We're stepping up this engagement, and we're going to see its effect over the coming weeks.'

Jay could almost see the thought forming in Gutiérrez's head – 'If you've got this all sorted out already, why did you hire me?' Had he really not figured out that he'd been brought in to appease the shareholders? He would either end up leaving in frustration, or being shunted sideways into a role that more closely matched his skills.

Gutiérrez said, 'And we pay these brand advocates?'

'Not with money. Their actions earn them free Pe products, commensurate with their effectiveness. We find it beneficial sometimes not to create something as tiresome and bureaucratic as a paper trail.'

'But this could be discovered.'

'It could,' Noonan interjected, 'in which case we fire some middle manager and say he was a rogue agent acting against the company's values.'

Smith and Thompson laughed, and Jay could see Gutiérrez trying to figure out whether this was a statement of fact or a company in-joke.

'Guys ...' Noonan was glancing at his watch. 'We're going to have to take this off-line.'

'Very well,' Gutiérrez said, 'but you can see I have many outstanding questions.'

'We'll sit down, just the two of us,' Jay said, 'and I'll show you how this all works.'

Clearly Gutiérrez was not one to be bought, not one to bask in the privilege of his position. His profile indicated a man of deep focus, not a multitasker. Jay would overload him with information, describing a multitude of SP's successful projects while steering round those he might find more troublesome. He would give the truth, just not the whole truth. Like the others, Gutiérrez would skirt the chasm and decide he didn't need to get any closer.

But enough of all this. Jay wanted to check the alert on his phone.

'So, there we have it, gentlemen,' he said, snapping the lid of his laptop shut.

Noonan stood. 'Thanks, all. Carry on.' He left, with his retinue in tow.

Jay was following right behind them – never be the last one to leave a room – when Gutiérrez tried to stall him: 'Mr Phillips ...'

'I'll book a meeting tomorrow,' Jay said. 'You can ask as many questions as you like. Will that be acceptable?'

'Yes.'

'Excellent. I'll see you then.' He departed, giving Gutiérrez no chance to respond.

He walked back to his office, went in through the badge lock, and mated his laptop with the docking station. The twin monitors blinked into life and showed him that the room's surveillance system had nothing to report. It never did – no-one else had ever been in here. He had overheard with amusement his colleagues' speculations about what his office contained: a colossal video wall linked up to the site's CCTV system, a gold-plated desk, a comprehensive library of porn. They would have been disappointed at the neatness, the minimalism. It was like anyone else's desk, just tidier.

He checked the alert on his phone and, yes, it was Henning. The ANPR system had picked him up. Two years ago, when Jay had asked a senior software manager if there was a back door into Britain's Automatic Number Plate Recognition system, the answer had been: 'Of course there is.' Pe had written the software, and it was always useful to have unofficial access for … testing purposes. You never knew when these things might prove useful. Late on Friday he had taken the liberty of logging the registration number of Wes Henning's Mini as a vehicle of interest, and rather than bothering the police with it, the back door meant that updates would be sent directly to him. Twenty-five minutes ago, Henning had passed one of the cameras in Strathurst town centre, his number plate had been recognised, and the information forwarded to Jay's phone. Since then, Henning hadn't –

No, wait: another alert. He was on the move again, driving up the A3 towards London. Now he was on a major road the alerts would come much more frequently. Jay tapped out an email to Brad:

From: DamonKane@xyz.com
To: Brad.Neill@daweb.co.uk
Subject: Game 6

WH is on the A3 near Hindhead going NE. Send K and G now.

He took the paper knife from its display stand – a gift from the head of the Tokyo branch – and turned it over in his hands while he thought. It was a beautiful object: an elegant, wafer-thin shard of steel, curiously pointless in a modern office. He wondered whether Katsuhiro-san would consider it vulgar to use the knife to actually open a letter. It was like the printer that stood, gathering dust, in the corner. Paper was crude, limiting, obsolete.

So, Keiran and Grant would get another crack at Henning. Were they up to the job? A delicious question. Grant was one of Jay's oldest and most reliable instruments, a devotee of the company's products even before they were called Pe. Given how much Jay knew about him, it was strange to think that they had never actually met. The closest they had come was when Jay had observed Grant from behind a one-way mirror during the pattern recognition experiments. Even back then, Grant had shown an admirable stoicism. He had been confined to a suite of rooms for a week, something many of the other volunteers didn't have the patience to endure. The electrodes attached to his scalp clearly bothered him – he would scratch around them and scowl – but he never took the device off. Amazing what people would put up with for a bit of cash.

The subjects' brain activity was monitored while they were shown certain symbols on a screen – including, critically, the new 'square-arch' logo Jay had proposed for rebranding the company as Pe. The suite of rooms was carefully designed to expose them to those same symbols, disguised in various ways. Jay had sat for hours behind that mirror, watching Grant, watching the confirmation of his theories: every time Grant went through a doorway there was a brainwave spike on the monitor.

The genius of the Pe logo – and the reason Jay had designed it this way – was that it repurposed the world as a subliminal advert for the company's products. Seeing the results, their CEO Piotr

Dolokhov – with the added ego-stroking incentive of having his first initial immortalised – needed no further persuasion to rebrand. Jay recalled with fondness the mockery the new logo had received from the press. It was too simplistic, too anonymous, a colossal waste of time and money. All free publicity. Meanwhile, Jay enjoyed a doubling of his salary, an increase in the value of his Pe stock, and free reign to create his own department.

Although Grant had been moved on to other, greater things, the research into symbols continued. There was still the tantalising possibility that they might create a Medusa: an image so arresting that the viewer could literally not look away. And if they could hack the human mind this way, what seeds might be planted while the drawbridge was down? The resistance to his work had been considerable, but wasn't that the case with all visionaries? Freedom was considered a right so intrinsic that it was impossible even to start a debate about its desirability. But give a man freedom and what does he do with it? Sits at a desk for eight hours a day, surrounded by people he doesn't like. Watches celebrities argue on television. Drinks himself into oblivion at the end of each week. For some men, freedom was a yoke. It was a kindness to give them purpose.

Grant and Keiran had purpose.

When news of a brother surfaced – one with that same, ideal upbringing – Jay knew he had to get them back together. It was an opportunity to extend his influence, Brad to Grant to Keiran. The network grew.

Jay flexed the paper knife in his hands, watching the shallow curve, the return to perfect straightness. It was amazing how far steel could bend. People thought of it as rigid, but in reality it was elastic. His phone buzzed again.

From: Brad.Neill@daweb.co.uk
To: DamonKane@xyz.com
Subject: Game 6

We're on it.

But there was more. Another alert had come through, triggered by audio from the microphones in Clive Goddard's house. The monitoring software had encountered the key phrase 'A-list'. A false positive? He had encountered them before. But on playing back the recording, it became unambiguous:

'What do you know about the A-list?'

He rewound to the last significant gap in the audio. He heard the opening of Clive's front door.

'Tina Derby! Good Lord. How long has it been?'

And a few seconds later:

'These are my friends, Alex and Tom.'

Very few things in life surprised Jay any more. Very few things.

So, Henning's wife and best friend weren't going to sit idly by while her husband was knocked off. Fair enough, but how the hell had they got as far as Clive in such a short space of time?

The paper knife felt different in his hands. Jay looked down and found he had bent the steel into a shallow v-shape. He regarded it for a moment, then tossed it into the bin.

Listening to the rest of the audio, it became clear that Tina was an ex-employee, and that Clive had known her when she'd worked for Pe. First Gutiérrez, now this. Jay had missed the presence of worthy adversaries. He had missed the invigorating possibility of failure. Alex, Tom and Tina might have to be added to the list of targets. It would represent considerable mission creep, but to recoil from a necessity was to curtail your own power, to defeat yourself before you had even engaged with your opponent. He had never been one to do things by halves. The man who pushed harder – who refused to accept the limitations others would impose on him – always won in the end.

He would send the details to Brad after the attempt on Henning's life had been made. No point confusing the poor man with multiple instructions. He played the recording again. This time he was able to be more analytical about it. The sound of Clive ejecting his visitors amused him, as did his soliloquy once they had gone:

'The gall of these people! And to think I used to trust Tina.'

Such a gloriously contrived piece of amateur dramatics, and proof that Clive knew his house was bugged.

Jay set up a meeting with Clive at 9:30 the next morning. Although he was at home, Clive would see the meeting request on his work phone. It would give him the chance to sweat overnight.

27

KEIRAN tried to flatten the sheets of paper against the coffee table, but the creases were stubborn. Though written in pencil, the words had not faded.

the terrible upbringing you had to endure

He stirred the spoon in his mug of hot chocolate. The fact that Henning had delivered a letter to him yesterday didn't necessarily mean he'd stuck around in Strathurst afterwards. Grant was right: he could be anywhere by now. And yet it was Grant who was still out there, combing the streets like an automaton.

you are a product of your past

There must be some clue here. There had to be a more intelligent way to get Henning than trudging around town for days, hoping for a lucky encounter. Something had to come to him – some insight, some piece of luck.

I never wrote that post on my blog

The note gave no answers, only questions. And this was how they got to you. Every question was a brick thrown at your conviction. Each one could be explained away, but there were so many that your instinct was to cover your head. Instead you should be standing firm.

women don't usually want to go out with murderers

If there was one piece of truth in the whole letter it was this. The thought had tormented him before, but Henning made it as fresh, as tender, as grazed skin. Nothing had changed – if Gemma was the sort of girl that was impressed by a man who would kill for what he believed, she was the right one for him; if she found the idea abhorrent, she was not. It was that simple. Why didn't this bring the whole issue to an end?

The spirit is willing, but the flesh is weak.

He had tried to imagine her as a member of DA but could not, in any realistic sense, place her in that kind of environment. Hardly surprising given that he had never seen a woman in a DA meeting. Gemma would be cynical of their philosophy. He knew this from the robust backtalk she used on awkward customers at the bar. He had once convinced himself this was a form of self-protection that would make her ideally suited to DA, but he had seen too much evidence to the contrary: the words of sympathy she offered the drunk woman who had just split up with her boyfriend, the giggling and gossiping that erupted when she went off-shift and met up with friends.

Even so, wasn't she closer to the DA ideal than most women? Yeah, right. Clutch at those straws.

He folded the letter up and put it back in his wallet. Hoping for some good news, he turned to the laptop and checked his shares. McMillan Cadieux and Pe were slightly up, MPMX down. When Grant had first mentioned buying shares, Keiran had felt intuitively that it didn't fit with DA philosophy, but any

206

exploitation of existing systems was fair game. It was dependence on them that was the problem. When these things were gone, they would fall back on other, more fundamental, skills. Still, it would be nice to experience a significant jump in share price for once – an unambiguous signal to sell. He had made a few quid out of it, true. There would have been more money to invest if he hadn't ploughed so much into the bunker and its contents. Surely they didn't need as much tinned food as Grant thought. It was beginning to resemble an underground supermarket.

A sound cut through the silence like an alarm – his mobile. It was Grant.

'Hello?'

'Where are you?' Urgency in Grant's voice.

'Not far from the flat.'

'We've got a fix on Henning. He's leaving town, in a car. We need to go after him right now.'

Keiran straightened in the chair. 'I'm ready.'

'No time to acquire another vehicle. We'll have to take yours.'

'The tank's full.'

'Bring it round the front. I'll be there in three minutes.'

*

Keiran kept his speed as high as possible, frustrated by the pockets of dense traffic, and shifting lanes frequently for whatever small advantage he could obtain. According to Grant, they were about ten miles from Henning. If he could average ten miles per hour more than their target, they would catch him in an hour, assuming he hadn't stopped by then. He imagined the kudos he would get from his DA brothers by ramming Henning off the road, writing off his own car in the process, reaching into the wreckage to break his neck …

Just before the A3 crossed the M25, Grant looked up from his phone and said, 'Go north. Come off here.'

He pulled into the slip lane marked 'M25 H'row'. Heathrow? Was Henning finally going to leave the country?

He asked the question that had been scratching at his mind ever since his brother had jumped into the car. 'So, how do we know Henning's on the move? Where is this information coming from?'

'Brad,' he said. 'Where else?'

'Yeah, but how is Brad getting it?'

Grant smiled. 'DA is more resourceful than you know. Have faith in your brothers.'

Not really an answer. He pictured a mysterious network of benefactors all pulling together to help him achieve his aim – people he'd never met, but who shared his philosophy. If he got this much help, would he be earning his Ascension? He imagined Hans, in particular, mocking it as valueless, like one of those honorary degrees they give away to famous people. But things were as they were. At this stage he couldn't afford to refuse the assistance. If it was a compromise, he would just have to swallow it. And … perhaps he wasn't the only one. Ever since their confrontation in the Tesco car park, Keiran had been thinking about Grant's Ascension. Why had he always been so reluctant to talk about something that should have been a source of pride? Why, when Keiran questioned how easy it sounded, had Grant lost his rag? Compromise; it had to be.

'Something funny, brother?' Grant said.

'Just looking forward to catching up with our friend Henning.'

Outside, the light was fading to the grey-purple of dusk. Keiran switched on the headlights. The traffic thinned the further north they went and he was able to put his foot down. With the M25 it was impossible to guess where Henning was going. It could be as close as the airport or as far as Scotland.

This part of the M25 always reminded him of their twice-yearly trip to the grandparents in Norwich. Dad had driven, with

Keiran and Grant in the back. It was years before Keiran knew the real reason the front passenger seat was empty – Mum didn't think Dad's parents took the church seriously enough, so she never came along. But he always insisted on taking the boys, and this was one of the few situations where he got his way. They sang on the journey, hymns at first, but as they got further away from home the music would shift to old pop hits – The Beatles, ABBA, The Police. There was a holiday feel to their visits, more than on their actual holidays. Granny and Grandad would bake them cookies, take them out to the park, play with them to the point of exhaustion. There was always a big plastic tub of toys there. As he grew older, Keiran became aware how meagre, how shabby, their grandparents' house was, but every time they visited, that plastic tub had new things in it. Their idea of sacrifice was very different to Mum's. And Keiran found himself willing to make sacrifices for them, too. Just as he did at home, he washed up when he was told, took the bins out when he was told. The difference was that he didn't feel any resentment; with his grandparents it seemed like a fair trade.

Idiots, every last one of them.

Dad was different in Norwich too. In fact, it was very simple: at home he was like Mum, in Norwich he was like his parents. He was a weak man, easily led. It was in Norwich that Keiran had loved him most. Huh. The tug of memory, the warmth of nostalgia. The past still had a powerful grip on him. How far he still had to go.

Dad never asked them to conceal from Mum what happened up in Norwich. He didn't need to. Their time away was a gift to his sons, and they would never do anything to jeopardise it. Coming home was hard, for Keiran in particular. Why couldn't they move to Norwich, and live with Granny and Grandad? Why? Why? This was the reason Grant held such power over him – he had seen him at his weakest, his most pathetic. He had seen him

209

whinge and cry. But things were changing. Perhaps they could be changed now. Right now.

'Tell me what happened to Dad,' Keiran said.

Out of the corner of his eye, he saw Grant look towards him. 'We've been through this before.'

'No we haven't. That's the whole point: we haven't.'

'It's in the past. A commitment to Darwin's Army is a commitment to the future – a leaving behind of the things that hold us back.'

'That's what you always say.' He cut himself off before the words could run away from him. 'But it *is* holding me back. How can I let go of it if I don't even know what *it* is?'

'The question you should be asking yourself is: how can this knowledge help me evolve?'

'Because whether I like it or not, I'm a product of my past. I need to understand what's happened to me so I can neutralise any feelings about it and concentrate on my future. I think this is part of my Ascension too. The path is straight, but there are many ways to the path.' He could do the DA quotations too.

Grant said nothing for several seconds. Usually there would be no pause before he came back with a retort, a rebuke. Keiran wondered, with an illicit thrill, whether his brother was getting just a little bit soft.

'All right,' Grant said. 'If you really wanna know.'

Keiran involuntarily filled his lungs with air – a gulp of triumph. Grant seemed too absorbed in preparing his story to notice.

'We were going to the supermarket for the weekly shop. I was already beginning my separation from them by this time, but I kept up the pretence. We were driving down this road and there was thick black smoke coming from one of the houses, so he stopped the car. There was a woman at the window, two floors up, trying to pluck up the courage to jump out, but the front of their house was all concrete, and it was full of junk – bits of

210

wood, an old bicycle, all sorts of shit. There was nowhere to land safely. Dad told me to stay in the car. He got the crowbar out of the boot, prised their front door off its hinges and went in. It took him a couple of minutes to reach the window and his face was blackened by the smoke. He persuaded her to climb out, hang off the frame and drop. Then he went back in.'

Grant stopped, as if that was the end of it.

'And then what?' Keiran said.

Grant shrugged. 'The fire brigade arrived and I told them what had happened. They went in and got him out, but he was already dead from smoke inhalation. They said I was right not to go in after him. The woman had twisted her ankle, but that was all.'

'Why didn't he jump out after her?'

'This woman told him there was no-one else in the building – she kept saying it over and over to the firemen. You figure it out.'

Maybe Dad didn't believe her and had to check for himself. Maybe she said something else to him that she didn't tell the fire brigade.

Grant said, 'For Mum, and for the church, it became this story of great and noble sacrifice. But you saw what it did to her. She couldn't admit the truth to herself.'

'But why didn't he just jump?'

'You know what he was like: the mood swings, the pills, the depression.'

But Keiran hadn't, not really. Their father had had 'episodes', times when he'd spent the day in bed, but Keiran had been too young to really understand what that meant. Grant made it sound so much more serious, so much more … medical. Keiran's puncture wounds started to throb again.

'The fact is,' Grant said, 'he decided not to go on, and wanted to check out in a way that tied in with their stupid obsession with sacrifice. None of them could see this for what it really was: nature's way of rooting out the weak.'

Keiran found himself gripping the steering wheel so hard he thought he might bend it. He didn't know what to think, what to feel. Why had he even asked about this shit in the first place?

Grant was looking out the side window, away from him. 'So, do you think this will help you move forwards, brother?'

'I …' He checked the traffic around him very carefully. He made an unnecessary lane change because it occupied his hands, his eyes, and at least a tiny fraction of his thoughts.

'With everybody around us increasingly insane and deluded,' Grant said, 'you can see why I left.'

Yes, leaving Keiran behind to care for their mother. No long tirades laced with scripture for Grant, no directionless fits of violence, no sitting in church with his hands clasped together while the congregation tried to pray their way to a solution.

'I had no idea at that time what you were going to do,' Grant said. 'It was your decision to stay with her or leave. I'm glad you took the right path in the end.'

'Yes,' Keiran said, eyes fixed straight ahead.

'There's no point thinking it could have been any different. He was never going to make it. He just wasn't adapted to the real world.'

'Yes.'

'We, on the other hand, have managed to break free of a difficult past. Despite all the disadvantages our parents lumbered us with, we've become as strong and competitive as anyone else in DA. You and I should be proud of what we've achieved, brother.'

'Yes.'

28

IT was the most stressful driving experience Wes could remember, worse even than his first driving lesson, where the instructor had directed him through central Strathurst in the rush hour so he could narrowly avoid hitting a pram on a pedestrian crossing. Every few minutes he had to remind himself of the facts: there was no tracking device, otherwise they would have followed him to the woods; they couldn't know where he was going unless the guy in the Merc looked under his car for the phone, and he had no reason to do that. Wes's Mini was just one vehicle among thousands, anonymous and untraceable. But his fear remained, impervious to any attempts at reassurance.

He wanted to be fresh for whatever awaited him at Enfield, stomach fed and bladder empty, so he pulled off the M25 at South Mimms service area and parked the Mini as near to the building as he could without taking a disabled space. He entered, taking in the seating areas and the shops that bordered them. It wasn't particularly busy at this time on a Monday evening, but there were still too many people, and dozens of places where his line of sight was broken by a wall, a coffee kiosk, a news-stand. He identified five exits. Most were at the front of the building, which consisted entirely of glass – far too exposed for a quick getaway. The best was the one at the back, the one marked 'Coach Park'.

After going to the loo, he emerged cautiously back into the main area and checked outside once again. The Mini sat there, patient and faithful – one of his last remaining links with home, to the life he had known and lost ... no: to the life that had been taken from him.

He picked up a sandwich from the Waitrose and queued. His view of the car was blocked by a flower stall, so he concentrated on the people in his range of vision instead, dismissing those with long hair or bright clothes, paying more attention to anyone closer to the 'Wanted' posters in his mind. Once at the front of the queue, he put his card next to the machine to make the contactless payment.

'Do you want to try again?'

For the first time, he paid attention to the assistant – petite, dark-skinned, polite. 'It hasn't gone through,' she said.

He inserted the card instead and typed his PIN, carefully. Invalid. No, it couldn't be.

'Have you got another card, or cash?'

He gave her a tenner, pocketed the change, then headed straight for the cash machine. It spat out both of his bank cards in quick succession. He stared at the useless rectangles of plastic in his hand. So, it was the government. Surely only they could cancel bank accounts. He was the victim of some anti-terror campaign in which the police had the power to do everything except catch the right man. And Darwin's Army were the channel through which the authorities carried out their dirty work. But that was nuts. It was the sort of paranoia he mocked on his blog. Used to mock on his blog. And yet it fitted the facts. He had been transported to another world – a simulacrum of the one he knew. It looked convincing enough, but under the surface nothing made sense. His life had become a Philip K Dick novel.

What could he do? He would press on through the falling dark to Enfield and try to *find* some sense. There was no other choice. Before going back out into the car park, he checked the Mini through the glass, to make sure everything was ... and there were Keiran and Grant, standing next to his car, trying to look casual. It was happening again. Grant leaned down, rested one hand on the wing, touched the tyre and straightened. The Mini settled a couple of inches. He folded something up and slipped it into his pocket.

Wes felt a fizzing sensation at the back of his head. How had they found him this time? How? He had been so careful. Well, it hardly mattered now; knowing his mistake wouldn't change anything. He had fucked up and they were going to kill him. If they could slip a knife into his tyres in a busy car park, they could do

214

the same to him when they came in here. In about thirty seconds' time. Keiran pointed to the side of the building. Grant took off in that direction, heading round to the coach park exit while Keiran himself went for the main doors.

Where could he go? One of the shops? Hopeless. The toilets? They would just wait him out. There was no time. Wes slipped behind the counter of the coffee bar. There were no customers queuing and only one barista – a man with a sharp nose and abundance of black hair who took a step back as Wes invaded his space. A badge identified him as 'Dmitriy'.

'Hey! What you think you doing?'

Wes went down on his knees so he was hidden from everybody in the building by the counter, everybody except this man. Dmitriy's eyes followed him down, like someone pointing a searchlight at him. Wes put a finger against his lips, then put both hands together, begging, praying.

'Man, I don't care what kind of trouble you in. You can't do this.'

Wes extracted his wallet, plucked out three £20 notes and held them out. Dmitriy froze. Wes put his hands together again – pleading, pleading – then thrust the notes at him.

'I see. You are criminal.'

They must be inside the building by now. Wes shook his head and gave him another £20.

'Wanted by police, maybe?'

Another vigorous shake, and Wes handed over another £20, his last banknote. Dmitriy's objections crumbled and he took the money. It disappeared into a pocket instantly and once again he became a bored service worker.

Under his breath, he muttered, 'You give me any trouble, I kick you out. If police come for you, I kick you out. You understand this?'

Wes nodded. On his notepad, he wrote a message, tore the page out and tucked it into Dmitriy's hand:

215

2 men: 20s, v short hair, black clothes. They will kill me.

'Who are you? James Bond? I tell you this: they ask me about you, I give you up.' He made a play of rearranging some chocolate brownies while he surveyed the room. 'Okay, I think I see one. He come through main entrance. He look around for someone. Looks like he in a hurry. He go towards –' he broke off.

How had Wes got himself cornered like this? By panicking, that's how. He should have gone through another of the front entrances at the same time Keiran came in. But he'd already decided that wasn't a good option. Maybe there were no good options.

Dmitriy spoke again, even quieter this time. 'Another one just came in through entrance to my left, went right in front of me. You get me into lot of shit, mister.'

The rucksack was still in the car. What had he been thinking, leaving it there?

'This is very exciting,' Dmitriy mumbled. 'Maybe too exciting for me.'

How much was £100 worth to this man? If he was on minimum wage, how many hours' work was that? What would he risk for it?

'One has gone to toilets. Other one in WH Smith. Now is your chance.' Dmitriy pointed off to his left. 'Use Coach Park exit. Good luck, Mr Bond.'

Wes poked his head above the parapet, and decided Dmitriy was right. He nodded his thanks as he went. Dmitriy patted his pocket and gave a crooked smile. 'Come back any time, sir.'

Wes ran outside and switched back. The path forced him away from the side of the building in a curve around some hard land-scaping. Once he gained the front of the building he slowed, aware that a sprinting man would be obvious to anyone inside who bothered looking. He felt for the unlock button on the key in his pocket and his Mini's lights flashed like a beacon. Damn it: another mistake. His wheel trims almost touched the tarmac; the tyres were slack and airless. He yanked the door open, grabbed the rucksack from the passenger footwell, shut the door, locked it. Looping his arms into the rucksack, he turned towards the building and squinted. They weren't coming out of the main entrance for him, but that didn't mean they wouldn't be doing exactly that within the next few seconds.

He took off across the car park, onto the grass, into the cover of trees. The ground dropped to a shallow stream. He splashed through it and climbed the other side, then fought his way through brambles until the trees came to an end, opening up onto a muddy field, rutted but devoid of crops. A hundred metres ahead of him was a cluster of farm buildings, off to his right the M25. It was exposed, and the darkness was not yet deep enough to conceal him if Keiran and Grant followed him through the trees – he would be a telltale silhouette against the sky. But staying here seemed the greater risk, especially if they had torches. He started off across the field. The mud clumped on his shoes, and after a few paces his feet had turned into lead weights. Although it slowed him, he forged ahead until he gained the cover of the buildings, at which point he allowed himself to look back. No-one. He carried on underneath an electricity pylon and turned left, parallel to the motorway and heading for the hedgerow that marked the start of the next field. He rejected the idea of crossing the M25: six lanes of fast-moving traffic could prove more lethal than any assassin. He continued east, counting on the idea that at some point there must be a road that went under the motorway. All the while, he urged the gloom to deepen.

By the time he got to the third field, that same darkness was a source of bitter frustration. The headlights from the traffic on the M25 were now his only source of light – shifting, pulsing and insufficient. He stumbled over the ground's invisible irregularities. Getting out of each field and into the next required him to walk the length of the hedge, up and down, before he found a way through and the mud was spattered up his jeans to knee-height. A dip in the ground caused him to trip and land on all fours. The soil squished between his fingers, his knees became cold as moisture seeped through the denim. He rose to a squat, but got no further. The traffic on the motorway hissed and grumbled like some gigantic black dog on the verge of attack.

If it was the government, he was screwed. Simple as that. He wasn't a trained spy or a hardened criminal. He didn't have super-human skills, safe houses to hide in, contacts to bail him out. They were powerful, resourceful, determined. Wes, on the other hand, was dog-tired, out of luck and ready to have his life back. A shame they weren't ready to give it to him.

On the near-black screen of his retina a series of images appeared. Practical jokes he had played on Tom, dancing the foxtrot with his wife, defeating his Wing Chun partners at chi sau – things that brought him close to people without the crutch of language. This life, so familiar until a few days ago, was now a distant country. He was like an old man stranded in a care home, his mind slipping between the days, between waking and sleep, the past now more real to him than the present.

One memory was especially vivid. An episode from his youth, impossible to forget.

He is lying in a concrete room, surrounded by splintered wood and plaster fragments, his ankle broken. The only light comes from the cracks in the ceiling through which he has fallen. It is dusk and will soon be completely dark. The first few flakes of snow are falling. He has played in the derelict factory before, but always with Scott and Martin. Neither of them had been available, and so he has come here alone. No-one knows where he is. Not his parents, not his friends. No-one has a reason to be anywhere near this place. Unable to cry out, he is beginning to wonder, to seriously wonder, whether he will die here.

And now history takes a detour. He doesn't find the length of steel pipe to bash against the exposed roof joist, using the pattern for SOS in Morse code – three dots, three dashes, three dots. There is no man walking his dog nearby to hear him, to investigate, to phone the authorities. He is still here in the factory. He has always been here, slowly cooling, slowly starving. His life from this point on – marrying Alex, setting up J+H with Tom, the liberation of blogging – is a fabrication, the fever dream of a dying mind.

What did he believe any more? They had stripped away his certainties, gagged him, cast him out into a hinterland of mud and despair. Maybe at this point he got to choose. Yes. This was the one thing they could not take away from him: he could believe what he damn well pleased.

He looked up at the sky. There was something he needed to do; he had known it for some time. He needed to purge any remaining suspicion of his wife. It was a cancer of the mind and he couldn't live with it any longer. Besides, his heart had never accepted her guilt. It was only what he had seen – mere evidence – that troubled him.

He would place his life in her hands. There. It felt good to do this. It felt noble.

Overhead, the clouds had thinned, revealing a few bright points of light. He recognised the 'W' of Cassiopeia. Some of these stars were so far away that the light he was seeing had been emitted centuries ago. Any one of them might be dead already, the news of its demise expanding through the universe until one day it reached the Earth and the light winked out. This is the way it would be for Alex. He would be lying somewhere, murdered, and she might not know until weeks or months later. If they disposed of his corpse thoroughly enough, she might never know.

A shard of anger lodged in his brain – not as a result of what they might do to him, but of the effect it would have on Alex. They had put her through enough already. If they continued to deny him the chance to reason or negotiate, perhaps his only option would be to kill them: Keiran and Grant and Brad and whoever else he discovered, up through the ranks, as high as he could get until he was caught. But where would this get him? They would brand him a terrorist, deny him any chance to tell his side of the story. He would be confined to prison for the rest of his life. She would visit him, but would she ever be able to forgive him? She abhorred violence.

A breeze stirred the nearby trees, prompting him to shiver. He stood, and rubbed his hands together to rid them of the worst of the mud. His skin was taut with cold.

Enough. Enough of these doubts, these speculations. What he needed was certainty, and he already knew where to find it. He would do whatever he could for her. She was the only thing that mattered; she was the reason to keep going.

Tuesday

ALTHOUGH Clive was early for the meeting, he was not surprised
to find Jay already installed at the head of the table, sat with perfect stillness, his fingers laced in front of him, thumbs touching –
the posture of a Chinese emperor, or the head of a crime syndicate.
It was the conference room with no windows. Jay had dimmed the
lights on his side, but kept them bright over the seat he offered to
Clive. So, it was to be an interrogation. Why not just use an angle-
poise lamp pointed directly at his face? In any other company
Clive would have lodged a complaint with HR. He sat, and immediately noticed that the seat seemed to be at an angle. Rather than
shuffle about and demonstrate his discomfort, he wedged himself
into one corner. To combat the desire to bite his nails, he placed
his hands on the armrests, imagining they were confined there by
steel bands. But this would make him appear tense, so he put his
hands in his lap instead. His fingers began fiddling of their own
accord, so he put them on the table and laced them. It was a
moment before he realised he was now mirroring Jay.

'Comfortable?'

'Yes,' he said.

So, Jay had forced him into untruth already. Maybe this was
all part of the process, like calibrating a lie detector before pro-
ceeding to the real questions.

Jay cultivated the appearance of a magician: twin sweeps of
sandy hair, a neatly trimmed Van Dyke, a wide-collared shirt the
same icy blue as his Medusa gaze. If, like a magician, he were to

conjure something from beneath the conference table, what would it be? A white rabbit? The Queen of Hearts? Clive's own testicles on a silver platter?

'What's this meeting about, then?' Clive said. 'You didn't put anything in the invitation.'

'I wanted,' Jay put both palms face down on the table and adopted a look of absolute solemnity, 'to have a few words with you.'

'Very well.'

'You've been a hugely valuable asset to this company,' Jay said, 'and Pe's success is, in part, down to your hard work. But there are people who are jealous of our achievements and want some of what we have. It's conceivable that they will try to compromise Pe through one of our senior employees.'

So, he knew about Tina's visit yesterday. This was a test of his loyalty – the faster he spilled the beans, the less suspicion would accrue.

'Three people came to my house last night,' he said.

'Is that so? Was one of these people Tina Derby, by any chance?'

'Yes. How did you know?'

'We've been keeping an eye on her.'

What twaddle. Jay probably hadn't even heard of her until yesterday. Clive was the one they were keeping an eye on. He remembered that June evening when he'd returned home after a ridiculously busy day at the office and noticed something different about the gravel on his drive. He had knelt down, ear close to the ground and sighted along the sea of stones. Ruts. Lots of them. Enough for several cars. He'd suspected ever since. He'd never found any of the bugs, but then he hadn't gone looking for them. The last thing he wanted was to let them know that he knew.

'I let them in because … you know, she was an old colleague.'

Jay nodded.

'I didn't give them any information, you understand. As soon as the conversation turned to work I refused to say anything. When they pushed, I showed them the door. You know I would never jeopardise the company.'

'I do.'

'It's been very good to me.'

'It has.'

Clive told him everything, and tried to convince himself that this confession was for the best, a kind of unburdening. But he could not ignore the sickly horror bubbling beneath the surface, as if he had eaten too much chocolate but was continuing to shovel it in regardless. He remembered Tina's time at Pe. She had always been warm, inclusive, quick to laugh. She had lifted the spirits of everyone in the workplace. Clive had started assuming his decoy personality around this time, but Tina had accepted that too. No questions, no disapproval. If she came to harm as a result of what he was saying, what on earth would he do? What could he do? It wasn't as if he had the luxury of choice. Choice was something from his past, something he seemed to have mislaid.

Jay nodded once Clive had finished his story. 'Yes. This is how they get to you: by claiming that something important is at stake. But did this woman – Alex – give you any proof that her husband's life was in danger?'

'No.'

'So it was an appeal to your emotions?'

'Yes,' Clive said. 'Yes, I see that.'

It was funny: Clive was more inclined to trust Alex, a woman he had met for ten minutes yesterday, than Jay, a colleague of years. And yet, in this moment, who was he cooperating with? The tyrant, the psychopath. It was a matter of survival.

'Do you have an alarm fitted to your house?' Jay said. 'Window locks?'

'Of course.'

'I don't want to worry you unduly, but it's important that your home is a place of safety and security. They didn't intimidate you? Threaten you?'

No, they hadn't threatened him.

'That's good. We don't need to involve the police, then. But if there's another visit like this, you should phone me directly. Will you do that?'

'Yes. Immediately.'

Clive tried to set aside the possibility that the life of Alex's husband really was at stake, that Jay was involved and that he, Clive, had done nothing to help her. Once again everything was upside-down, every attempt to do the right thing subverted, as if he was destined to be this man's pawn. Why couldn't life be simpler? Why could he not be sitting by the open fire in his mother's cottage in Devon? Why could he not still be growing up with his brothers, excelling at school, his childhood extended indefinitely? His father's absence and his mother's strict nature did not seem like hardships now. He would trade his current life for his youth without hesitation, because no matter how many arguments there were, how many punishments, there was always love and a kind word at the end of each day. She was straight as an arrow. With her, life had purpose; it had certainty.

'You are a fascinating character,' Jay said.

He paused for a long time, giving Clive the opportunity to wonder what he meant by it. Was it a reference to the profile they held on him, to the motley collection of misinformation Clive had fed into it over the last couple of years?

'Indulge me,' Jay said. 'How long have you known?'

It was an open-ended question, a strategy to get Clive to confess to anything that was on his mind. How long had he known what? That Jay was an utter bastard? That Tina and her friends were interested in the A-list? That he was gay?

224

'You know what I mean, of course.' Jay said.

'I'm sorry, you'll … have to be more specific.'

Jay smiled. 'It's the thing you're thinking of right now.'

He had seen people buckle and confess to Jay – a spontaneous admission that seemed to come out of nowhere. He had wondered at it before, but now he saw how it worked: they did it because Jay was in their head, because he already knew what he wanted them to admit. Why keep secret the thing that was obviously no longer a secret?

'You're going to –' Clive's throat caught and he tried to hide behind a cough. 'You're going to have to tell me.'

'Oh, dear. It seems so unnecessary, so … indelicate to have to spell it out.'

Clive said nothing – the one act of defiance he could allow himself without incurring punishment.

'Very well,' Jay said. 'You've always valued plain-speaking, as any good man of science should. I'll come straight out with it: you're a homosexual.'

And so it was true: Jay really did know the contents of other peoples' heads. Was it the profile? Had they found some way to filter out the falsehoods and get to the core of who he was? Or had the information come from elsewhere? Rob, perhaps, or even Giselle. It hardly made any difference. Jay had found his way to the truth. The man truly was a sorcerer.

'It will, of course, be treated with the strictest confidentiality,' Jay said.

It was an odd way of phrasing it, like it was a company secret, or a terrible lapse of judgement from Clive's past that he was prepared to overlook. It was typical of Jay, to simultaneously be so insightful about human nature and yet somehow utterly miss the point.

Jay continued: 'At Pe we firmly believe that all employees have the right to live free from prejudice. But … you'll forgive me if I say that I cannot speak for those outside the company.' He paused for effect, like all the best orators. 'Like your mother, for instance.'

So, here it was at last. Trust Jay to frame the threat so delicately. He was the gentlest of murderers. What right did he have to use his sexuality against him? Jay, of all people: a man Clive could not imagine engaged in any act of love. A man who probably considered sex a compromise if it involved more than one person.

But Clive's disgust was impotent, and swamped by his sense of despair. He had heard that pills were the best choice. A hundred paracetamol and his 21 year old Courvoisier should do the trick. He'd been saving the bottle for a special occasion, but no such event had been forthcoming in the last couple of years. But could he? Really? He no more had the courage to kill himself than he did to club Jay to death with the conference phone in front of him, which would have been a far better use of his energies. He already knew what would happen – he'd forget the pills and just drink the brandy. Was he becoming an alcoholic? Quite possibly.

This was all so wrong. He was a man of intellect. He shouldn't have to dirty his hands with the machinations of these bloody, fucking … Why could he not have stayed in that research lab in Cambridge? Why?

'I've taken enough of your time,' Jay said. 'You've put my mind at rest and I can't thank you enough for that. Pe can rely on you. I can see that very clearly.'

He stood, nodded pleasantly, and left the room. Clive unclasped his hands and found that his fingers ached. He placed his palms over his eyes, but, deprived of any visual stimulus, his mind conjured an image of Jay's face, his hypnotist's eyes. He felt the urge to get up and just walk out of the building. He didn't know where. Back to Devon perhaps, to the warmth of that fire, to the embrace of his mother and her firm, dependable kindness.

If only. This picture of her belonged in his past now. Jay had taken it away from him, like a parent prising open a child's fingers to remove a favourite toy.

30

WES swooped under the black Mercedes and sawed through the duct tape with the steak knife he'd stolen from the pub. They'd treated him well at the Painters Arms considering he turned up looking like he'd just climbed out of a sewer. He had taken his shoes off before entering; perhaps that's what had persuaded them not to turn him back out into the street. And how had he rewarded their hospitality? By slinking away early in the morning without paying for his room or last night's meal. By stealing their cutlery. There had been no other choice – his worldly wealth now amounted to £1.21 in cash.

The phone fell into his hands and he retreated down the street, keeping an eye on the house's bay window. He stopped at the junction with another residential road, and sat on a length of pedestrian railing at the edge of the pavement. He peeled the remainder of the tape off the phone, wiped the road muck off on his jeans, and switched it on. It still had 18% charge. He enabled mobile data, and logged into his webmail, hoping for something from Alex. *Yes*:

From: countessdragula@freemail.com
To: countdragula@freemail.com
Subject: Where are you?

Wes,
Please, please, please reply. I need to know you're safe.

Love,
Alex

He could hear her saying it. He could see her lips moving. She was out there – living, breathing, waiting for him to return. He would dance with her again. He would feel the weight of her hair, like a bolt of cloth in his hand as he brushed out the knots. He would write witty notes and leave them for her to find in the fridge, the car, the airing cupboard.

The email contained no evidence of her innocence, but he would not be dissuaded. Last night, in a quagmire next to the M25, he had made his decision to trust her. He would stick with it.

He read the email again. Its urgency implied she had tried to contact him before, but there were no other messages. Wait a minute ... He checked his spam folder and there was another one, sent two days previously:

From: countessdragula@freemail.com
To: countdragula@freemail.com
Subject: Urgent information

Wes,
Tom and I are now free of the people who've been watching us. We're on the run and we've been doing some digging. Too much to explain here, but we think Pe – the electronics giant – might be involved.

We don't know how much credence to give this at the moment, but couldn't pass up the opportunity to tell you.

Will keep you up to date.

All my love,
Alex

Gone on the run? Oh, for Christ's sake. Why couldn't she just sit tight at home? She could have pretended not to notice the goons outside the house while feeding him any information she uncovered. He looked up at the rows of houses, their roofs like terracotta pyramids against the grey of the sky. It was never going to happen. She had once said that the difference between him and previous boyfriends was that he encouraged her to indulge the myriad curiosities and obsessions that plagued her mind. She was never going to sit by when there was a puzzle to be solved. What he hadn't expected was that she would put herself in this much danger for his sake. She was an idiot. She was a heroine.

He read the message again. His phone had been a Pe model. So had Keiran's. He had blogged about the poor quality of their software updates, about the difficulty of synchronising the calendars on his PC and phone. But that couldn't be the reason for all this. For God's sake, he'd written worse about other people, other companies. Besides, what he had said was simply the truth: there were problems with their software. He had just told the company to pull their finger out. The problem was that, in this heightened state of paranoia, every little coincidence looked significant. Alex's email offered no proof, yet it seemed more than just a possibility. It also seemed an improvement on his previous line of thinking: given the choice between being pursued by the government or a powerful multinational, he would take the latter any day of the week.

The sound of a front door closing made him look up. For a moment the black wool beanie threw him, but it was definitely the right guy, a leather jacket stretched tight across those huge shoulders. He locked his front door, a toolbox dangling from his other hand. Wes slid off the railings and hovered near the edge of the nearest house. The man climbed into his Merc, reversed it onto the road, and drove off in the opposite direction.

Wes tapped out a reply to Alex's email:

He picked the last of the dried mud off his jeans. The sun made
a brief showing through an otherwise cloudy sky. Several other cars
left from the street – people setting out on their commute. Nine
o'clock came. It would get no quieter. He sauntered up to the door
and set to work with his paper clips. It was an old lock, and stubborn, but eventually it yielded to his manipulations. A brief check
of each room confirmed there was no-one else in the house. He
was getting good at this. If J+H didn't survive as a business, maybe
he could fall back on professional housebreaking.

The place was in need of decoration, but exhibited the same
psychotic neatness as Keiran's flat. A vague smell of mould permeated every room. A couple of things gave Wes clues as to the
man's character: a calendar of topless girls adorned a kitchen cupboard, and the spare bedroom was stacked with electronic items
– TVs, phones, PCs – all in their original boxes. This last discov-
ery made Wes nervous that the Merc might return at any time
with another batch. But the man had taken a toolbox with him.
Was the selling of stolen goods just a sideline? Fingers crossed.

He kept the kitchen door ajar to provide a quick escape into
the garden if he needed it. A phone charger next to the
microwave provided him a convenient place to plug in his

mobile, which would be fine as long as he remembered to pick it up on his way out.

It was the toast rack that made Wes freeze. It was being used to hold utility bills – three of them, unopened. All were addressed to an Oliver Robson. Wes didn't recall an Oliver from Keiran's diary, nor from the list of contacts he'd copied off Keiran's phone. He definitely had the right house – the Merc had been on the drive; the bald guy had come out the front door. Perhaps there was another layer of authority between Keiran and Brad. Or it was a fake name, like the one Keiran had used with Marcus. Or Brad had been promoted, or demoted, or had strayed from the one true path and been tossed into a river. Whatever. Nothing changed the fact that Oliver had spoken to Keiran and Grant. He was still a part of this.

Wes concentrated on the PC: an old tower case computer stowed under a table in the dining room. It was password protected, and resisted his few half-hearted attempts to guess his way in. He checked the desk drawers in case the password was written down, but found only stationery, sticky tape, a book of stamps.

His hopes of a quick operation – break in, pick up some crucial evidence, flee – evaporated. But he had been in this situation before, with Keiran's laptop. Trepidation was not the way to get what he wanted. He had to stay for as long as it took, give himself the time to think of a solution. A few minutes of calm contemplation, and it came to him. It was the operating system that was password protected, not the computer's hard drive. Using the screwdriver blade of a penknife he found in the kitchen, he dismantled the PC and removed the solid-state drive. He then unpacked one of the dodgy PCs from the spare bedroom and started it up. It welcomed him with open arms and invited him to set it up.

The thing took its sweet time, during which Wes raided the kitchen, taking only items that were unlikely to be missed: a bag of crisps from a multi pack, a tangerine from an overflowing bowl.

Once the PC had finished, Wes shut it down, removed the cover and attached the hard drive from Oliver's PC as a secondary storage device. Liberated from the steel cradle of its host, it was no longer in charge of proceedings; it was just a mass of data waiting to be read. He started the PC and began sifting through it, trying to determine what might be useful, when something leapt out at him – a plain text file called 'passwords'. It couldn't be … yes, it bloody well could. No encryption, no other security at all. Oliver had assumed that since his operating system was password-protected, he could store all his other passwords on it with impunity. Wes opened the file, ignoring the details for his Amazon account and the numerous suggestive websites such as dirtydutch.com. There was one marked 'DA' – the name and password for an email account. In the kitchen he typed the details into his phone, and within seconds a bunch of terse, cryptic emails appeared. Bingo.

The last couple of messages gave him a taste of how things were being coordinated. They were all addressed between a Damon Kane and Brad Neill. So, yes, Brad was Oliver's pseudonym. He should really be writing all this stuff down.

From: DamonKane@xyz.com
To: Brad.Neill@daweb.co.uk
Subject: Game 6

Did you catch him? From now on, we will co-ordinate the game via email – it's too slow and clumsy to keep meeting up.

From: Brad.Neill@daweb.co.uk
To: DamonKane@xyz.com
Subject: Re: Game 6

> K and G failed to catch him. Last seen at south mimms services on
> the M25. He won't be using the car any more. He's now on foot.

So, if the police became interested, the whole thing could be passed off as an elaborate version of hide and seek? Well, this game was about to get a lot more interesting now he could use his phone to read every email Damon and Brad sent to each other.

He searched the internet for 'Damon Kane' and 'Pe', but it yielded nothing of any relevance. Either Alex was on the wrong track with Pe, or Damon Kane was another pseudonym. Or both. While he was pondering this, an email came through from Alex. He couldn't tap the screen fast enough.

From: countessdragula@freemail.com
To: countdragula@freemail.com
Subject: Re: Where are you?

Wes,
Thank God you're safe.

The Pe connection is complicated. We've enlisted Tina, an ex-employee of Pe, who helped us find your name on a top secret database called the 'Dubai A-list'. We're going to see the man who manages these databases at his home tonight. We've tried to get information from him before, but we weren't very successful. Wish us luck.

All my love,
Alex

It was like an injection of adrenaline. Amazing, how different things felt this morning compared to last night. There was light and hope and progress. There was trust – fresh and newborn.

233

There was a distinct lack of mud.

He tidied up, putting everything back where he'd found it. The urge to get out of the house was strong, but as he was finishing off, he knew he might be squandering his one chance here. If Oliver was a nine to five man, Wes still had hours left. Best not to waste them. He started a systematic search of the house, checking under every surface, behind every piece of furniture, between the pages of every book. The task was made easier by the fact that Brad was neat and tidy, owned few possessions, and wasn't exactly big on reading. Wes expanded his search, trying to find loose floorboards and search for hidden compartments in drawers and cupboards.

It was behind the plinths at the bottom of Brad's kitchen units that Wes found the sealed envelope – A5 in size, white and bulging. His policy had been to leave everything untouched, but this was too great a temptation. He opened the flap. Inside was a stack of £20 notes totalling perhaps £1000, a passport for 'David Smith' featuring Oliver's bulldog face, and another sealed envelope marked 'Urgent', stamped, and addressed to the National Crime Agency, Queen St, London. Wes opened that too, and removed a single folded sheet.

I know who is responsible for murdering these people:

There followed a list of eight names, including Wes's own. He sank to the floor and propped himself up against one of the cupboards. How many of these people were already dead? Was he the first, the last? Was DA intending to start on another round, emboldened by their success, once he was gone?

He didn't do it himself, but he gave the orders. He goes under the name Damon Kane but I hired a private detective to find out his real name: Jay Phillips. He needs to be put away for a very long time.

Don't try to contact me. I'm already somewhere I can't be found. I need to protect myself.

An informer

Breathe. He had to breathe.

So, this was Oliver's get-out-of-jail card. Clearly, in an organisation which championed the individual above all else, trust didn't feature very highly. Wes copied the names into his notebook. He wrote each one with solemnity and hope. Seven other people. Christ. He hoped every last one of them was on the run, proving as much a pain in the arse to DA as he was. It seemed unlikely. How many of them, when the moment came, had been able to arm themselves, or rely on years of self defence training? How many of them were the targets of other members' Ascensions, long since gone, cases unsolved by the police?

He fanned the wad of twenties and it took on the appearance of a Wes Henning compensation fund. Taking three notes off the top, he put them in the blank envelope, wrote the address of the Painters Arms on the front, added a quick note of apology, and slapped on a stamp from the stationery drawer. The letter to the NCA went back into its original envelope. Using some of Oliver's sticky tape, he sealed both envelopes shut and put them, along with the remainder of the money and the passport, into his coat pocket.

He continued his search, but found nothing more and accepted this was about as good a find as he could expect. He put everything back, scoured the house to make sure he'd left no obvious signs of his presence, scooped up his phone – now fully charged – and finally, *finally*, he allowed himself to leave.

With his new-found wealth he indulged in a cappuccino at a nearby coffee shop, and made use of their Wi-Fi to search on 'Jay

Phillips' and 'Pe'. This time there were matches. An abundance of them. An article from *Bazaar: The Marketing Magazine* featured him discussing the effectiveness of advertising that bypassed the rational mind and appealed directly to the emotions. Elsewhere it was revealed that 'Pe as you go' was one of his creations – a phrase that 'made consumers think about our brand even when they're talking about our competitors'. So, even if he wasn't involved in murder, he was at the very least a prize wanker.

A more recent article made it clear he'd left marketing behind to become 'Director of Special Projects' at Pe. Wes could not conceive of a more euphemistic job title. It throbbed with Orwellian undertones. Pe were based in Reading, not that far away, but he was pretty sure that getting into their offices was a non-starter. Breaking into a house with a cheap lock was one thing, full scale industrial espionage was another. Still, he had to go there, if only to find out what his next step might be. Perhaps the receptionist could be persuaded to give him some useful information – his home address, maybe? He could claim that he needed to post something to Phillips at home.

It was the start of a plan, and the journey to Reading would give him time to refine it. He set off for the train station, pausing only to deposit David Smith's passport into a public bin, and to drop the envelopes addressed to the Painters Arms and the National Crime Agency into a post box.

31

THE back of Tina's car was not a comfortable place for a woman of Alex's height. And waiting for Clive's car to pass the end of the road was not a happy occupation for a woman of her impatience. Normally she would have found a way to pass the time with her phone, by playing a game, or texting friends. But no, she'd been persuaded to abandon it on a supermarket shelf behind a tin of mulligatawny. She looked off to her right, past the five bar gate to the fields and hedgerows beyond. It would have been great to get out and stretch her legs, just for a couple of minutes.

Her mind wandered to what she had witnessed last night. At 12:30, unable to sleep, she had gone to Tom's room. The door, though heavily sprung, hadn't quite shut. She had knocked very gently, then pushed the door open. She heard them before she saw them, two voices of different pitch – rhythmic, wordless. Then, in the darkness, a snapshot of Tina's naked back rising above the edge of the duvet, Tom's fingers curled around her ribs. Alex let the door close as quietly as she could and retreated, blushing furiously. God, he didn't waste any time, did he? And why was the door ajar? It was almost like he wanted to be found out.

Back in her own room her anger soon collapsed. Why shouldn't they, if that's what they wanted? She was envious of what they had tonight, that was all. She imagined Wes in bed with her, the warm weight of him pressing down, from chest to open thighs. She touched herself, but soon abandoned the venture. It wasn't physical gratification she wanted, it was his presence, his nearness. Instead, she used the second pillow as a prop and imagined lying across him, a simple embrace, the river of her hair thrown across his chest. She loved the way he played with it, combing it, wrapping it round his fingers.

It was something he had done from the early days of their dating – those stumbling, hesitant beginnings when uncertainty was the rule. Initially her parents had been uncertain about Wes, but they were soon charmed by him. People just had to get used to the way Wes communicated. And when he did, it was because there was something worth saying, something heartfelt or funny or profound. Wes had liberated her from the social imperative for prattle. He gave her room to be herself.

237

She remembered a ring in a velvet box, a tiny message on a sliver of paper threaded through it:

I am yours, if you want me.

She did then; she did now. And if that meant more arguing about children, then so be it – she would not hesitate to choose it over the terrifying void that was her present situation. She didn't know what the answer was for them, what the conclusion would be. That was something for another day. Right now, she just wanted him.

She had woken at seven, concluding with surprise that, yes, she must have slept after all. Over takeaway coffee and croissants they had worked out how they were going to kidnap Clive. Tom drew a rough layout of the house, which Alex and Tina adjusted according to their memory of the place. They drew arrows on it, like a battle plan.

After that last, terse email from Wes, she had regularly gone back to the computer in the hotel's lobby to check for new messages, but there was nothing. It chipped at the foundations of everything she had thought about him last night. Was it not obvious that she needed to hear from him again? At four o'clock that afternoon, impatient to be getting on with things, they had set out for Clive's.

Tina sat up in her seat and started the car's ignition. 'That was Clive's Audi.'

'Give it a couple of minutes,' Tom said.

Tina drummed her fingers on the steering wheel, rocked back and forwards. 'Now?' she said finally.

'Now.'

Alex and Tom ducked down below the level of the windows – no mean feat for a car that small – and Tina pulled onto the road towards Clive's. She parked on his drive, pulled the handbrake and killed the engine.

'Wish me luck,' she said, got out and rang the bell.

After a few seconds Alex heard the click of the latch and Tina's muffled voice.

'Clive, I am so sorry about yesterday.'

Remember to wring your hands, Tina. Tony Blair convinced a nation to go to war doing that.

'Tina,' Clive said, 'I really can't talk to you.'

'I wanted to apologise by inviting you out for a meal, just the two of us. I know a lovely place in –'

'No, look, I'm sorry, I –'

'Please, Clive, I feel awful that I put you on the spot like that.'

'I appreciate the apology, but I really can't –'

'Now!' Tina shouted.

Alex and Tom leaped out of the car. As soon as he saw them, Clive tried to close the door, but Tina already had one foot inside. As they reached the entrance, Clive yielded to their superior numbers. They entered the hall and Clive backed away down the central corridor towards the study.

Tina advanced after him, hands held out flat in placation. 'Clive, this is unbelievably important and we really can't take no for an answer.'

His eyes were wide, his mouth set in a line. Just how difficult was this going to be? Alex was about to add her calming voice to Tina's when she heard from outside a car's engine, increasing in volume, followed by a spray of stones as it skidded to a halt on the gravel. Through the wide open front door, she saw the two men with crew-cuts – Kavanagh and Groves – abandoning their vehicle and charging towards them.

Her breath seemed to desert her. 'It's the … it's the two from the …'

They had to slam the door shut. But that would mean going straight towards them. No – it was already too late. Alex grabbed at Tom and started to run. He didn't need any persuading to stick with her. Tina was still following Clive into the study and

Alex didn't want to join a traffic jam so she took another route. Avoiding the lounge – which, she remembered, had only one exit – she pulled Tom in the opposite direction and they stumbled into the dining room. Skirting the table, she headed for the door on the other side of the room, which opened into a vast kitchen. She passed a staircase on her left and an island of kitchen units on her right, heading for a door that led into the back garden. She twisted the handle and yanked, but it didn't open. It was a mortise lock. No sign of a key.

'Keep going!' Tom yelled from right behind her and she abandoned it.

There was no choice but to turn left again down the corridor that led to the study. This was no good: they would be trapped in a pincer movement, but with Tom breathing down her neck there was no time to think. Clive was coming towards her from the study, probably heading for the same back door she had tried. Did he have the key? Finding his way blocked, Clive opened the corridor's only other door. For a second, Alex entertained the hope that it was another exit out to the garden, but as Clive disappeared inside, she caught a glimpse of tiles and a towel rail. Clive slammed the door, and a *click* told her he'd locked it.

Ahead of her, at the other end of the corridor, Tina stood with a wooden chair in her hands, thrusting the legs at Groves and yelling, 'Back off, shit-for-brains!'

Alex turned and Tom collided with her. Kavanagh was right behind him. There was no way round. Tom turned to face Kavanagh, and his fists went up into a boxing pose. Chivalrous, but Alex felt a wave of panic rising up to engulf her – Tom was no fighter. Kavanagh feigned a blow to the face, and as Tom's hands went up, he piled the other fist into his stomach. Tom's defences crumpled. He hunched up, trying to ward off the blows with his hands and elbows. It wasn't a winning strategy, but still he blocked the corridor to prevent Kavanagh from getting to her.

'Stop it!' she yelled. 'We'll do whatever you want!'

But this *was* what they wanted – to keep punching and kicking until all three of them were bloody and broken and defeated, until they yielded Wes up to them. She glanced over her shoulder to see the chair being wrenched out of Tina's grasp and hurled backwards into the study. Groves punched her in the face and Tina staggered in an effort to stay upright. Alex turned back in time to see Tom's head whip round, his hair following a fraction of a second later – the result of a blow from Kavanagh. He grabbed Tom's arm by the wrist and slammed it against the corner of the wall. Alex heard the bone snap. Tom might have cried out in pain as he hit the floor, but it was drowned out by her own scream.

They stood no chance against these two. None. She had never spat at anyone in her life, but she spat at Kavanagh now. It was a good shot, spattering his right cheek, and Kavanagh's whole body turned ninety degrees, as if absorbing the impact from a bullet. When he turned to face her again he was smiling and Alex realised that her defiance came at a price. He would now feel justified in doing anything he wanted to her. Absolutely anything.

A blur from the right. Kavanagh was shunted into the door Alex had tried to open, the back of his head breaking one of the panes of glass. It took a Alex a moment to grasp what had happened. It was Wes. How? It didn't matter – it was Wes. The two of them grappled, rotating round each other. Wes landed a palm-strike on Kavanagh's jaw, sending him back against the kitchen counter. Instead of following the blow up, as she knew he was trained to, Wes stepped back towards her and Tom. Keeping his eyes on Kavanagh, he reached behind him with one hand. She brushed her fingers against his, wanting to hold them, but releasing immediately so he would have both hands free to fight. Wes pointed a finger at his opponent, then drew a line across his

241

own throat.

She turned around. Like Tom, Tina was sitting on the floor. Groves was fending off two more attackers – a bald black man and a Chinese woman. Alex had met them a couple of times – Wes's sifu, Ant, and his wife, Xiaoying. One of Groves's eyes was already puffed up; blood poured from his nose and down his shirt. With a wild swing of his arms he broke free of Ant, and backed away a pace while fending them off with an outstretched hand. With the other, he drew a flick-knife and pointed it at eye level.

'Is this what you fucking want?' he said. 'You and your bitch?'

Wary of the knife, Ant and Xiaoying nevertheless kept up the pressure. They tried to flank him, but Groves backed out of sight, down the corridor that would take him to the front door. He would be funnelling them both into the range of the blade.

'Keiran,' Groves shouted, 'we are going!'

Alex turned back to Kavanagh – Keiran? – who said through gritted teeth, 'He's here. He's right fucking here.'

Wes beckoned to him with one finger, invitation and mockery in a single gesture. Alex wanted to tell him to let them go, but her voice had deserted her.

'We are *leaving*!' Groves said in a growl.

Keiran backed up through the kitchen and Wes followed, testing his defences all the way. They disappeared round the staircase and Alex heard the intruders forced further back until the front door was shut on them. It was possible to breathe again. She took the air in with great gulps. She started towards the front door, then became aware of Tom, curled up and nursing his arm.

'Tom,' she said, and found she was almost inaudible. She tried again. 'Tom?'

He looked up, just enough to make eye contact. There was a cut above one eyebrow. His mouth was open, wet and pink and downturned, all the teeth showing. A string of saliva hung from his lips.

'We're going to get you to a hospital.'

He sank back over his broken arm, and she ruffled his hair. Tina padded over, unsteady on her feet. Blood from her nose was dripping off her chin, a trail of tears from one eye joining it like a tributary.

'Tina?'

'I think I'm okay,' she said, but her voice was tremulous. 'Is Tom … ?' Her eyes widened and she knelt in front of him.

Alex put a hand to her mouth. She had been sandwiched between the two of them, and in just a few short seconds they had ended up like this. She had not asked these people to defend her. Look what it had cost them.

Wes reappeared and she collided with him, crushed him, bent her head over his shoulder so her lips were by his ear. But there was no need to say anything. She felt through fabric, through skin, that everything between them was all right.

'They're gone,' Ant said on returning from the front of the house. 'Xiaoying's keeping an eye out to make sure they don't come back.'

He crouched down to see how Tom was doing. 'Okay, let's have a look at you. It's okay, I've done first aid.'

'How did you know?' Alex asked Wes, once she felt able to release him.

On his phone he showed her an email he had intercepted between Damon Kane (who?) and Brad Neill (who?), instructing 'K' and 'G' to watch Clive's house in case Tom and Alex returned. He had given them an address and Wes had used it to find her.

'And you assumed from my email that we were coming here?'

He nodded.

I texted Ant, asked a big favour. We met at Twyford station, came here, hid, watched the house. Only had to wait 5 mins.

He reached down to put his fingers on Tom's shoulder, and Tom's good hand came up to grasp them. They shared a wordless moment, needing nothing from each other but the reassurance of touch. When Tom released his hand, Wes wrote again, and showed his pad to Alex:

Should've come quicker.

'You couldn't, Wes. Clive wouldn't have let you in. And they would have been waiting for you.'

He shook his head, eyes fixed on Tom. She touched his arm, drawing his gaze.

'I'm glad you came when you did.'

I emailed you, told you not to come here.

'How was I supposed to receive that? You told me to get rid of my phone, remember?'

Why did you come back here?

'We're here to –' she lowered her voice, looking first at the toilet door, then at Ant and Xiaoying '– to kidnap Clive.'

Wes raised his eyebrows.

'It was Tom's idea.'

Wes gave his that-explains-everything look.

'Tina thinks he might know why all this has happened.'

Tina was holding the red wad of Tom's handkerchief up to her mouth and nose. 'I'm Tina,' she said, her voice nasal. 'Nice to meet you.'

She held out a hand to shake, but hesitated as she saw a smear of blood across her palm. Wes took it anyway, enfolded it in both of his hands, nodded his acknowledgement and thanks.

'You're welcome,' she said.

Alex turned to Ant and Xiaoying. 'Can you two take Tom to A&E?'

'Of course,' Ant said.

'Should one of us stay with you?' Xiaoying added.

'No, no. That's fine. You've done more than enough for us

already. And we're leaving straight after you.' She turned to Tina. 'Do you want to go with Tom?'

'I …' Tina looked pained, shook her head. 'You'll need me to help with Clive.'

Ant and Xiaoying helped Tom to standing, his broken arm cradled carefully against his chest. Wes drew him into a half-embrace, nothing too tight. Prompted by this, the others gathered round him in a huddle.

'Very touching,' Tom said. 'Thanks, all. Now can I go to hospital, please?'

On the way to the front door Ant said to Wes, 'You need to go to the police with this.'

Alex knew from Wes's nod that he had no intention of doing any such thing. Could Ant see this? Probably not.

Once they had gone, Alex returned to the toilet door. It was rustic and slightly ill-fitting, but solid enough to withstand a battering ram. Now, how did they get Clive to come with them peacefully?

It was like telekinesis: the latch clicked, the handle dipped, and the toilet door opened. Clive brushed something off his jacket and stepped out.

32

THERE were spots of blood on the kitchen flagstones. The Regency armchair Clive used in his study lay on its side with one leg snapped off. The sanctity of his home had been violated. This was something to be angry about.

'Clive?' Alex said.

Tina was not her normal, bubbly self. The beginning of a black eye and the crusting of blood around her nostrils made her look haunted and upset. A scruffy, unshaven man stood next to

Alex.

'Clive?' Alex said again. There was a patronising tone in her voice that irritated him.

'Yes?' he said crisply.

'Erm ... we, uh ... need you to come with us.'

'I see I'm still thoroughly outnumbered.'

All three of them were frowning. He walked through the kitchen towards the front of the house and they followed him uncertainly.

'You'll have to manhandle me out of here.'

The time he had spent sequestered in the downstairs toilet had made things abundantly clear to him: given the choice between staying here for Jay's hired thugs to return or going with the friends of an ex-colleague of whom he was rather fond, it was entirely logical to prefer the latter. He had no idea what they intended for him, but it was clear this was his least worst option.

'I won't go without a struggle,' he said, opening the front door.

And so he found himself squashed into the back seat of Tina's rust bucket as she drove out of Twyford. She made a lot of turns, and much use of her mirrors. Did she know where she was going? Ah, no – this was to throw off any potential pursuers. Good thinking, Tina. Eventually they arrived at a chain hotel so anonymous that Clive immediately forgot its name. He was led down a featureless, echoing corridor, and the four of them crowded into a room. Tina sat on one of the double beds and encouraged Clive to take the room's only chair. Alex filled the kettle from the bathroom tap and plugged it in.

She said, 'We're going to have a cup of tea and a chat.'

Out of the corner of his eye, he saw her husband quietly turn the lock on the door. The kettle was suddenly full of angry stones. The sound jolted him, as if he had been sleepwalking and was now forced into wakefulness. How had he ended up here? How had he got himself into this situation? Three pairs of eyes

246

were turned on him, but Alex's husband was the one to watch. He would be the one wielding the pliers. *Stop it.* If it came to violence Clive would crumble. He knew this, even if they didn't. He might be able to maintain his dignity now, but all that would go out the window with the first smack across the – *stop it.*

'I'm sorry for what's happened today,' Alex said. 'We didn't want it to be like this.'

It was a scene from any number of trashy movies – the good cop, bad cop routine. When her husband finally did speak, his voice would be a bellow of fury. How had he fought off Jay's hired thugs? With those fists, of course.

Between his front door and Tina's car. Between her car and the hotel. These had been his opportunities to make a run for it. Why hadn't he? Now they had him trapped. There was no way to get past them to the door; he turned towards the window instead. It was ajar, but fitted with one of those security thingies that prevented it opening more than a few inches. On a branch outside, a blackbird danced about, vaunting its freedom. He could yell for help and hope that someone came before he was silenced. And after that, what? Go home and wait for those psychopaths to turn up again? Go into work tomorrow and face another interrogation? Run back to his mother with his tail between his legs, only to find that she already knew his secret and that her door was forever closed to him?

Alex leaned forward. 'This is very important. We need to know about Dubai and the A-list.'

He felt the hangman's trapdoor give under his feet.

In that oh-so-gentle voice of hers, Alex said, 'We need to know the truth, Clive.'

It was the interrogation with Jay all over again. He couldn't go through this a second time. He wouldn't.

'The truth? Well, yes. Why not? Now I'm basically a dead man, we might as well have the truth, mightn't we?' Strange that while the noose tightened he could feel so loquacious.

'Clive –'

'I'm gay,' he said. 'There! Does that shock you? Does it?'

He addressed the question to Tina, who stared at him, open-mouthed. Yes, she was shocked all right.

'It's true. Clive bats for Dorothy. He's a friend of the other side … you know what I mean. He *likes men*. Didn't see that one coming, did you?'

Tina said, 'Well, it had crossed –'

'You're picturing me picking up men in a bar heaving with drunkards and thumping music, or engaged in some sordid fumbling in a public lavatory, aren't you? Nothing could be further from the truth. You people and your bloody judgemental attitudes. All I want is a romantic relationship with another human being. Is that so terrible? Well, it turns out that, yes, it is. And I've spent all this time poisoning my profile, and now I find it's been a colossal waste of effort. All that time practising in front of the mirror. All that time constructing a convincing … But since Jay knows, and he's willing to use it against me, my only option is to ruin my life before he ruins it for me, deprive him of some of his vast power, which is a pointless exercise anyway because although I gave up any notion of Catholic faith when I was fourteen I actually, *actually* believe I'm working for Satan. This is a man who knows what I'm thinking before I do, who keeps a silver platter somewhere with my … "No, Clive. Surely work isn't that bad," you say. Yes, it is. You have no idea. You don't know what I have to do every day. That hard-nosed bastard you think I am? It's a fiction. In reality I have a phobia of melon seeds and that hideous frothy slop from the vending machine Rob calls coffee. I have to treat people like shit so management will have some kind of respect for me, and I have to watch them piss all over Giselle's career because all human compassion has been optimised out of the system. And I hate myself for doing it, but I have to do it anyway. Have you any conception how exhausting that is?'

They were all looking at him as if he were mad. And, of course, they were right – he was mad, the outlier in the data set.

'Well, you'd be mad too if you'd been through what I've been through. My life is a lie. My entire life is a lie. Why do other people get to do whatever they want? Why am I not allowed the things that everyone else takes for granted? Why do all my plans fail to … I've even managed to leave the Courvoisier at home! See? Nothing ever goes right. All I ever wanted was to be me. Why can't I just be me?'

He looked down at the carpet as if he might find some answer hidden in its tiny grey tufts. What an embarrassment he was. At some point during his tirade he had stood up. Now he tried to sit back down, but he couldn't even get that right. He missed the chair, bruising his coccyx and ending up on the floor. He made no effort to get back up. This was where he belonged: on the floor.

He felt a hand on his back. Through the blur, he saw it was Tina. Alex's husband, his face a mask of concern, offered a wad of toilet paper to dry his face. Clive didn't understand. What was this? After such an unhinged, incoherent confession, how could they show anything but contempt for him?

In the wake of all this emotion he experienced a moment of abrupt, and ironic, clarity: in spite of all the data, all the algorithms, all the analysis, other people had always been incomprehensible to him.

*

After the tears he felt a blankness, as if his personality had accidentally been deleted.

Alex went out to get them a takeaway. Her husband – Wes, he gathered from the conversation – took a great stack of twenties out of his pocket, peeled three off and pressed them into her

hand. With only two of them remaining, this was his best opportunity to escape, but he found he no longer had any desire to.
Until he knew where to go, why not stay here? He felt the urge
to speak, less to ingratiate himself with his abductors than to
demonstrate that, in spite of all that gibberish he had spouted, he
was still capable of civilised, rational discourse.

'You're not used to this kidnapping lark, are you?' he said.

Wes shook his head.

'Aren't you supposed to have me tied up in the corner, eating
nothing but ...' He stopped himself.

Wes grinned. Time to change the subject.

'You ... don't say a lot, do you?'

Wes showed him the first page of his notepad.

Clive was aware he was gawping. Wes wrote:

It's OK – you can talk.

But now, of course, he couldn't think of anything to say.

Alex returned with food, paper plates, plastic forks. Clive was
accustomed to handmade cutlery and linen napkins, to a china
plate set on a drop leaf Edwardian table. He was also used to eating alone, but here they shared each dish. And what a restorative
it was. By the time they were polishing off the rogan josh, Clive
was fumbling his way towards acceptance, and had made some
decisions: (1) there was no going back to his old life; (2) these
people had treated him well and he would help them; and (3)
rather than give in to despair, he would do his best to reinvent
himself – a sort of Clive 2.0.

'What I told you earlier,' he mumbled, with some mortifica-
tion, 'that wasn't exactly what you were after, was it?'

Alex stifled a smile. 'Not exactly.'

'Yes. Well ... yes.'

'Clive, we never meant to put you in danger. If you could just
give us some hints, something that won't –'

He shook his head. 'I can't abide doing things by halves. My company is involved in some deeply questionable activities, and although it was never my intention, I have … enabled them. For that, I must bear some responsibility.'

He had always assumed that his achievements in life would be academic or technical, but the more he cast himself in the role of whistle-blower, the more he liked it. What, after all, do you do with a life? Something decent. Something good. Of course, there was still the distinct possibility that Jay would get him before this was all over. And so he would have to go into hiding, throw himself on the mercy of the police. By all rights he should have hated these people for forcing him into this situation, but he didn't. He couldn't bear his life. A change was long overdue, and it was almost a relief to have the decision taken out of his hands.

They told him what had happened and what they'd managed to discover, piecing the whole together between them. Alex spoke for Wes where she could and he corrected her by pencil and gesture, shorthands evolved after their years together. What they told him was outrageous. And entirely plausible.

'Clive, how does your work fit in with this?' Alex said.

'So, yes … My work at Pe combines personality profiling – based on extensions of the Myers-Briggs and HEXACO models – with game theory and machine learning algorithms to create a behavioural prediction engine.'

They were staring at him.

'In … uh, simpler terms: we collect lots of information about people, put it in a database, then use software to draw conclusions about their opinions, tastes and probable behaviour. The name Dubai comes from DB/AI – a database connected to an artificial intelligence. Technically it's not accurate, but the name stuck. Pe harvests data from any and every source available. One use for this is to design more effective advertising campaigns and target them at the right demographics – the sort of thing every company does. But over the years our methods have become

251

much more sophisticated, and the scope has expanded drastically. If we relied on employees to process all the data it would take forever. Obviously it's all done by computer; it's the only way. This sort of thing works well when you're dealing with a huge batch of people, but with individuals it begins to fall apart. Assumptions and simplifications are necessary, and they come back to bite you.'

'Give us an example,' Tina said.

'Very well. You might post on a social networking site something like, uh … "As you know, I hate Pe's products." Our AI can parse a sentence like that, and draw a conclusion. But what if you make a statement like that ironically? You might say this to a friend who knows you mean the exact opposite. If Pe just used this information to decide whether to email you a marketing flyer, then it's pretty harmless. But things have gone beyond that … way beyond that.'

Alex said, 'But surely most people have their social networking set to only share posts with their friends.'

'Yes, that's what they tell you, isn't it? It's all nice and private and secure. And only the police are supposed to have access to the national CCTV network. And GPS tracking is supposed to be anonymous. But … deals are struck, donations are made to political parties.'

'Huh,' Tina muttered. 'Follow the money.'

'Quite.'

'So who's in charge of all this?' Alex said. 'Who's responsible?'

'Jay Phillips is your man.' How deliciously thrilling, to drop his boss in it. 'You've heard of him?' he added, seeing Wes's reaction.

He's calling the shots in Darwin's Army. He gave the order to have me killed.

'Oh, good Lord.'

'So,' Alex said, 'he's using this cult to carry out his orders.'

Why?

Wes stared at Clive with an intensity he had only ever seen from Jay himself. What might happen when two such single-minded people collided? He made a mental note not to be there when it happened.

'I – I can only speculate. Much of what Jay does is secret, even from his colleagues.'

Wes gestured him to continue.

'Jay is exceptionally clever. Everything he's achieved has been from his own initiative and theory and hard work, but he's never had the benefit of a proper education. I'm sorry, I know that sounds pompous, but it's a very important point. He doesn't think critically. He misinterprets statistics, cherry-picks results that fit his world-view. And the force of his personality is so strong that he pushes this view of the world through. He believes what he wants to believe, and he makes other people believe it too. But truth isn't something you can fabricate. I've tried to warn him of the mistakes that might be made, but he sees this as academic procrastination. He insisted – against my advice, I hasten to add – that I create a list from the database of the people who are most detrimental to Pe. This is called the A-list – the Anti-Pe list. There's a P-list too, for people who are Pro-Pe.'

Alex turned to her husband. 'But what could you possibly have done to get onto that list?'

Blogged critically about Pe's software updates.

Wes wrote this with a sardonic smile to show that it wasn't to be taken seriously.

'That could be it,' Clive said.

Wes's expression morphed into incredulity.

'How influential is your blog?'

'It's got a lot of readers,' Alex said. 'It's been mentioned in the mainstream press. But still …'

Wes's mouth opened and closed, as if he were gasping for air.

'I know it sounds ludicrous, Mr Henning, but if your blog posts coincided with dips in the company share price … You see, this is what I'm saying: he thinks he's being rational and scientific, but correlation is not causation. He gets these ideas into his head and … And, of course, he's a psychopath. He's not troubled by mere morality. For him this is just the exercise of power. And they keep giving him more of it, and he's not the sort of person who is going to say, "thank you very much, that's enough".'

Wes tried to express his indignation on paper, but ended up striking through the page, tearing it off, crumpling it. He got up and started to pace the room.

'Wes?' Alex said, a note of caution in her voice.

'Look,' Clive said. 'I had no idea he'd gone this far. You have to understand that this is not the *company's* policy. They let him do what he wants and they turn a blind eye. As long as his methods are effective, that's all they want to know.'

Wes was shaking his head.

'I'm sorry, Mr Henning, but you have to understand that to Jay, you are just data. We are all just data.'

Abruptly, Wes ceased his pacing, sat down on the bed and wrote: *Where does he live?*

Clive gave him the address. 'But please be warned: I cannot express to you just how terrifying and ruthless this man is.'

Wes's head was down, his elbows on his knees. He gave no sign of having heard. He took out his phone and began tapping intently. He consulted Alex and Tina, tapped some more. After a few minutes, he came back with a note for Clive.

Your help means a lot. Sorry about the kidnapping.

Tina gave him an unexpected hug. 'Thanks for your courage, Clive.'

In the light of the terror he had experienced today, he knew it was ridiculous for her to say this. Then there was the reflex of his work persona, who would accept the compliment while knowing it to be false. Finally, there was the new and astonishing realisation that it might actually be true. Was he courageous? What defined a person, after all – what they felt or what they did? By pretending courage in his work life, perhaps the lie had become a reality.

Clive 2.0.

He looked at Tina, at Alex, at Wes. They had either condemned him or set him free. Maybe both.

'We should phone Tom,' Tina said. 'See how he's doing.'

Wes nodded.

'Yes,' Alex said, 'but I need to send an email to Fraser first.'

Wes gave her a look of puzzlement.

'He's the journalist I mentioned – the one who's going to blow this whole thing wide open.'

33

GRANT'S eye was a slit between two pillows of swollen tissue. Keiran asked if he wanted to see a doctor, just on the off-chance.

'It's nothing.'

That's why they had retreated, was it? Over nothing? Grant didn't, however, refuse the use of Keiran's sofa, or the bag of frozen peas for his eye, or the hot cup of tea. Keiran's own injuries amounted to a minor cut on the back of his head.

Keiran said, 'I was *that* close to Henning.'

'We were outnumbered.'

'His technique was sloppy. He was distracted by his wife. Another minute and the job would have been done.'

'We had no choice,' Grant said.

Yes they had. And, anyway, what was this about 'we'? It was Grant who had made the decision to pull out. Keiran should have overridden him. The question was: why hadn't he? Because it would put his brother in more danger? Because at some deep level he didn't want to go through with any of this? He probed at his feelings, trying to reach under the façade of strength to find out what was really going on. So hard to tell. What was undeniable was that Grant had not showered himself in glory. The fact was as tawdry and delicious as gossip. He was, quite literally, sitting on the reason. It was there in his pocket – the knife. Keiran had been surprised when Grant had produced it and slashed Henning's car tyres at the service area, more so when it made its second appearance as a weapon.

'Brother, I think there's something we should –'

Grant was taking his phone out. 'I need to contact Brad.'

He started tapping in the message. Was he phrasing it in a way that shifted all of the blame to Keiran? If he went to the kitchen area he could pass behind the sofa, steal a glance. No, Grant would know what he was up to. Better just to come out with it.

'What are you writing?'

Grant finished, put the phone down, stared at him. Had he heard? Of course he had. It was the sort of stare that until recently would have induced shame in Keiran, a realisation that he had acted in a way unworthy of Ascension, but Grant didn't look like such an authority with half a bag of frozen peas over his face.

How could he open a conversation about the knife? *Mum, guess what Grant did?* He could guess Grant's justification: it wasn't a one-to-one fight; the normal rules didn't apply. But if the rules could be bent, why couldn't they be broken? A sniper rifle would be much more effective against Henning, and the result would be the same. Perhaps after Ascension he would be told that the purity of the hand-to-hand fight was impractical in the real world, that it was nothing more than a test. After all, animals on the African savannah didn't abide by the Queensberry Rules.

The mobile pinged.

'Brad?' Keiran said. 'What does he say?'

Grant glanced at the message, then pocketed his phone.

'Seriously,' Keiran said, 'I need to know.'

'Let's just say he's less than happy.'

'Did you say anything about Henning and his mates turning up?'

Again, nothing from his brother. It was Grant's way of making him seem naive and overeager. But Keiran wanted to talk. It was necessary. He would make his brother communicate.

'How did Henning and his friends know we were going to that house?'

He waited for an answer, or at least some productive speculation. It was like Grant had given up.

'It's Sean and Jamal,' Keiran said.

'No. The order came to my phone, direct from Brad. They can't have known about it.'

'It's them. I know it is.'

'I'll pass on your concerns,' Grant said, but made no further effort to use his phone.

This was pointless. Grant was shutting him out.

Keiran microwaved dinner for them both. Grant ate with an almost comical slowness, and as soon as he put his plate down he lay back on the sofa and said, 'My body needs to heal.'

Keiran gave him the spare duvet and pillow, and left him to it. Grant made no requests and gave no thanks. In the past Keiran had taken his brother's silence for a stoic thoughtfulness. Now it seemed less noble, more like resentment. Thinking he might have an early night too, Keiran went to the bedroom, checking his phone on the way.

From: countdragula@freemail.com
To: k95734@wigwam.net
Subject: New information

257

Keiran,
Hello. Wes Henning here.

First of all, let me be absolutely clear: if you ever lay a hand on my wife, I will kill you. If you ever lay a hand on any of my friends again, I will kill you. This is not a threat – it's a simple fact.

Now, down to business.

I've been doing a bit of digging concerning Darwin's Army, and I've come up with some interesting information. Your boss is called Brad Neill, right? Except that isn't his real name. His real name is Oliver Robson. I know this because I've been to his house in Enfield.

From your diary, I gather you don't know who *his* boss is, but I do. For DA purposes he goes under the pseudonym Damon Kane, but his real name is Jay Phillips. He's a businessman working for Pe Corporation. I've attached a couple of his communications with Brad/Oliver. I've also attached a photo of Phillips from the internet, just so you know who you're working for.

How did I find all this out? With a bit of cunning and an enquiring mind. You don't ask enough questions. If you did, you would see the truth – you're being used.

He was falling into it again – paying attention to what Henning had to say. A stronger man would have deleted the message unread, sure of his position.

A phrase came to him from another world: 'He that hath ears to hear, let him hear'. Twice in his life he thought he understood these words: once, when he was a child, trying to bind himself to his parents' faith; and later, when he was leaving the church and had used it ironically as a justification for opening his mind to a

258

wider world. It was strange. It remained truthful even when used against the faith that had produced it. It could be used to justify belief in one thing, or its exact opposite.

He closed his eyes and rubbed at the bridge of his nose. On the blank screen of his eyelids he saw the bright pulse of Grant's blade, of Gemma's smile. There was no way he was going to get to sleep. Vodka would have helped, but he wouldn't risk touching that while Grant was in the flat. Keiran needed evidence to counter Henning's claims, something he could point to and say, 'That. That's why I believe what I believe.' And it had to be something he'd discovered for himself, not something he had been fed. By anyone.

Back in the lounge, he saw that Grant was already asleep on the sofa. Keiran retreated back down the corridor, slipped on his shoes and coat, and left the flat.

He drove to the Henning house, went round the back, and slid the patio door aside. The furniture remained in disarray. Books were still strewn over the floor where he and Grant had left them. A chaos of words – covers and spines and open pages staring up at him. Upstairs, at the desk in the spare bedroom, he sat down and switched on their laptop. He tried the last password on the list he'd discovered when he and Grant had searched their house. He was a little surprised when it let him straight in. Of course, Henning was a Refuser, fundamentally trusting of his fellow man, believing that everything in his house was safe because it was behind a locked door.

There was a folder called 'blog backup'. He opened it and double-clicked a file at random. The web browser opened, displaying one of Henning's blog posts about a best-selling author in Japan who had turned out to be a computer program. Keiran performed a search in the folder for the phrase 'darwin's army'. No matches. To make sure he was doing this correctly he performed the search again, this time on 'japan', and the previous blog post duly appeared. Perhaps the apostrophe had confused it. He did another search on 'darwin'. Nothing.

So, Henning had been home at some point and deleted just this one blog post about DA from his backup so he could claim he'd never written it? He'd done this because he knew Keiran would come to his house and search for it, even though he'd never mentioned this backup in any of his communications?

Keiran's mouth was dry, as if he'd been dehydrating for hours and was only just realising it.

The blog was well known. There would be other people linking to the article on the internet. Again, he tried a test with the Japan article, searching the internet for 'japan author mute henning'. He scrolled down the list of results and there they were: references to that very article. He performed a similar search for 'darwin's army mute henning', then 'darwin mute henning', then 'army mute henning'. No links to the blog post about DA. So DA had managed to erase every page from every website in the world that had linked to the article? But if that was possible, why didn't governments or corporations do the same thing to suppress bad news? There was only one plausible conclusion: Henning had been telling the truth. He genuinely hadn't written it. It meant someone had interfered with Keiran's laptop. It meant someone was using DA to knock off people they didn't like. Was Grant's Ascension also a murder by proxy? Were all of them?

Elbows on his knees, Keiran struggled with a bout of dizziness, a sensation that the world was rotating, with him at its pivot. He had felt this once before, when Grant had come back into his life and first told him about DA. He lurched into the bathroom and splashed water on his face. In the mirror he didn't quite look like himself – there was something … Of course, the mirror gave a reversed image. Only a photograph would show him as he truly was, and he hadn't been photographed since his youth. Strange that what he saw in the mirror every day was not what other people saw. Beyond the image of his own face, the bathroom was also reversed, and this world, too, seemed to be rotating. He tore himself away from it, sat on the lid of the toilet and ground his palms into his eye sockets.

Time passed. How much was difficult to tell. He almost felt that he might have slept. At any rate, when he opened his eyes again the dizziness had abated. The rotation had stopped. He got up and went down to the lounge. As he was about to slide the patio door aside, he noticed a figure sitting outside on one of the plastic patio chairs. He knew who it was from the silhouette. The figure rose from the chair, came through the patio door, slid it shut behind him.

'You thought I was asleep,' Grant said.

'Yes.'

'What are you doing here?' Despite the eye injury, Grant looked fresher than he had a couple of hours before.

'Listen,' Keiran said. 'Listen to me. Henning never wrote the article.'

Grant tilted his head to one side.

'It's the truth,' Keiran said. 'Let me show you.'

'I've already seen with my own eyes that he did.'

Keiran shook his head. 'Someone must have tampered with our internet.'

'Who would do that?'

'The person who's using us as a way to kill him.'

'Listen to yourself, brother.'

'Someone is controlling us. I can … prove it.' Could he? Was there enough to convince Grant?

'No-one controls me. I am the freest person on earth.'

'You're telling me,' Keiran said, 'that there's no possibility we're being had, that you don't even need to ask the question.'

Grant tilted his chin up. 'I am free from the influence of others. That's what it means to be in Darwin's Army: a rejection of

261

society's collective delusions.'

Enough. Enough of these proverbs. Keiran pointed at his brother's wrist. 'Why the Pe tattoo, then?'

'That was from before. All men come to the truth from somewhere else.'

'But you've never quite got round to having it removed, have you?'

Grant's jaw muscles tightened. Keiran was seeing another tattoo – a Celtic tribal pattern. If DA really was a sham, it would free him up to make another life for himself, a life with her, the sort of life Wes and Alex Henning had, before some bastard had come along to destroy it.

'Tell me, Grant, why are there no women in DA? How are we supposed to keep going if we can't reproduce? What are we supposed to do, rape our way to victory? Recruit the offspring when they grow up?'

'You,' Grant was shaking his head, 'have strayed.'

'DA is not what we think it is. If I show you what I've discovered, you'll believe it too.'

'There is nothing to see but the Harsh Truth. Nothing you show me could possibly shake –'

'What? Your faith?'

Grant said nothing for the space of three breaths – loud, strong breaths. Then: 'Why did you give Henning the information for his article, brother?'

'What!?'

'Had you arranged to meet him here?'

'What the fuck are you talking about?'

'I figured out why he keeps escaping. All that shit about Sean and Jamal is just a diversion, isn't it?'

'Wait a minute. You're the one who insisted on retreating from that house. How was I supposed to get him with you dragging me out the door?'

'You never were going to get him. You told him we would be there. All you had to do was act out a little scuffle with him until I was injured enough to call the whole thing off and "rescue" us.'

'Oh, you rescued us, did you? What, like you rescued our father all those years ago, *Christian*?'

He had said too much. Grant's teeth came together and the knife was in his hand. 'He was weak.'

'He was our dad!'

The knife shook, but he didn't lower it.

'Put it down.'

'So you can have a fair fight?' Grant sneered. 'The only thing that matters is who survives.'

'What are you going to do – stab me in the back? Is that what you did with your target?'

Keiran stepped back from Grant's lunge, hollowing his stomach so the blade didn't reach him. Simultaneously, he reached out to test whether he could grab the hand, twist, disarm, but the knife was already withdrawn. So Grant was the pinnacle of evolution, the teller of undeniable truths, the master of hand to hand combat? He was as flawed as Keiran. He was just better at papering over the cracks.

Keiran had always backed down in the face of his brother's determination. Well, not this time. He was sick of it. He would prove himself on his own terms, free of the influence of DA, of his brother, of anyone. He was familiar with how Grant fought with his hands, but had never faced him with a knife, not even the wooden substitute they sometimes practised with in DA. Keiran ceded ground while he looked for a way to neutralise Grant's advantage. He could back up to the front door, feel for the handle and let himself out into the street. But no, it would be locked. And perhaps that suited his mood anyway. No more retreat.

He stopped just before the lounge doorway and took the opportunity to reach out and grab a bottle from the little dining table. It was tall, like a wine bottle, but he remembered from his previous visit that it was empty, and had once contained apple juice. He smashed the bottom off on the edge of the table and held the jagged end out in front of him. His brother's advance stopped. Keiran tried a series of feints, each a different length. Grant yielded a little with each, back towards the patio door. Yes – with the injured eye, he was struggling to gauge distances. Keiran felt the fire in his blood and pushed harder.

Grant's foot came down on the corner of a book, upsetting his balance. Keiran thrust at his face with the bottle, trying to make his brother fall, drop the weapon, accept that he was at a disadvantage and seek a truce. But Grant was already recovering from the stumble, his hand thrown back against the wall, pushing himself upright. Having glanced down at the book with his good eye, his blind side was towards Keiran. He couldn't have seen it coming. Keiran did – he saw it happen very slowly, but not slowly enough that he could command his arm to pull back. The glass tore out Grant's throat.

Grant's free hand went to his neck, but the darkness bubbled out between his fingers. He took two tottering steps backwards, bounced off the patio door and fell face down. Keiran abandoned the bottle, knelt, turned him over. The carpet was already soaked.

'Brother,' he said.

Grant said nothing, could say nothing. He was choking wetly on his own blood. He stared up at Keiran, his eyes perfect concentric circles – iris, cornea and orbit.

'Grant.'

He felt something against his side, and looked down to see Grant trying to force the knife between his ribs. But there was no strength in his fingers; the knife was slipping through his hand.

'Grant.'

The fingers uncurled. The knife came free.

34

THE email from Brad came through at eight o'clock, while Jay was at home, dumping his plate and cutlery into the sink after a meal of liver and bacon. The cleaner would deal with it. What was her name? Anna? Amanda? He could never remember. He retired to the lounge area, threw himself onto the chesterfield and checked his phone.

From: Brad.Neill@daweb.co.uk
To: DamonKane@xyz.com
Subject: Game 6

More bad news. K and G failed to catch A, T or T. W turned up with friends and stopped them. K and G are still active, but G is sub-optimal.

This was unexpected. Jay stared up at the exposed roof beams and white plaster high above. This was the advantage of an open-plan barn conversion: a big space for big thoughts. Like: how had Henning known to turn up at Clive's house? Had someone tipped him off? Not Keiran or Grant, obviously. If they had not demonstrated their competence, they had at least shown commitment. Brad, then? No, he was loyal as a lapdog. Who else had access to the information about staking out Clive's house? Only Jay himself. This only left the lines of communication. The instructions had travelled from him to Brad, then from Brad to Grant, both times via email. Could Henning have intercepted them?

Jay took the stairs two at a time up to his mezzanine office. He brought up a map on the PC and centred on Henning's last known location – South Mimms services. Not so far from Enfield. He played the audio from Brad's house at nine o'clock that morning, the point where Brad should have been at work. Footsteps on a hard surface, scrapes, a clank. Someone was definitely there. He heard the rumble of drawers being pulled out on their runners, one after the other, the hollow *clop* of cupboards being closed. It wasn't Brad; it was the sound of someone methodically searching the place. Fast forwarding through the audio, he thought he heard typing. How Henning had cracked the security on Brad's computer was a mystery, but it seemed he had found a way. Clever boy.

The audio from Clive's house was much louder. Jay tutted. Keiran and Grant's clumsy violence would do nothing to help him keep a lid on things. And then another surprise – the Hennings had kidnapped Clive. Of course. They would now be at leisure to question him, and Clive would need little persuasion to blab – he was not a difficult man to interrogate. Jay had to assume the worst: that he would tell them all about Dubai, about Jay Phillips, about the creation of the A-list.

How refreshing fear was, how cleansing. Jay had often worked at his best when spurred by fear. It was the ultimate motivator. He had to hand it to the Hennings; they had performed way better than any of the other targets. So: options. He could use the email kill switch, erasing every record of every DA email that had ever been sent. It would also force him to send instructions via text or phone call, channels over which he had far less control. Or he could meet with Brad and give orders face to face. No: clumsy, slow. He would keep the email open for now.

The evidence for the creation of the A-list existed in only two places: a secure server at Pe in Reading, and on this very PC. Clive would tell them this, knowing that Jay did much of his work from home. And given this information, it was likely that Henning would go for the easier option – breaking into a private house rather than a high security company building. Instead of protecting himself against an intrusion of his home, perhaps Jay should be encouraging it.

A plan began to blossom, and the more he thought about it, the more it appealed to him. When he was sure of the details, he typed an email to Brad:

From: DamonKane@xyz.com
To: Brad.Neill@daweb.co.uk
Subject: Game 6

It's clear from what happened at the house that W and A have been communicating all along, and that they arranged to meet there.

I'm up in Birmingham on business tomorrow, travelling back some time on Thursday afternoon. It's going to be fairly intensive, so I won't have any time to devote to the game. Keep it running in my absence.

After sending it, he picked up the phone. Things were getting too messy. It was time to put an end to this.

*

They met just outside Reading train station. Niall was dressed in a duffel coat, leaning against the statue of Edward VII. He nodded in recognition as Jay approached.

'Tomorrow morning, 8:30,' Jay said. 'These coordinates.' He passed Niall several sheets of paper with the details.

'Tomorrow *morning*? Giving us how long to scout out the site?'

'Sunrise is at 7:37. I've included a floor plan.'

Niall folded his arms. 'Perhaps you don't understand how this works. This is not a case of booking a conference room so you can have a business meeting with your colleagues.'

'I understand this is short notice, which is why I'm going to pay you 50% more than the sum we agreed.'

'You fuckin' people.'

This was a good sign. Niall needed to show his displeasure so that when he accepted, he wouldn't seem to be caving in. He was a proud man, one who needed to appear in control. Jay was happy to let him maintain that illusion. Jay was not the one trying to rustle up the funds to send his daughter to a private school.

'So where might this be?' Niall said.

'Three kilometres from here. A barn conversion. The nearest neighbour is a couple of hundred metres away. Read the paperwork. Everything you need to know is there.'

Niall leafed through the pages. The job was contained, clean, simple. He would not turn it down.

'For this,' Niall said, 'for the short notice, we want double. One hundred percent extra.'

'Seventy-five.'

'Done.'

'Good. If I need you to act, I'll send you the codeword "Indigo" by email. That will be your signal to go in. I don't want anyone coming out of that house. And I want the full clean-up – bodies and blood removed, all spent ammunition casings accounted for, and I want the place burned to the ground. But I do not, repeat not, want you to do *anything* until I send the codeword.'

'Understood. Indigo. It says here "between one and four people".'

'I'll give you an exact count nearer the time.'

'Armed?'

'They may have knives, blunt instruments. Nothing more than that.'

'Piece of piss.'

'Listen,' Jay said, 'it may not happen at all.'

'Then you'll be paying us the standard retainer for every day we're on call. Plus that seventy-five percent.'

'Of course. Is there any other information you need from me?'

Niall shook the paper. 'I don't *want* to know any more than this.'

So: that was that. Even though it was his own initiative, the simplicity of it surprised him. What stopped ordinary people from doing this sort of thing all the time? Lack of money? Lack of imagination? He turned to go, but said in parting: 'Oh, and Niall?'

'Yeah?'

'When I say I want the site clean afterwards, I mean it. Nothing for forensics to pick up on.'

'You do not need to tell me how to do this.'

Jay smiled and left. He liked the way Niall bristled whenever his competence was questioned. It reminded him of the time he'd first approached him with the proposal, and prodded him as a test of his seriousness.

'You're using all the right words,' Jay had said, sitting in the grubby kitchen in Croydon, 'but how do I know that you'll be able to do the job when the pressure's on?'

'You think we can't do what you're asking? You'd better come with me.'

Niall had driven him to a warehouse where he unlocked a strongbox full of assault rifles.

'SA80s, kindly donated to us by her Majesty's finest.' He took one out, sighted down the barrel. 'Semi- and full auto. Thirty round capacity.'

Other boxes revealed pistols, silencers, Semtex.

'We don't have rocket launchers or helicopter gunships. Is that a disappointment to you?'

'I think this will be fine,' Jay had said, 'but I do need to meet your men.'

'Of course. They've all been vetted by me personally – they're trustworthy, experienced, and absolutely fuckin' lethal.'

Jay had been suitably impressed when he'd met them. No-one felt the need to show off how tough they were, yet each could talk at length about his combat experience and demonstrate his effectiveness. Jay had reiterated that he may never need their services, but if he did, he would make it worth their while. At that point, Niall hadn't even haggled on price, making Jay wonder whether he should have struck a harder bargain. Interesting how cheap a person's life was – such a tiny fraction of his department's annual budget.

*

On returning home, Jay disabled the burglar alarm and, with the help of a ladder, removed the prominent red box from the front of the house. It left a discolouration against the woodwork, but they were unlikely to notice it. Back inside, he set up a tiny camera with a motion detector and pointed it at his desk. He tested it with a wave of the arm. A notification was sent to his phone and he was able to see the live video. Finally, he backed up his PC to an external hard drive, then formatted the entire computer, wiping it clean of all data, the operating system, everything. The main unit was located in a small cupboard built into the desk, which he closed and locked, pocketing the key. That would slow them down.

Preparations complete, he poured himself a generous Laphroaig, lounged on the chesterfield and looked around at the too-familiar vista of his home. He supposed he could rescue some possessions from it before Niall and his crew arrived to torch the place, but for the life of him he couldn't figure out what. His eyes fell on one of the original abstracts he had hung to break up the space. It had been a costly piece. The art dealer – whose sales techniques Jay had studied with interest – assured him it would appreciate in value. He had bought it not because

270

he saw anything in it, but because in time he might. Years of gazing at it had shown him that these explosions and smears could be anything he wanted them to be. At that point he had concluded that he – the viewer and interpreter of the work – was the important one, not the artist. These paintings merely confirmed the potency of his own imagination. He could find something similar in a log fire or a pattern of clouds. The artist profited, true, but had relinquished his authority, his power to influence.

Nothing about the house was ideal, now he thought about it. The location of the staircase was awkward, the view from the conservatory not all it could be. Let it burn. The prospect of starting again from scratch was quite appealing. His mind was his home – a palace more opulent than anything that existed on Earth.

He would hold an emergency press conference, feigning shock and confusion in front of the country's journalists. When asked why this had happened, he would suggest that his only enemies were business rivals. He would state his commitment to stand firm in the face of this kind of intimidation, like a politician condemning an act of terrorism.

But an itch of unhappiness still troubled him. It wasn't how close the Hennings had got to him; it was that they had forced him to call on Niall. The inelegance of the solution offended him. Once used, the ultimate backup plan ceased to be an ultimate backup plan. They had made him tarnish it.

Death was a concept that had always interested him. When considered from a purely scientific point of view, life and death were really not that dissimilar, just a minor difference in the arrangements of clusters of atoms, the difference between a running computer and one with the power unplugged. Granted, it could be argued that death would cause suffering and was therefore to be avoided. But after death there was no more chance to feel anything. Was it worse to experience a fleeting moment of pain and die, or to go on living, with all the suffering that might entail, only to die in the end anyway?

It wasn't like any of these peoples' lives were significant. They weren't achievers and pioneers, people of audacity and innovation. And soon they would be gone. He would erase their inconvenient knowledge the way he had erased his computer's hard drive.

Wednesday

35

ALEX and Tina insisted on coming with him. Wes had tried to argue them out of it, but not too hard. After the trials of the last few days, having support from others was a welcome novelty. They stood near a footpath sign, looking plausibly like walkers who had stopped to discuss their route. Despite being late October, the day had the bright clarity of spring, roads and leaves wet from recent rainfall. Out of the drab greyness of the last few days, suddenly everything was fresh and vibrant, as if newly created.

They had left the car in the village and continued on foot to where the buildings became sparse and the green undulations of the countryside began. It gave a vantage on Jay Philips' house – half-concealed by a stand of trees, but with a view of the driveway. The man certainly liked his privacy, which was pretty ironic, given what he had put Wes and Alex through. There was no-one out here except for a couple of workmen examining a broadband cabinet, their van parked nearby.

Tina climbed a couple of rungs up a five bar gate to get a better view, and Wes felt Alex's fingers meet his. He turned to her and saw that she was afraid. He nodded reassurance, knowing it was what she needed. For her sake he hid his own fear. Did she know that this was a two-way process, that he was drawing as much strength from her as she was from him?

They had drawn strength from each other last night too. Alex had phoned Tom, who had just arrived home, his arm now in a cast. Then they had emailed Fraser, who had replied not two minutes later, insisting on more information about their 'very promising leads'. So they wrote a longer email, giving him everything they had – all the details they were able to cobble together from their separate discoveries. Finally they had sunk back on the bed in their hotel room, surprised that there now seemed nothing left to do except get some sleep. He hadn't expected that they would make love. But fatigue seemed to be no impediment, and somehow it happened anyway, as if their bodies had decided independently of their minds that the need for sleep should be postponed while this vital thing happened. Wordlessly, she fished the condom out of his wallet. He was grateful – this was not the time for a discussion about children. This was for them, and them alone. She straddled him, loosed her hair and let it fall around them, enveloping. Their rhythm was slow, lazy. There seemed to be an unspoken agreement that if they never reached the destination, that was fine: the journey was enough. But they did. They tuned out the rest of the world. He had always encouraged her to talk during sex. She said nothing profound; that wasn't the point. She breathed the words into his ear, gifting them, making him believe, if only for a few moments, that they were his.

'There he is,' Tina said. She gulped in a lungful of air and blew it straight back out. 'Let's get this done.'

On the road that headed out towards the village, Jay's Jaguar was gliding by. While Tina was climbing down, Alex turned Wes's chin towards her and kissed him – a hasty improvisation that landed somewhere between his mouth and cheek. He squeezed her hand.

Tina said over her shoulder, 'Are you two lovebirds coming?'

The house was a strange mix of the old and the new – a timber-framed barn conversion where the modernisation had been taken too far. The conservatory did not blend in, its ruthless geometry at odds with the imperfect lines of the barn. It was an unwelcome growth, a carbuncle.

'No burglar alarm,' Alex said.

'Maybe if you're this rich,' Tina said, 'you just replace anything that goes missing.'

The front door was designed to blend in with the wood, but on closer inspection it was brown uPVC. The lock was digital, so picking it was out. They went round to the back door, but faced the same problem. No matter. This side – further away from the road and the rest of the village – offered them a better opportunity. Wes shrugged off his rucksack. He fished out the blanket they'd borrowed from their hotel and the crowbar they'd bought at a hardware store this morning for just such breaking-and-entering activities. Alex and Tina held the blanket over the glass upper section of the door, like two conjurer's assistants, while Wes performed his crude magic.

The wail of an alarm. He was sure it would happen. But no, after the crash of glass into the house there was no sound. He reached in, found the handle, and opened the door. They used the blanket to sweep aside the glass, then entered through the kitchen area. The place was even more open-plan than it looked from the outside. The downstairs was essentially one huge space, combining the kitchen, dining area, and a lounge that maintained some sense of separation from the rest by virtue of being sunk into the floor. The ceiling above them presumably marked out the bedrooms, but beyond the kitchen area it opened up and he could see all the way up to the rafters. At the other end of the building was a mezzanine with a desk and shelving – the study.

'Bloody hell,' Tina said, gazing upwards. 'How many times could you fit my flat into this?'

Wes strode across the floor and went straight up the stairs to the study. The mezzanine gave a commanding view over the rest of the building. Bookshelves lined the walls, and a sturdy oak desk gave a huge working space, empty except for a keyboard, mouse and two large monitors. He traced the cables from the screens to a hole in the back of the desk – there was a locked compartment for the PC itself. As the others came up the stairs behind him, he tapped the box with one knuckle.

'I'll look for a key,' Alex said.

Wes shook his head and held up the crowbar. They had smashed their way in; no point aiming for subtlety now.

He had to give Jay credit for buying quality furniture. Alex winced as the sound of tortured timber reverberated off the walls, but there was no other way to do this. Besides, it was very satisfying. By hammering away around the latch, then bracing his foot against the box and yanking with both hands on the crowbar, he was finally able to splinter off enough wood so that the lock had nothing left to latch against. The PC sat inside, LEDs glowing – it had been left on.

Tina produced a screwdriver from her pocket. 'Shut it down and let's get the hard drive out.'

He switched on the monitors but instead of the expected login screen, he was presented with two lines of stark white text on a black background:

Booting from hard disk...
No operating system found.

That wasn't right. What was the use of a computer without ...?

'Shit,' said Tina quietly. 'He's wiped it.'

Alex's head jerked towards Wes. 'S-so, what does that mean? He knew we were coming?'

The email about Jay being away on business – it was bait. He had found out that Wes was reading his email. They had been played. Tina took a breath in order to say something, but the words never left her lips. From somewhere beneath them there came a click and the sound of rubber seals releasing. It was the front door. Wes motioned them to get down, and they flattened themselves against the polished wooden floor of the mezzanine. The staircase was their only exit, and it would be blocked within seconds. Having been defeated at Clive's house, their adversaries would come in harder. Grant had used a knife to fend off Ant and Xiaoying. What would it be this time? If it was a gun, they would basically be targets on a firing range.

He looked at Alex. She turned her head slowly towards him. This time, he was sure, the veil had slipped – she would see in his face the curdling dread, the terror, the desperation. If only he could give her something better. If only they could be outside, walking in the woods and fields, enjoying a simple day together in what might be the last truly warm sunshine before winter took hold.

Alex's lips parted. She mimed three familiar words – tongue to roof of mouth, teeth on lower lip, mouth formed into a circle. She said nothing, but he could hear it all the same. His fingers tightened on the crowbar.

36

ALEX was closest to the edge of the mezzanine, her face up against the railing. With her chest pressed flat against it, would the floor act as a soundboard, amplifying the thud of her heartbeat? It was hammering away, but the gaps between the beats seemed enormous. Time had elongated, like an elastic band stretched to the point of snapping.

The front door closed and she heard footsteps beneath her – a light step, almost inaudible. She was the only one of them who could see over the edge. The top of a head came into view, black hair in a pony tail, the shoulders of a white T-shirt. Not Keiran or Grant; nor the other two from the silver car. Thank God. She saw a container full of plastic bottles set down on a side table. She put her hand over Wes's and stood up. His eyes widened, but she held a finger to her lips and set off down the stairs before he could stop her.

'Hi!' she said. 'You made me jump.'

The woman was just beginning to hide a look of surprise. She was pale, with heavy eye liner and a pierced eyebrow. Over the T-shirt she wore an apron.

'You've come to do the cleaning? Did my brother not tell you?' Alex positioned herself so the woman's gaze was drawn away from the violence they had done to the back of the house. How thoroughly had they swept aside that glass?

'Tell me what?' A London accent, East End.

'We don't need the house cleaned today.'

'Really? Why's that?'

Because we like it messy, because Jay has decided to fire you; think, think, think.

Alex said, 'I haven't introduced myself. I'm Jay's sister, Gertrude.'

She held out a hand, and after a moment's pause the woman shook it.

'I'm sorry,' she continued, 'Jay has never told me your name.'

'Hannah.'

'Hannah. Nice to meet you. The things is, we're preparing for a party tonight, so, as you can see, there's really no point tidying up until it's over.'

'But he'll want the house clean for a party, won't he?'

'No, no. We've got a lot of things to ... to set up, and you'd only be in the way. It's okay, you'll still be paid; you don't need to worry about that. Think of it as a bonus for all your good work.'

Hannah's eyes narrowed. 'You're sure? He didn't say anything about this.'

'Well, it's a bit of a last minute thing. You know how spontaneous Jay is.'

278

'So, I've got the morning off?'

'Yes! I'm sorry about this. He should have told you earlier, but you know how he is: busy, busy.' Alex handed her the container of cleaning products and ushered her towards the door. 'You just go out and enjoy the day.'

How patronising she sounded. It didn't matter, she told herself, as long as the woman left. At the front door Hannah stopped and turned round. Oh, for goodness' sake, couldn't she just *go*?

'I think he could do with a party,' she said. 'He's too serious.'

Alex smiled. 'You know, that's exactly what I said to him.'

'Well, I hope it's a good one.'

'Thank you. It's a beautiful day out there.'

'Yeah, a bit cold, but at least the sun's out, eh?'

Alex saw her out and closed the door behind her. She watched through the window as the woman got into a tiny green hatchback and drove off.

'All clear,' she said.

Wes bounded down the stairs, grasped one hand, put the other round her waist, and drew her into the first few steps of a waltz.

Tina was leaning over the railing of the mezzanine. 'Gertrude?' she said.

'First thing that came into my head.' Alex laughed, but it was short-lived. 'Do you think she bought it?'

She detached herself from Wes, then took Hannah's position and looked towards the back of the house. A couple of shards of glass and the edge of the broken window were visible, but maybe that's because she was looking for them.

'I tried to prevent her from seeing the back door, but … she could be phoning the police right now.'

'She could be the scout,' Tina said. 'If he knows we're here, she could just be the precursor to the big guns.'

'We need to get this done, right now.'

'Okay.' Tina ran her hands through her hair. 'So, this PC isn't necessarily a problem. If he's done a normal format – fingers crossed – we can still get the data back off the hard drive. You see, the computer doesn't actually ...'

She trailed off, seeing that Wes was nodding vigorously.

'You already know this?'

Another nod.

'Really?' Alex said. 'We can get the data off even if ...' Then she realised that she already knew this too. Tom had mentioned something about it, back when all this had first started. She felt giddy with relief. 'Then why are we standing around, talking? Get that hard disk, now. I'll stay down here and keep a lookout.'

She sounded unlike herself – impatient and demanding. If Wes noticed, he didn't show any sign of it. He was already halfway up the stairs before the words were out of her mouth.

37

KEIRAN'S opportunity lay in the hundred metres between Jay's parked car and the six-storey glass façade of the Pe building. He didn't look for a parking space, just abandoned his vehicle, undid the seatbelt, threw the door open and started running. Jay was striding towards the revolving door, tapping at his phone. More orders for Brad? More lies? More deception? Keiran pulled him round and slapped the phone out of his grasp. It hit the ground with a *clack* and skittered to rest under the wheel of a parked car. He expected to see fear on the man's face, or at least surprise. The eyebrows rose, but settled again within seconds, and the face assumed the look of intensity and assurance he'd seen last night in photos of this man on the internet.

A reflection off the curve of a bottle. A glint of steel. Something yielding, tearing, torn.

The plan was to get the first words in, to assert himself, but Jay was first to speak. 'So, here you are at last.'

'You're Jay Phillips.'

'Correct.'

'You're also Damon Kane.'

'Yes. And you are Keiran Lowry.'

Keiran opened his mouth to demand some answers, but again Jay spoke first.

'Before I say anything else, let me tell you that I understand your anger. What I have asked of you is no small thing. You deserve – you have earned – an explanation.'

Ah, and it would be so tempting to believe there could be such a thing – a key to making sense of it all, the balm for a rioting mind. After all that had happened, did Jay actually think he could provide that?

Jay's eyes moved in the direction of the fallen phone. 'Before I give it to you, I need to send a message.'

An inward rush of air. Dark droplets falling. A collapse.

'No.'

Jay didn't move. 'Your confusion is understandable –'

'I'm not confused.'

But it was a lie, a habitual answer, something that came from living too long with certainty. Now there was choice, and on its heels came doubt, just as the Doctrine said. He had come here with a purpose, and once again the hard light of reality showed him that nothing was as it seemed. He needed someone to tell him his plan was sound. He was dependent on others. He was weak.

Jay said, 'I've been waiting for one of you to find me. It's a … test, of sorts, and I have to say you've performed brilliantly. I can now reveal to you the true nature of your work in DA.'

How could this possibly be true? He had failed, over and over, to kill Henning. In what way could this be considered a brilliant performance? Unless the point wasn't to kill Henning at all. But that made no sense.

Enough of this. Answers. He would get answers. 'Who's your boss in DA?' he said.

'I have no boss in DA.'

'You're in charge?'

'Yes.'

Now he could go on the attack. 'Are you the one who wrote Henning's article?' But before Jay could answer, another thing occurred to him, and it was out of his mouth before he could stop it. 'You wrote the Doctrine?'

'All these things will be answered, but more importantly, they can be put into context. You have to see the big picture to understand. I will show my trust in you, Keiran. I want you to go to my house. You followed me here, so I know you know where it is. You will have to be quick.'

No answers, only more commands. Jay was trying to divert him, the same way Henning had.

'I'm not going anywhere.'

'In answer to your question – yes, I wrote the Doctrine,' Jay said. 'I wrote it because it was true, and it is my guiding principle as much as it is yours. It is scientifically proven. It has been since Darwin wrote the foundations for it in the mid-1800s. The only difficulty is in accepting it.'

The words played themselves out in Keiran's mind, like a recording:

Life or death: the only question
Adaptation: the only truth
I will cure myself of the burden of choice, for it tempts me to weakness;
deliver myself from the illness called love, for it makes me dependent.

282

There is one path and one choice.

I will take it.

The survivor evolves.

The evolver survives.

'Look me in the eyes,' Jay said, a kindly father imparting his wisdom. 'Look me in the eyes and tell me the Doctrine is false.'

He couldn't. He couldn't just come out and say it. The Doctrine had been his entire ethos for the last two years. And yes, he had felt the crippling burden of choice in a world awash with contradictory information; yes, he had felt the weakness of love, the delicious, terrible weakness of it. The creed of his parents was wrong – he knew that with absolute certainty – and the Doctrine was the solution.

Almost as if it had been designed that way.

Unthinkable that he had yielded his life to false teachings, not just once, but twice. Unthinkable. And yet he was thinking it.

A clawing. The sound of bubbles. An almost familiar face.

Grant. Jesus Christ. Grant.

There was no more guidance. Not from anyone. He was free, and all the world was spread out before him. It was terrifying. A man couldn't live like this, adrift of everything. There had to be something to believe in, on his own terms, in his own way. It was that four-letter word in the middle of the Doctrine that had always clawed at him. He recalled Henning's letter, the line 'love is the solution, not the problem'. Henning, with his wife and his business and his house and his money. Henning, with his wife. His wife.

The weakness was also a glorious kind of strength.

He said, 'I'm in love with a girl called Gemma.'

'No,' Jay said. 'You desire her sexually. You know this is the truth.'

Keiran clenched his teeth. 'No. I love her. She would hate me for what I've done, but that doesn't mean I don't love her.'

This man's control over him depended on adherence to the Doctrine; on a group of people who secluded themselves from the rest of the world, just like his parents' church; on the collusion of his own brother. And the Collapse? It was not some nebulous event in the future, something that affected all mankind – it was personal, individual. And it had already happened. He was living in the aftermath of it. He had prepared for nuclear war, for economic meltdown, for pandemic, when all along he should have been preparing for this, for *now*. He had squandered his present for an unknowable future.

'Grant is dead,' he said.

Jay paused for a moment. His expression betrayed nothing, but the delay before his next words suggested a frenzy of thought.

'Then I can understand your emotion, but you must be strong, and not submit to the temptations of sentimentality. He died in service of the Harsh Truth, and he did it willingly. You must have your revenge. It is even more important that you kill Henning now.'

'You don't understand. *I* killed Grant.'

He saw Jay's mouth open, and waited for the clever reply, the twisting of the facts, the master manipulator's trump card. In thinking these things, he realised he had become immune to them. Jay's lips closed, unused. Keiran could see his chest rising and falling, rising and falling.

'Why have you done this to us?' Keiran said.

'As I said, the reasons are very complex. Come to my office and I'll explain.'

'No. Tell me here. Tell me now. Tell me the truth.'

Jay bolted for the building. Keiran matched him for the twenty paces it took to ready Grant's flick-knife. He grabbed Jay's collar and yanked him to a halt while punching the blade through his back. Jay tottered. Keiran withdrew the knife, spun him round and thrust again, up and under the ribs, towards the heart. Jay clung to him with ferocious strength and whined like an animal in his ear so loudly that Keiran had to jerk his head aside. He felt something warm and liquid against his leg. The grasping arms lost their strength, went limp. He let the body fall.

There were people around him, people who had arrived here for work, near but not near. He should escape. That's what murderers did, wasn't it? They had getaway cars, accomplices. They had plans. All Keiran had was a vast sense of fatigue. This was not a beginning. This was not the chance to start a fresh life with Gemma. It was an ending. He sat down on the paving slabs, not two metres from the damning evidence of how unsuited he was to this thing they called civilisation. He didn't understand the world. He had tried, he had tried so hard, but its truths had always eluded him. He looked up at the Pe building – six storeys of polished glass. Inside it he imagined a giant machine made up of people and computers, networks of electricity and conversation. But it might be full of packing foam for all he knew. It might be empty. From here he couldn't see anything of what was inside. It was a giant mirror, its internal workings obscure.

'I've got shares in this company,' he said in wonderment to a man with a moustache who was just exiting the building.

The man back-pedalled, almost crushing himself in the revolving door in his desperation to get back inside. There were more people now, but they were further away, a circle expanding, like a ripple on the surface of a pond. Keiran was alone in an oasis of his own making. Some things never changed.

After a while – who could tell how long? – he became aware of flashing blue lights, of people shouting orders. It prompted an image from his memory; no, from a story. He saw, in his mind's eye, a fire engine, an upper storey window, empty except for the belching black smoke. *Empty.* Long, long ago he believed he had broken with his past, with his parents, with his old life. But he saw now the harsh truth. He had become his father. He had sacrificed himself for the sake of a stranger.

Epilogue

38

Pe Executive Killed in Rush Hour Stabbing

A senior executive of Pe Corporation has been stabbed to death in the car park of the company's headquarters in Reading.

Jay Phillips, 32, was killed in front of horrified colleagues arriving for work on Wednesday. The murderer has been identified as Keiran Lowry, 26, of Strathurst.

John Bevilacqua, a programmer at the company, witnessed the incident. 'I was just popping back out to my car when I heard a shout. Jay was on the ground and a man stood over him holding a knife. There was blood everywhere. He didn't try to escape. He just stayed there until the police arrived and gave himself up.'

On searching Lowry's flat, police discovered another body, identified as Lowry's own brother, Grant, who was a devotee of the company and had a tattoo of the Pe logo on his wrist.

Lowry has confessed to both murders, but police say his motives remain unclear. Links with terrorist organisations have not been ruled out.

Pe's founder and CEO, Piotr Dolokhov, issued a statement from his home in San Jose, California: 'This is tragic and incomprehensible. Why would anyone want to do such a thing? Jay's work was innovative and he had unbelievable drive. He will be sorely missed. We are stepping up our security worldwide in response to this cowardly attack.'

Head of UK operations, Daryl Noonan, said: 'We are all in

shock. Jay was a brilliant mind and a respected colleague. He was dearly loved by all who worked with him and will be impossible to replace. He had no family; he was married to the company. His father died when he was just two months old and he grew up in poverty. He was the epitome of the self-made man.'

A man from Enfield has also been arrested in connection with the investigation.

*

Wes,

I expect I'll be in prison by the time you read this.

You were right. I could say I'm sorry but I don't think that will mean much.

Here are the rest of my diaries. I don't know what you'll do with them but I knew I had to send them to you. You're the only person who ever tried to understand me.

Keiran Lowry

*

Dear Mr Henning,

I am given to understand that your recent experience at Strathurst police station was not all it could have been. It is therefore my duty to apologise for any distress that may have been caused. Please rest assured that our officers take their duties very seriously and that every effort will be made to rectify any misunderstandings regarding your case.

As a gesture of good will, I would like to offer you a free tour of the station so we can demonstrate our commitment to combating crime.

Regards,

Chief Inspector Hugh Simmons

*

Clive Goddard
Tollgate Cottage,
New Road,
Twyford.

Dear Alex,

Thank you for your letter. There's really no need to apologise for the kidnapping. On the contrary, it's probably the best thing that's happened to me in years. There are times in life when one needs a boot up the posterior.

My life has changed immeasurably in the last few weeks. Alas, as predicted, my mother has stopped talking to me since I came out. I've decided to put myself through the ordeal of writing to her once a month and keeping her abreast of developments in my new life. It's up to her whether she decides ever to reply. I hope that some day she will see the light. Be assured that I don't regret the decision – it had to be done. My life seems to be working its way through the elements of a Greek play. At Pe I did hubris and hamartia. I've now moved on to catharsis.

With regard to Pe's database, about which you so rightly show concern, I may have done something rather rash. I created a little program that pollutes the database by randomly shifting the metrics away from their true values, so the whole thing becomes less accurate over time. The process should be slow enough to be imperceptible. If it runs for long enough, the whole database will be mangled beyond usefulness.

Dangerous? Why, yes. But that's the new Clive! And anyway, even if they could pin it down to me – and I've done my homework on that count, I can assure you – I'm wagering that Pe don't want to call the police and say that someone has ruined their intrusive and sinister database. I've also left the company, so with luck the blame for this – or at least the blame for not spotting it – may fall on the head of my successor, which would delight me no end because he's a scheming weasel.

In the grand tradition of spy novels, I'd appreciate it if you could burn this after reading. But please do write again. If I don't reply immediately it's because I'll be in Sweden for a couple of weeks visiting Lars. 'And who is Lars?' I hear you ask. Lars is my first attempt at internet dating. He's a professor of behavioural science at Linköping University. I can only hope that the dating website's database is more accurate than Pe's is about to become.

Wish me luck!

Yours,

Clive

*

From: fraser@standish.co.uk
To: countdragula@freemail.com, countessdragula@freemail.com
Subject: Re: Hard Drive

Wes/Alex,

Tina and I have been looking over the contents of that hard drive. Fascinating stuff. It appears that Mr Phillips didn't hijack this Darwin's Army group – he created them in the first place. There are very detailed notes on how it's organised, its principles, how it functions, how people are kept in line. It is a quite brilliant fabrication.

Don't for a moment suppose that I'm expressing approval, merely astonishment at the work and ingenuity that has gone into its creation. The police have assured me this will all be considered as part of their investigations, but how much attention they will afford to data on a stolen hard drive that has technically been deleted remains to be seen.

You must curb your expectations of what will come of this. Pe will, of course, deny all responsibility. They will say that Jay was acting alone, a rogue agent, and now he's dead, everything is wrapped up. Pe get to control the narrative at the moment because one of theirs was killed. My own investigations will take longer but give a truer account.

If you have any more information, you know where to send it.

All the best,
Fraser

P.S. Apologies for my little outburst over the diaries that Lowry sent to you. I quite understand why you didn't want to open them. It's just that they could have proved *such* a goldmine of information. I do hope the police give proper attention to their contents.

P.P.S. There is more to go through on the hard drive, for which I need Tina's help. She is, however, proving unusually difficult to contact at the moment. I understand she's currently shacked up with your friend Tom. I don't suppose you could encourage her to put her knickers back on for five minutes and drop me a line, could you? We have important work to do.

*

The house is silent.

It's a little larger than their previous place, and situated towards the eastern rather than the western side of town. The lounge is spacious, and contains a new three piece suite. On the coffee table is an A4-sized box containing scraps of paper on which various messages have been written by hand. At the bottom, hidden under layers and layers of newer notes, lies a sheet of thick writing paper bearing a longer message, its ink blacker, its letters more carefully formed.

Illustrious and esteemed wife,
    I've been thinking. This might explain the grimace of effort

you've noticed on my face over the last couple of days.

I feel humbled that so many people have risked so much to help me. I've always been an outsider, but after all they have done for me I feel more a part of the world than ever before.

The last week has been bewildering and terrifying. But that terror has kept me alive and it's given me a new perspective on things. Fear has been a constant throughout my life, perhaps more than for most people. I'm afraid of being alone. I'm afraid of not being able to communicate with people. I'm afraid of passing on my wonky genes to a son or daughter.

But the difference is this: the prospect of being murdered is a true, useful fear because it helps keep you alive. The others are not – they're stifling, limiting fears. I can't think of many instances in my life where I've regretted doing something that scares me. On the other side there is always something worth having.

I've come to the conclusion that while fear might be a good reason to do something, it's rarely a good reason <u>not</u> to do something.

Let the future be what it will. I'm still afraid, but I'm ready. Let's put a bun in the oven.

W

Up the stairs are two bedrooms. In the smaller of the two, the walls are painted yellow and decorated with silhouettes of elephants and storks. Between these creatures, painted by hand, in every conceivable colour, filling every gap, are words, words, words. On top of the wardrobe is a small camera, a baby monitor. It points at the corner of the room, but there is nothing there to see, only four rectangular impressions in the carpet where the cot used to be.

Outside this room, on the landing, a bookshelf takes up one wall. Among the paperbacks, sandwiched between a book on pregnancy and a Wing Chun manual, is a copy of *Crime and*

Punishment, its top edge coated with a fine fur of dust. Halfway through, the corner of a page is turned down.

Across the landing is the master bedroom. From the doorway can be seen a double bed, unmade, its bottom sheet rippled, its dove grey duvet tangled. The curtains are open wide. Light pours in. Only on entering the room fully does the extra piece of furniture becomes visible. Round the edge of the door, within arm's reach of the double bed, is the cot.

Along the landing and down the stairs, there is the rasp of a key in a lock, a click. The front door swings open. Wes and Alex and Grace are home.

Acknowledgements

THANKS to the following people for reading the novel in its entirety and providing useful and much appreciated feedback: Loree Westron, Scott Smyth, Joan Smith, Gail Loose and Neil Edmunds. For valuable comments on the early chapters I'm grateful to: Ruby Cowling, CM Taylor, Chris Hammacott, Wendy Metcalfe, Carol Westron and the late Eileen Robertson.

Thanks also to the Arvon Foundation and their tutors, who commented on parts of this novel or on my writing in general: Naomi Alderman and Joe Dunthorne, Ed Docx and Alice Jolly, Jon McGregor and Helen Oyeyemi.

For specialist knowledge, thanks to Paul Thomas and Duncan Hobbs. All errors are the author's responsibility.

Most of all, thanks and love to my wife Helen for her unflagging support. Her perceptive comments (on many, many drafts) have been crucial in shaping this book.

The typefaces used in this book are Adobe Garamond Pro and Myriad Pro by Robert Slimbach. With the environment in mind, the typesetting is designed to use 20-25% fewer pages than most equivalent books. The cover design is by The Art of Communication (artofcomms.co.uk).

No AI was used in the production of the text or the cover.

If you like this novel, please recommend it to (or buy it for) a friend. A personal recommendation is still the surest, warmest, truest way of finding a good book.